Also by Erin K. Rice:
On the Way to Someplace Else
www.erinkrice.com

First Fountainhead Print Edition, August 2009
Copyright © 2008 by Erin K. Rice

All rights reserved under International and Pan-American Copyright Conventions. Published in the United States by Fountainhead Print, Texas.

This novel is a work of fiction. Any references to historical events; to real people, living or dead; or to real locales or places of business are intended only to give the fiction a setting in historic or contemporary reality. Other names, characters, places of business, corporations, locations and incidents are either the product of the author's imagination or are used fictitiously, and their resemblance, if any, to real-life counterparts is entirely coincidental.

Book design and layout by Stephen Cullar-Ledford
www.cullar-ledford.com

Library of Congress Control Number 2009906912
ISBN 978-0-615-30741-1

Printed in the United States of America
10 9 8 7 6 5 4 3 2 1

For Alice

WHAT HAPPENED ON SMITH STREET

A NOVEL **ERIN K. RICE**

For Rebecca and Samantha, the glorious Sisters Fite.
Thanks for pushing me off the cliff.

PROLOGUE: MAY 2007

"It's an incredible opportunity."

Amanda steadied herself as the surge of nausea that always followed those words worked its way up her throat. She watched her hand place the wine glass carefully atop the white tablecloth. It seemed to float in front of her, as if it belonged to someone else at their table; someone just out of eyesight. Finally swallowing the sip of merlot she had taken before Matt's announcement, she smiled brightly at her husband.

"I'm sure it is. When do you start?"

Matt had been waiting, tense. He exhaled the full capacity of both his lungs slowly, hoping Amanda would not notice. She sat, still as the Dead Sea, studying him. Looking for any indication that he, himself, did not believe the statement he had just voiced. His eyes, his hands, the corners of his mouth.

"Honey? When do you start?"

Matt raised a glass of water to his lips, barely wetting them before he set it down.

"Two weeks from Monday," he responded, at last. "Two weeks. And you'll be back in Houston. You'll like that, right?"

Back in Houston. Amanda pondered the notion even as she nodded. It had been fourteen years. Would that prove long enough?

"It'll be great," she told him, although she doubted very much that it would. Very much.

JULY 2007

MONDAY, JULY 23

Matt is bored. It's not a complete surprise; Vantage is an insurance company, after all. But he had been recruited as a fresh thinker, an agent of change, an innovator who would help drag the staid and stable firm into the latest version of the new economy. But in the two months since he has joined the company's M&A team, he has done little other than teach himself the finer points of risk management as it applies to property, life and casualty insurance and how Vantage has steadily increased its market share in those product offerings under the innovative leadership of John Allen Wallace III.

He doesn't even know why they have an M&A team, in fact. There is limited access to leveraged capital for acquisitions, and it's very unlikely that Vantage would ever merge with a competitor — even cosmetically, to mask a take-over and allow the acquired party to save face. He considers raising the issue with his boss, Frank Riley, the vice president of M&A; but he doesn't want to come off as a whiner. And he can't talk to Amanda about it. She would never express "I told you so" in words, but the look in her eyes would be enough to grind what little ego he currently has left down to a nub. So he sits at his cubicle desk, day after day, monitoring the status of competitors. He watches their stock prices, their earnings reports, scrutinizes every press release, looking for signs of weakness or even just change. It is the most mind-numbingly tedious job he could ever have imagined for himself, and he had fought like a tiger to land it. He pushes back from the desk and ambles to the coffee bar; he needs a shot of caffeine to make it through the final two hours of the day.

"Hey, Matt." It is Kendra, the department's summer intern. She will start her senior year at The University of Texas in a couple of weeks. It cannot come soon enough for Matt. She has followed him around all summer, perching on his desk, waylaying him at the coffee bar and making a general pest of herself at every opportunity. The attention is great — she's ridiculously hot — but she is also the daughter of Stan Firestone, Vantage chief technology officer. And beyond that, he's pretty certain Amanda would literally eviscerate him if she caught him straying. And yet somehow make him enjoy the process from start to finish.

"Kendra. What's up?" Matt selects a coffee pod from the dispenser and pops it into the single-serve machine.

"Oh, nada. Working on anything exciting today?" She is waiting for her microwave popcorn to finish popping. Four empty and otherwise useless coffee filters stand ready at her elbow.

Matt laughs out loud, a short, barking sound. Then he looks at her seriously. "I could tell you; but then I'd have to kill you."

She giggles as the microwave timer sounds. She busies herself distributing an even amount of popcorn into each filter. "Want some? It's kettle corn."

He shakes his head. God did not intend popcorn to taste like cotton candy. "No, thanks. You ready to head back to Austin?"

"Yes! I leave next weekend. I can't wait." She pauses, a slight frown on her pretty lips. "My dad is giving me, like, a huge going away party on Saturday? Do you want to come?" Another hesitation before she adds, "And your wife, too, of course." Although the prospect of introducing gorgeous Matt Parsons and his wavy dark hair to her girlfriends all alone is tempting beyond belief.

Matt smiles a little as he tries to envision Amanda surrounded by college students enjoying their last weekend of summer. "I think we have plans. Sorry. But thanks for the invite." His coffee is ready and he grabs the cup and heads back down the hall. "Have fun," he calls to Kendra.

At his desk once again, he wakes up the monitor and toggles to the stock tracker. He keys in the ticker symbol for one of the firms he is following and then grimaces at the screen. The wrong company; he had fat-fingered the letters. He re-keys the letters and then takes a closer look at the firm he had errantly summoned, before hitting the enter key again. Fox Trade. An online brokerage system that provides discount trading for individual investors who think they can outmaneuver the pros. The top document in the news section is a warning on Q3 earnings. Matt's brain starts churning. Vantage needs access to capital; Fox Trade is built on the concept of creating capital. He clicks the link to open the document, and starts reading. Two hours later, when he should be packing up for home, his eyes are glued to a spreadsheet model and his coffee stands, untouched and cold.

WEDNESDAY, JULY 25

Amanda is bored. So far, she has attended six interviews for executive director positions at local nonprofits. Attended, because the opportunities were so limited in scope that she could hardly be more than physically present for the conversations. Even so, two of the agencies had contacted her for follow-up interviews and one had offered her the job on the spot. In Amanda's careful estimation, that was a very bad sign. She had declined the job offer and put off the second interviews for another week so she could reassess her situation. Perhaps it was time to get out of nonprofit and take a fresh look at the commercial arena again. The Houston job market was in great shape, and she could probably find something interesting and financially rewarding in renewable energy or high tech, if she spent a little time exploring the fields.

She scans the online postings again and sees a basic repetition of the same type of jobs that have been listed since she and Matt arrived in late May. She had spent the first month in town searching for the perfect house and found one in The Heights. Not a Victorian-style, recently constructed knock-off, but an actual Victorian-era Arts and Crafts, complete with generous porches but absent of the gingerbread and filigree that mark the Queen Anne and Painted Ladies styles. She is extremely particular about her architectural periods. The second month had passed with Amanda painting and furnishing the house, right down to the switch plates and door knobs. She had spent immeasurable hours at Adkins in Mid-Town and had found the exact knobs to restore the few that had been replaced with the DIY special. That shiny brass had made her brain hurt when they toured the house. Matt had laughed at her, but she didn't care. Some things simply had to be done the right way. After the house was furnished and restored, she had turned her attention to the garden. The heirloom roses planted by the previous owner were a nice touch, but they had been left to grow wild across the back fence. Amanda had driven to Brenham to meet the experts and learn the proper way to care for her new babies. It was worth the trip. The elderly woman who lives behind them had been so delighted she invited Amanda for tea, and it had become a weekly engagement.

But now, three months into Matt's experiment at Vantage, Amanda is running out of projects and running out of patience. If she cannot find some way to stimulate her brain, she fears for her very sanity. And it simply will not do to seek her father's help, although it would take only one phone call, either to his own HR department or that of a colleague or rival. But Amanda does not want to join the Texas Tea Party — her sarcastic nickname for the oil business when she was an outspoken teenager. As ever, she wants to do this without anyone's help; that's how her father had raised her, after all. When he had been present. She refreshes the screen one more time, just in case she has missed something. And there it is. A new entry at the top of the list: Curator and Executive Director, Houston Commerce Museum. She opens the posting and reads the description, feeling her blood start to churn at last.

FRIDAY, JULY 27

John Wallace is bored. After twenty-two years at Vantage — eleven of those as CEO — he is finding it difficult to justify getting out of bed each day. And it has only gotten more difficult since he turned fifty last year. His life has not gone as planned; at least not as he had understood the plan. He had known since he was old enough to add a column of numbers that one day he would succeed his father as head of the largest insurance company in the southwestern United States. He had known that, with the job would come a big office, a fast car, a gracious home and a huge salary to support the only lifestyle he had ever led. And, as he had grown, he had come to understand that certain responsibilities would also come with the title; he got that part, too. But he had not counted on the tedium of it all, after so many years. Nor the daily worry that accompanied his every move; the staff that lurked in the shadows, waiting for him to take a false step or issue a statement they would have to manage or perhaps retract.

In the industry, he is regarded as a Goliath. His competitors are both envious of his company's success and grateful for his willingness to lead the way in even the minor innovations the field has allowed in the last few years. Their "you first" attitude is as flattering as it is frustrating; doesn't anyone else have the *cojones* to try something new? It wasn't as if the changes were earth-shattering. Most had to do with operational improvements, not new market entries. He longs for the pace of the nineties, when he had guided this turgid insurance company so swiftly through the acquisition waters, like the shark people had considered his doppelganger in the early days of his leadership. Not anymore; not with interest rates pounded down and stock prices through the roof for the unlikeliest of companies; companies that didn't even bring an actual product to market. Web services, search engines, outsourcing firms.

He stares out the window of his office, studying the bayou as it runs its course fifty stories below. Muddy and sluggish, just like his industry. *What we need*, he thinks, *is someone who just doesn't give a damn about protocol.* Someone who is young and brash enough, with just the right touch of greedy impulsiveness, to overstep some bounds and shake things up. Energy was doing it, even after the disaster that had rocked the industry six years ago. And the technology sector based its entire existence on that principle. *Why not us?* But he knows the answer; it's been the same for years. Too much risk is bad business, in his business. And policyholders think the company makes too much money off them as it is. He looks back at his computer monitor. Maybe it's time for him to retire.

The intercom on his phone beeps, followed by the voice of Melissa Kemper, his assistant. "Don't forget your lunch with Harry today, John."

"Right," he replies. Harry Lexington, chairman of the board of the Wallace Family Foundation. He is on fire about the new curator for the Commerce Museum and looking for someone to share his enthusiasm. John rises from his chair and leaves his office, waving briskly to Melissa on his way to the elevator bank. Maybe the museum opening will rouse him out of the lassitude that has taken hold over the last few months.

AUGUST 2007

WEDNESDAY, AUGUST 8

The Wallace Family Foundation office is a Post-World War II brick house in the Hyde Park section of Houston. Amanda pauses briefly before entering the building, almost wondering if she should ring the doorbell. It is her first meeting with Margaret Wallace since the final round of interviews for her new position. Amanda had left the interview certain that she would never hear from the foundation board again, but the board chair had called her that afternoon to extend the offer: Curator and executive director of the Commerce Museum of Houston.

"Your background is certainly notable," Margaret tells her when she takes a seat across from her at the massive Country French desk.

"Thank you."

"And you made a strong impression with our foundation board during your interviews."

Amanda nods once in thanks. Clearly, the opinion of her background and her performance is not shared by the foundation's executive director, sitting a few feet in front of her at this moment.

"So I'm certain you will do nicely at the museum," Margaret continues. "It's a new concept for the city, to have one so far outside the District. But the board was drawn to the location for some reason."

Amanda knows exactly what that reason is, but she does not say a word. "I'm honored to have been charged with its success," she says, once she has determined Margaret is finished politely airing her dismay with the board's choice.

"And of course you will meet with my husband to discuss the financials. That is an absolute requirement; that he has complete access to how the museum is spending his money."

"Of course. I'll contact his assistant to schedule a meeting."

"No need; she will contact you. Melissa is very thorough."

Amanda nods.

"I'm sure it goes without saying that his reputation in the community is riding on the success of this venture. People outside of

Houston think the city is an eye-sore." She pauses for a moment to let the force of her words settle before adding, "And much of it is. So this is our chance to show what a vital role we have played in the nation's commercial history."

"Absolutely," Amanda says with just the right level of tempered enthusiasm.

Margaret looks at her sharply. Apparently, she was not finished speaking. "How we learned our lesson from the crash of the '80s and diversified into technology. And, of course, the debacle with what happened on Smith Street."

Amanda merely nods again this time in response. She has never heard this euphemism for the headline-dominating crash of the once-massive energy company. It troubles her, this manner of limiting the event and its consequences to simple geography. As if it could never happen again.

"Before you meet with Mr. Wallace, I'll have to see your one-year plan. I'd like that by the end of next week."

"I have it with me today; I can leave a copy here for your review and comments."

Margaret draws a sharp breath. "Well," she says. "That would be fine. I'll review it and provide my comments by Friday."

FRIDAY, AUGUST 10

Balaji Anand is conflicted as he takes his seat at the afternoon staff meeting. The rest of his team is chattering happily about the Fed's recent injection into the capital market, seeing it as a stabilizing force in what is only a mildly uncertain financial period. But Anand thinks it is a sign of growing trouble, and so he is torn between his two obligations to Vantage. His first is to seize opportunities to make money for the company. His second is to mitigate the risk inherent in those opportunities.

He clears his throat softly and the chatter ceases. "I'm sure you've all seen the latest out of Washington."

Nods and murmurs of agreement around the table.

"What do you think, Carlo?" He turns to the young man at his left.

"It's a good sign," Carlo Capelli asserts. "The situation is similar to the aftermath of 9/11. Investors are nervous, the Fed opens up the markets a little bit; money starts flowing again. We stand pat."

Anand nods thoughtfully. "Thomas?"

Thomas Sessions shakes his head. "I don't know. All these subprime lenders going belly-up; it's hard to say where it will end. I mean, as economic Darwinism, it's a good thing. But I don't like seeing the government too involved in the economy."

More nods and sounds of concurrence.

"Do you think they're really going to bail out the homeowners?" This from Meg, a summer intern and the daughter of Vantage CFO Larry Foote. "And is it good or bad if they do?"

"I think it will happen," Anand says, his voice tired. "And then the gates are open. Like Thomas said, who knows where it will end?"

Carlo leans forward, earnest. "But our portfolio is still good. We're diversified."

The room is quiet. They all know this meeting is a formality; it will be up to Anand in the end. He surveys the faces at the table, gauging how committed each person really is to the words he or she has spoken. He finds concern but confidence at each turn. They are looking to him to make them feel better about the future. But Carlo is only half-right about the diversity of their portfolio. Literally half, in fact. A full fifty percent of their assets are tied up in derivatives; the rest is indexed. Anand is not certain that is enough. He knows that he can cover some losses with shorts in the near term. On balance, they should come out okay, as long as the situation doesn't get any worse overall.

"Okay," he says reluctantly, as if they have twisted the word out of him with a hot poker. "We'll hang in a little longer."

FRIDAY, AUGUST 17

"I think the time is right," Matt says, walking confidently into Frank Riley's office.

Frank puts down the report he was perusing. "For Fox Trade?"

Matt nods eagerly. "They're teetering on the brink. But we need to pull the trigger soon — this weekend, if we can. We could announce it on Monday before the market opens."

Frank studies the young man carefully, looking for the telltale signs of excess enthusiasm that accompany bad deal-making. Matt's stance is relaxed, his eyes steady. His arms hang loosely at his sides, feet still. Amanda has coached him endlessly on this. *Don't overstate your interest, no matter how excited you are. People will write you off immediately if they think you can't control your emotions.* But if he can pull this off, it will make his career at Vantage. Amanda can get the museum going and then hand it over to someone else; they can start a family. And he will be able to give his family what they need *and* want, not merely what he can manage. He feels himself slipping into a trance about the future and forces himself to remain in the moment.

"Well, Matt," Frank says slowly, opening his calendar. "What are you doing this weekend?"

"Nothing," Matt replies evenly. "Not a damned thing."

"Wrong," Frank corrects him. "You're buying Fox Trade. I'll have Stephanie rally the troops and order dinner."

# # #

Frank's M&A team assembles in his private conference room. "We're moving quickly on this one, for a change," he tells them. "Matt is running point; he's been watching Fox Trade for the last few months as they've tried to dig themselves out of the hole created by the mortgage mess."

Knowing glances are exchanged around the table. Since January, half a dozen subprime lenders had filed for Chapter 11, leaving their creditors holding a big bag of worthless paper. Fox Trade, like so many upstart, Web-based companies, was backed almost entirely by one these creditors and had been hemorrhaging cash ever since, going deeper into debt as company leaders managed to convince lender after lender that they were victims of a temporary "market correction." It was a miracle this conversation hadn't taken place sometime in June or July.

Stephanie Ames, Frank's assistant, enters the room, pushing a cart filled with barbecued ribs, brisket and chicken, along with potato salad, cole slaw and beans. Nobody moves to help her as she pops plastic lids off the side dishes and peels back foil covers from the entrees.

"Anything else?" She asks briskly, surveying the credenza to make sure they have plenty of bottled water and plastic cutlery.

"Might be a good idea to order some coffee, too, Steph," Frank replies, his voice cordial. "If you don't mind."

"Not a problem," she chirps. "Will you need me to stay tonight?"

Frank shakes his head. "No, but tomorrow is likely. Can you manage it?"

"Not a problem," she repeats, heading toward the kitchen to brew a fresh pot of coffee.

SATURDAY, AUGUST 18

"I'm thinking sixty-five cents on the dollar," Matt ventures.

Frank closes his eyes and thinks for a minute. He opens them and looks around the room. Rachael is asleep, hand against her cheek, sneakers tucked underneath the sofa on which she is curled. Phil is asleep with his head on the conference table, the side of his face spread against an open folder of Fox Trade financial data. He hasn't seen Thomas or Pete in hours but thinks they are passed out under their desks. He and Matt have been awake for at least 36 straight hours.

"How much does that leave for negotiating?"

"About a nickel or so. Low enough to whet their appetite for more, but high enough to discourage other suitors and keep the state government and shareholders off our backs."

"Seems reasonable." Stephanie breezes into the conference room with fresh coffee. "And you've run the regulatory traps?"

"I put Rachael on that. She feels good," Matt answers. "At least, she did twenty minutes ago, before she fell asleep."

Frank sighs. "Okay," he says. "Let's make the call."

"To Fox Trade?"

Frank laughs. "To JW," he says. "He kind of likes to know when we're planning to drop a couple of billion dollars."

Matt shakes his head, as if he had been asleep, too. "Oh, yeah. Man, I must be even more tired than I thought!"

MONDAY, AUGUST 20

"He's ready for you now, Amanda."

Amanda stands and smoothes the front of her skirt. She is still piqued by the need for her visit with John Wallace. She has work to do; what possible interest could the CEO of a company the size of Vantage have in her plans for the museum? His sponsorship could be no more than a tax shelter, after all. She is treating the visit as a necessary formality — get in, get his blessing, get out — so he will feel good about the pile of money his company had donated to the effort. But Matt's pestering that morning had nearly put her over the edge. What was she planning to wear? Wasn't the blue shirt back from the cleaners? It was just so perfect with her eyes and hair. She had threatened to cancel until he relented and left for work.

"Thank you," she says, belatedly, realizing she has not moved since standing.

"Are you nervous?"

"A little," Amanda replies, although she is not; but this is what Melissa wants to hear. She is frustrated to be spending time away from work in order to placate a man she expects to be the perfect mate for Margaret Wallace — over-involved and under-appreciative.

"Don't be," Melissa urges. "He's been looking forward to this all day."

"He has?" Her surprise is genuine.

Melissa laughs. "Oh, yes. He loves local history. It's his hobby."

With that, Amanda is ushered into John Wallace's office and finds him seated — not at his desk, but in a leather armchair — fiddling with his Blackberry.

Melissa clears her throat. "Amanda Parsons is here, John."

"Oh!" He presses a button and sets the phone on an accent table, standing to greet her. "Forgive me; I was texting with my son."

Amanda smiles at this. "Not at all," she insists. "Do you need a minute?"

"No, I'm finished." Hand extended as he faces her.

She takes the hand and shakes it firmly, one pump, and then releases. He is not what she expected, even though she has seen his photo inside the cover of the Vantage employee magazine that is mailed to Matt at the house. Tall and lean, a shock of dark hair offset by brilliant green eyes. The photo does not do justice to his eyes, she notes. And his face is angular and youthful, much livelier than the serious pose suggests.

"Thank you for meeting with me, Mr. Wallace," she begins. "I know your schedule is tight."

"It's my pleasure," he responds, sweeping his open hand toward the chair next to his. "I've cleared my afternoon. Will you sit? And please call me John."

Cleared his afternoon? For this? She sits, cautiously, on the edge of the chair.

"We've made a tremendous amount of progress on completing the opening day exhibit." She opens her portfolio and withdraws a printed spreadsheet. "I brought our most recent financials, so you can see where your contribution is going."

He takes the sheet but does not look at it. "I'm sure it's all fine," he says. "I'll look at it later. I thought —" he hesitates.

"Yes?"

"I thought maybe you would show me some of the actual pieces — or at least photos…layouts…?"

"Well," she says slowly. "I have a floor design, and a few photos. Nothing like what you'd see in person, but it should give a flavor."

He is looking at her intently. "Can I see it in person?" Leaning forward in his seat, elbows on his knees. "That's what I'd really like to do."

"What? Now?"

Now his hands drop to his knees and he pushes himself up from the chair. "Yes, why not?"

Why not? Other than the fact that there is nothing to see, no reason.

"It's still very much a work in progress. Most of the pieces are still off-site. You'll have to envision quite a bit."

He is standing in front of her. "I've been credited with a fair share of vision, in the past." His voice is ironic, and Amanda remembers the view from the office in which she is sitting.

"I suppose you have," she concedes, standing along with him.

"So let's go."

He follows her to the door and then opens it for her.

"Going out for a bit, Melissa," he calls over his shoulder. "I'll be at the museum if anyone needs to know."

In the lobby, John taps the button to call the elevator, humming contentedly as they wait. Amanda cannot imagine a more awkward situation. So much for get in, get his blessing, get out. She clears her throat; it sounds like thunder in the empty space. He looks at her, amusement plain in his face.

"How old is your son?"

"I have three, actually. Twenty-five, eighteen and fourteen."

"You have a twenty-five-year-old son?"

He smiles. "Well, thank you."

Amanda takes a deep breath to prevent her face from flushing. The compliment was intentional on her part, but the undercurrent in his response was unexpected. "Which one were you texting?"

"Oh, that was my eighteen-year-old, Rob." The elevator arrives, empty.

"He's a freshman in college?" Amanda steps into the car.

"Senior in high school; he's actually not quite eighteen yet." He frowns a bit. "September birthday. Messes up everything for school, but more so for girls, I think. With boys, they just get an extra year to grow; good for sports, anyway."

The doors close.

"Do you have kids?"

"Not yet," she says. "Someday." She finds his stream-of-consciousness style of communicating unusual for a man of his position, but she likes it. It gives him a quality of authenticity.

"How old are you?" The elevator stops. Two people join them.

"Thirty-two." Doors close again.

"Plenty of time."

Amanda nods.

"Melissa tells me your husband works here?"

"Yes. Matt Parsons." She offers no more than this, not knowing who has joined them. And, the door has opened again. Three more people step into the car.

"Matt Parsons," he repeats. "I'll have to look him up."

Amanda is silently frustrated. This makes five people now who have heard John Wallace mention her husband's name on the elevator; the major artery of corporate gossip.

At last they reach the ground floor and step out of the car. John walks quickly to the revolving doors and steps into a section. He pushes backward against the partition and moves just enough to open the wedge in front for Amanda. Once she enters, he propels them both through the shaft.

"I didn't know it was possible to hold open a revolving door for someone," she observes when they both emerge on the other side.

"That's why they gave me the big desk." His grin strips the words of conceit.

Amanda smiles; she had not expected him to be funny. "So now I know."

They walk wordlessly, silenced by the heavy traffic and construction noises. John spies a company Town Car parked at the curb and hails it. "Washington Avenue, someplace near Heights. You don't mind if we walk a bit, do you?"

"Not at all," she says again. "This is handy." Nodding at the car.

"Yeah, handy." His voice is sardonic, as if he uses the service to fulfill someone else's need.

The ride is silent; John has fished his Blackberry from the clip at his side and become engrossed in another round of text messaging with his son.

"College visits," he mutters, by way of explanation.

Amanda nods and turns her attention to the activity outside the car. The driver lets them off at a convenient corner and John sends him to wait at a coffee shop down the street, placing his order for a large coffee of the day and asking him to return at four o'clock.

"Here we are," he announces, when they stop in front of the museum. Pride is evident in his tone. "It's perfect, isn't it?"

"Yes," Amanda agrees. "It is."

She would have agreed even if decorum did not require it. The Commerce Museum is housed in a former bank, erected in 1925. One of the few historic buildings near downtown that has not been razed to accommodate lofts or a Starbucks — or a new bank.

"Have you been inside yet?"

He shakes his head. "I was waiting for you — well, for the curator," he qualifies. "I wanted a thorough tour at my first visit."

No pressure, she thinks.

"Did you know that Bonnie and Clyde robbed this bank?"

Amanda touches a spot on the corner of the building. "Bullet hole, right here."

A guilty smile from John. "I guess you would know, wouldn't you."

"Well, I *should*, anyway."

Inside, the old bank is a mess. Amanda cringes inwardly when she sees it with fresh eyes, but she steps confidently into the array of sawhorses, plywood and two-by-fours.

"This will be the reception desk," she says, waving her arm at a centrally located pile of lumber, much of which is still covered in plastic. "Although the exhibits will begin just inside the door." She points behind them to several more bundles of wood.

"And," she continues, removing another set of papers from her portfolio, "we've selected lighting and other interior fixtures consistent with the period of the building, rather than going neutral. So, the installations will change, but the building will be true to its own heritage."

"Good call," he comments. "How about your office space? Did you get the delivery from Vantage?"

"I did," she says, smiling. "Thank you for that. I'll be very comfortable." She leads him to the rear of the building. "Just through here, and big enough for me and a couple of volunteers, as we need them."

Her office is appointed in the same décor as the conference rooms on Vantage's executive floor. "I feel a little guilty, honestly," she continues. "A nonprofit really shouldn't have things this nice."

John shakes his head. "We were remodeling an old conference room, updating it for new A/V equipment or something. I was told we couldn't use this stuff anymore." A smile. "So why not put it to good use someplace else?"

He walks to the small conference table and takes a seat. "Let's see some items for opening day. Are you ready to share your plans for permanent installations?"

Amanda pauses at her desk to gather additional materials and sketches, and then joins him at the table, her mind racing. She has never seen a corporate donor so involved in the details, but she believes it is genuine interest, rather than a need to control.

"You have about an hour left?" she asks, as she takes a seat across from him. He might have cleared his afternoon, but she was certain he worked well into the evening.

"About," he confirms. "How much can you show me?"

She takes a thoughtful breath. "How about the opening, for starters, and then maybe the first year. If we still have time, we can talk about permanent installations, although I'll cover some of that in our first year plans."

"Okay. Go."

"We launch on October 18, as you know, and that corresponds nicely with the beginning of the NBA season." A quick look to gauge his reaction. "And sports are big business. I'm working on a commitment from the media relations team at the Rockets to have a starter on hand at the opening."

"I like it. Who are you trying to get?"

"Jones."

John smiles. Not the most popular of the starting five, but a local boy. "Good call."

Amanda narrows her eyes in appraisal. He gets it. She is relieved. "I think we'll get him, too; he doesn't garner a lot of requests for appearances."

A nod at this. "Even better. I like your thinking on this."

"I've made arrangements already for some artifacts from the team — as well as the other major clubs in town. Some items will be on loan, and others will become part of our permanent installation on sports and commerce. I should make it clear that we don't intend to turn this into a sports memorabilia display, though. The focus will be economic impact. So artifacts will include ticket stubs from significant years, stadium seating diagrams, gate receipts — even concessions and ancillary staff." She pauses. "It's all information that exists in the public domain, but it has never been presented collectively. I think visitors will be surprised when they see the dollar amounts and realize how many people are employed by the franchises — and then how those employees fit into the consumer market in Houston."

John is watching her face as she speaks. Her expression is earnest but serious and she looks him in the eye; not at the ceiling, not at the walls around them. Her hands lie still on the table in front of her. She believes completely in what she is saying and has no need for dramatics to communicate her enthusiasm. The foundation board was right; she has both the vision and the sense to make it all happen. And, he understands this is exactly why Margaret doesn't like her. Margaret has never been able to join vision to sense; the result is an authoritarian yet disorderly approach to everything in her life, including him.

He clears his throat and his mind. "You have a contact at the Sports Authority?"

"I do, although it might be helpful to have someone at Vantage to make a few more introductions."

"Of course," John nods emphatically. "I'm sorry you don't have that already. Get in touch with Dave Galvan, my head of Public Affairs.

He'll pass you off to Grace Kim, but she'll take good care of you. She knows everyone in Houston."

"Thanks. I'll get his number from Melissa."

He gives her a bemused look. "I have it." The Blackberry makes its third appearance and he scrolls through the contacts. "Here, I'll send it to you. What's your number?" She gives it to him and hears the answering buzz from her cell a few minutes later.

"Done. What's next?" He speaks rapidly but not tersely, and Amanda finds herself warming to this man her husband has described as a shark. Maybe in the Vantage Tower, but certainly not here, in her little museum office. She likes him. Amanda doesn't like many people; and never at the first meeting.

"We're going to rotate feature installations on a monthly basis. This will keep us fresh and draw some repeat visitors."

He is nodding again. "And your plan is to retain key pieces of those exhibits in the permanent installations that they fit?"

"Exactly," she agrees. "We'll begin each area with a small set of pieces and then add to those pieces as we grow."

"So your first year will be exciting," he notes. "What do plan for an encore in year two?"

She smiles. "The low points of commerce in Houston."

"Oh." He says the word slowly, extending it until it vanishes into silence. He eyes her with new appreciation. "Very good. How far back will you go?"

"I was thinking of starting at 1900, when Houston took the financial spotlight away from Galveston, after the hurricane. I thought one-hundred years would give us plenty of fodder for a few boom-and-bust cycles. And then our third year we might back-track to the 1800s and spend some time there."

"Good." He looks at the stack of papers in front of her. "Can I see the sketches?"

"Of course." She moves to slide them across the surface of the table but he stops her.

"No, no. I'll move." He slides into the chair at her left and studies the first sheet. "Nice."

They pore over the sketches together, looking up every so often so Amanda can help him locate the section of the building represented in the designer's airy strokes. Through it all, he nods and makes comments, until at last, his eyes shift subtly to his watch and he sighs. Four o'clock.

"The big desk calls," he says, standing and offering his hand. "I can't tell you how much I've enjoyed this preview. You've done a great job, and I can't wait to see it in person."

"Thank you, John. I appreciate your time. It was...unexpected and very pleasant." She stands with him, stacking the papers they have scattered across the table.

As he passes through the office door, he turns and asks, "Has my wife been in your hair much?"

Amanda smiles. "Her input is so valuable," she says. "I wouldn't have been able to do any of this without her."

He laughs out loud, actually halting in his steps to enjoy the moment. "You're good," he tells her, the corners of his eyes crinkling with joy. "You're going to be very successful here, I think."

And with that, he leaves her. Amanda takes several deep breaths and steadies herself against the edge of the conference table as the air settles back into place after his departure.

# # #

"So, how was it?"

Amanda has rehearsed the answer to this question all afternoon, beginning the moment John Wallace had left the museum, and ending the moment Matt had asked it.

"It was fine," she says.

"Did you give him the report?" Matt had spent a lot of time making it just right the night before, although Amanda could easily have done it herself.

"I did," she replies. He is looking at her expectantly. "He didn't have time to review it just then, though."

"Oh." He is deflated. "Of course not. You didn't get much time, then?"

"Well, actually, he spent about an hour with me. Maybe a little more. We went to the museum."

Matt puts down his chopsticks. "John Wallace, the CEO of Vantage Property, Life and Casualty, went to the unopened Commerce Museum in the middle of the day and then spent an hour with you there?"

She nods.

A grin spreads slowly across Matt's face. "That's fantastic, Amanda! Freaking fantastic!"

"You don't think it's odd?"

"Odd?" Matt snorts. "Hell, yes, it's odd. But who cares? You had uninterrupted access to one of the busiest men in the free world — when Washington needs financial advice, this is who they call. What did you talk about?"

Amanda looks at him blankly. "The history of commerce in Houston and how we intend to bring that to life at the new Commerce Museum?"

"Shut *up*." His eyes are wide.

"And his kids, a little bit. And…"

"And?"

"You."

"You mentioned my name to John Wallace."

"He said he would have to look you up."

Matt rises from his chair.

"Where are you going?"

"Bed," he says simply. "I have to go to bed. I can't take anymore."

She thinks he may actually be glowing. He spins around.

"Come with me," he says.

"But…" She looks around the table.

"I'll take care of it in the morning. Come on." He starts to dance. "Come on, shorty."

Now Amanda smiles. He is impossible to resist when he gets his groove on, as silly as it looks. She stands up and moves to follow him.

"Let's go make a baby, baby."

Amanda stops, cold. Her smile fades. "Matt."

"What?" He honestly seems to have no clue.

"I can't get pregnant *now*," she seethes. "I'm just getting started at the museum. And you're never home before eight o'clock. Nice environment for a baby."

His shoulders slump. "I'm sorry. I wasn't thinking."

Her face is like ice. "Thanks for pointing that out." She walks swiftly by him and climbs the stairs, feet heavy on the wooden treads.

"Mandy?" He stands, helpless, at the bottom of the steps. "I'm sorry," he calls after her, but she is gone. He walks back to the table and clears away the take-out boxes, mentally cursing himself as he works.

SEPTEMBER 2007

MONDAY, SEPTEMBER 3

Vantage PLC Announces Acquisition of Fox Trade
Deal to open new investment and growth opportunities.

HOUSTON, Sept. 3, 2007 – Vantage Property, Life and Casualty (NSE: VPLC) today announced it has reached an agreement to acquire ailing online trader Fox Trade for a purchase price of $12 billion.

President and CEO John Wallace cited the move as confirmation of the firm's aggressive new growth strategy. "This move adds a sharp new tool to our set and will provide the flexibility we are seeking to further broaden our earnings and return to investors," he said. "The rise in both companies' stock proves the market is energized about the possibilities this creates."

Vantage shares rose $.15 on the announcement. Fox Trade shares rose $.11.

Vantage PLC is a North American leader in insurance and financial services, operating across the United States, as well as in Canada and Mexico. Vantage services commercial, institutional and individual customers via widespread property-casualty and life insurance networks. Vantage is listed on the National Stock Exchange, with the ticker symbol VPLC.

_{This press release contains forward-looking statements concerning future economic performance and events. It is possible that Vantage PLC's actual results and financial condition may differ from the anticipated results and financial condition indicated in these projections and statements. Vantage PLC is not under any obligation to update or alter its projections and other statements as a result of new information or future events.}

WEDNESDAY, SEPTEMBER 5

Matt chews at his lower lip as he keys in the new numbers, pausing in mid-stroke to look back at the worksheet on his desk and make sure the figures match. It's a big increase in his contribution, but he feels good about it. Amanda will be worried, he knows. But people who come from old money just can't comprehend what it's like to see an opportunity for a quick win and pass it up. He supposes it isn't a good sign that the two of them have such different ideas about investing, even if their goals are essentially the same. But in his mind, he is simply balancing out her conservative nature.

As he clicks the *submit* button, Amanda appears in the doorway.

Figures, Matt thinks.

"Hey, babe. What are you working on?" She has entered the room with the day's mail.

Matt tries to keep his voice casual. "401(k) contribution."

Amanda shuffles through the stack, dropping coupons and flyers into the recycle bin. "Making a change?"

"Yeah, I'm rolling more of it into Vantage stock." Good; she's distracted.

She looks up sharply. "Are you sure that's wise?"

"Well, sure. I've been studying the last few years of growth. The stock is still climbing. You always invest on the way up, right?" A pause. "And we're young enough to take on a little more risk."

"That's true." She lowers her eyes to the mail once again. "But diversification is still important. Remember what happened." She catches herself before she completes the sentence, surprised at how easily it almost came through her lips.

"That was different," Matt insists. "That was because all the leaders were crooks."

Amanda looks at him again, her expression frank and a little condescending. "You don't really believe that, do you?"

"Of course I do. I read all the articles."

"Yes, no bias there." She laughs.

"I know, you think it's all a big conspiracy, perpetrated by the media and the Justice Department."

"And you think it's one perpetrated by the company's leadership." Her voice pedantic now; something Matt hates. "We both have our conspiracy theories. With one important difference."

"What's that?"

"Mine's right."

He grins at her. Such a know-it-all. "Well, here's how I see it. I'm directly responsible for yesterday's stock bump. As long as I keep doing what I do, I control my own fate. Is that enough personal accountability for you?"

There is a certain, crazy logic to this argument, but Amanda still doesn't like the move — or his arrogance, for that matter. She will take another look at her own portfolio with her father's adviser. See if she can spread it out a little bit more to compensate for Matt's cowboy approach. Her father had built a tidy sum following the simple principles of dollar-cost-averaging. It was old-fashioned but effective.

"I guess it'll have to do," she concedes.

MONDAY, SEPTEMBER 10

Amanda taps the sensors on her abdomen compulsively and then sets the chronometer on her watch. She takes off from the edge of her driveway at an easy pace, running in time to the first and slowest song on her *Thirty Easy* playlist. Thirty minutes; it doesn't matter how far, just enough to stretch her legs after the fifteen miles she had run in Saturday's group training session. She is still seething over Matt's behavior the previous day; she needs a steady thirty-minute run to work out some aggression. It was supposed to have been a casual, Sunday-afternoon barbecue with some colleagues, but he had slipped back into graduate-school mode, where he had used her as his personal hand-stamp to the forbidden kingdom every weekend. Whether it was a cocktail party at the dean's house, a clam-bake with the cool kids or an invitation to a networking breakfast, he had offered her up like a post-embargo *cohiba* to the ranking male in attendance.

She always thought he would outgrow it when he graduated; or maybe when he landed his first job. But school is three years behind him now, and he is on his second corporate gig since earning his MBA. And yet there he stood in Frank Riley's meticulously landscaped back yard, arm draped around her as he sang her praises — all the while making it clear that he must be a serious player if she — *she* — had chosen him. She likened it to the old gag with the one-hundred dollar bill connected to a fishing line, then placed on a sidewalk to lure some patsy into reaching for it. When someone bit, the line was tugged and the money moved just out of reach. Of course nobody had ever been foolish enough to make a play for her, and she sometimes wondered what Matt would do if it ever happened. Or whether he would even notice at all. Someone is bound to call his bluff, some day. And if he doesn't grow up soon, it might be Amanda, herself.

She stops to allow a car to pass through a four-way stop, glancing at her heart-rate on the display. She is going too fast. It's time to turn back; she has defeated the purpose of the run. She'll grab a shower and then head to the museum. It has quickly become her safe haven.

Matt never visits; he couldn't care less how she spends her days or what impact it has on their life. She knows he is just biding his time until he can push her to have a baby and complete the picture he has painted in his mind.

He hadn't been like this when they met; at least she hadn't thought so. He was shy, charming, self-effacing. And beautiful. Dark hair and smoky blue eyes on top of a frame that was right out of a men's cologne advertisement. And smart; the top of his section, always the team leader. It doesn't fit with the person he has become: uncertain and needy. She trots up her driveway as the sky begins to lighten. He'll get it sorted out, she knows. It's the new job. The new city. Even though she regards Houston as a bottom-feeder, she supposes it could be intimidating to someone who is trying to carve out a niche for himself.

"Matt?" Her voice echoes off the wood floors. *More rugs*, she thinks. *And maybe some drapes.* She'll run by Pottery Barn this weekend, if she gets a chance.

"Matt?" Still no answer. He probably went to the gym before work.

She passes through the kitchen for a glass of water and stops short at the breakfast table. A plate of fruit, some granola and a rose from the garden greet her. A note rests under the rose.

Oh, Matt. What did you do?

Amanda slides the note out and flips it open.

Sorry I'm such an ass. You deserve better. At least the granola and fruit are sweet. And the rose, but don't eat that — it only smells sweet. Like you. P.S. Yogurt in the fridge. I didn't know when you'd be back.

She shakes her head and smiles. And so he lives another day.

WEDNESDAY, SEPTEMBER 19

Anand's concern is growing. He doesn't like the Fox Trade deal at all, and he has told anyone who will listen. Frank Riley, head of M&A; Larry Foote, the CFO. He had even considered making a call to Steve McAllister, chief operations officer, but he had stopped himself. He has a family to feed, too, after all. But he seems to be the only person at the company who is paying attention to the Fed right now. And he can connect the dots, even if nobody else can — or wants to connect them. When people default on their mortgages, the lenders can't stay in business. When the lenders can't stay in business, they default on their loans. The whole thing sets up a domino effect, with the lenders' creditors next in line for collapse. And at some point, Vantage will be a domino in the series. It's just a matter of when they will topple.

The overt response from both Larry and Frank had been simple: *Eyes on the prize.* He knows what this means; he has to find a way to manage it without letting anyone know he is managing it. He has found some companies that he can sell short with the portfolio his team had set up to decrease the cycle for ROI. Already at the very peak of the company's overall risk profile, he could push it a little farther without upsetting much. Of course, that also meant he wouldn't be impacting much, either. He needed something else, something outside Vantage but still close enough to redistribute the funds on the sly.

He pinches the bridge of his nose; his sinuses are killing him. Allergy season never seems to end in this city. He sighs and moves the mouse to clear the screen saver from his monitor. A message catches his eye.

The Commerce Museum IS *History*

The new Commerce Museum will open next month. Largely funded by John Wallace's own family foundation and Vantage itself, it seems little more than a tax-free coffee can for Wallace's annual, million-dollar bonus and a vehicle for him to stroke his own ego. He smiles as he opens the e-mail. *What a stupid tagline.* He could not care less about the museum and its promise to "celebrate the role Houston has played in the commercial history of both Texas and the nation." But Anand could certainly use a coffee can at the moment. And he knows exactly how to game the system and get his hands on the foundation's portfolio without anyone noticing. That skill set is what had gotten him hired, after all.

FRIDAY, SEPTEMBER 28

Vantage PLC Reports First Quarter FY2008 Results
Leadership Credits Solid Investment Management

HOUSTON, Sept. 28, 2007 — Vantage Property, Life and Casualty (NSE: VPLC) today reported adjusted earnings of $1.15 per share for the first quarter of FY2008, compared to $.95 adjusted earnings per share (EPS) earned in the same period last year. Adjusted earnings exclude the impact of special items. On a Generally Accepted Accounting Principles (GAAP) basis, the company reported a net gain of $1.72 per share in the second quarter of its fiscal year 2008, compared to earnings of $1.05 per share in the same period last year.

President and CEO John Wallace commented on the firm's recent announcement to purchase failing online investment broker Fox Trade and how it impacted the stock price. "We're seeing a positive response to our acquisition strategy," said Wallace. "That, plus our increase in revenues in all sectors, has created a net effect that will allow us to continue our aggressive stance in the development of additional financial products, just as it will facilitate our entry into new markets."

Details regarding specific operational units are available on the company's Web site and will also be discussed in an analyst conference call on Wednesday, October 3, 2008 at 10 a.m. Central Standard Time.

Vantage PLC is a North American leader in insurance and financial services, operating across the United States, as well as in Canada and Mexico. Vantage services commercial, institutional and individual customers via widespread property-casualty and life insurance networks. Vantage is listed on the National Stock Exchange, with the ticker symbol VPLC.

This press release contains forward-looking statements concerning future economic performance and events. It is possible that Vantage PLC's actual results and financial condition may differ from the anticipated results and financial condition indicated in these projections and statements. Vantage PLC is not under any obligation to update or alter its projections and other statements as a result of new information or future events.

OCTOBER 2007

MONDAY, OCTOBER 1

Amanda's ash blond ponytail swings behind her as she runs along Allen Parkway in the mid-morning sun.

"Slow down, lady!" Grace is huffing behind her. "There is *no* way I can keep pace with you *and* talk about the museum calendar."

Amanda decreases her pace a bit. "Sorry," she says. "I get a little focused on my time."

Grace shakes her head. "Figures. Look at you."

Amanda rolls her eyes. "Look at *you*."

"Yeah, but I can't talk and run. I should have known you'd be one of those annoying types. Although, you've figured out how to deal with Margaret Wallace, so I can't be too harsh," Grace reasons.

"It's not difficult, Grace," Amanda asserts. "I'll let you in on it, but don't tell anyone else."

"Seriously?"

Amanda nods; Grace doesn't have the finesse skills necessary to pull it off, so there is no harm in telling her. "Here it is: Be extremely selective in the information you share with her. Listen silently to every comment. Do not react to anything. When she finishes speaking, agree with everything she said. Give her a project — nothing too big. And then, after she leaves," Amanda pauses and shrugs. "Do it all the way you know it should be done."

"And wait for her to bust your ass when she realizes you were just humoring her?"

"Oh, no." Amanda laughs. "She cares about results. She can convince herself that a good outcome was all about her input, no matter what the truth is."

"Damn," Grace breathes. "You're good. I wonder if that's how John deals with her."

"What do you think the Wallace Family Foundation is all about?" An ironic smile. "Charity?"

Grace laughs. "So it really does begin at home! Okay, duly noted. I will give it a try."

"Oh, mm-mm," Amanda chides. "You can't just try it. You have to commit. Sort of like running." She smiles.

"Yeah. All right. Let's talk about the museum. What's the latest?"

Amanda shifts gears smoothly. "We have commitments from all the major sports franchises in town to make appearances when their seasons begin."

"I'm still not getting the connection," Grace interjects. "Why do we want to remind people that sports are about money?"

"Because it's true, and when your city hosts the Super Bowl and the MLB All-Star game within five years of each other, your city makes a lot of money. And the investment in the infrastructure to host those events puts you at the top of the list for other, similar events. In a sports-crazy city like Houston, that pays dividends all over the place."

"Oh. Again, *damn.*" Grace looks at her suspiciously. "Maybe you should leave the nonprofit stuff to someone else and come work for Vantage."

Amanda laughs out loud. "No, thanks. Anyway," she continues. "We'll have our feature installation dedicated to the sport of the season for the next month and then we'll reduce the size and move select pieces into the permanent sports area. Basketball will be first, as of the opening, and we'll replace it in November with retail, featuring the Thanksgiving Day Parade — from the old Foley's through the Macy's acquisition. Retail will carry us through the holiday season. And in January, our feature installation will shift to the technology sector. The Rodeo is February; energy is March; we'll pick up sports again in April, when baseball season starts."

"What, no hockey?"

A wry look from Amanda before she continues. "So, as each feature moves to its permanent installation, we build up the collection for those sectors. At the end of our first year, we have a great basis to build for the future."

"And John was down with this?"

"Yes." Amanda smiles. "He was down with it and into it. It was nice."

"I see." Amanda detects a curious lilt to Grace's voice but says nothing. "Back at Vantage," Grace says as they pass under I-45 and cut through Sam Houston Park. "Coming inside to shower and change? I got a guest pass for you."

"I think I will," Amanda accepts. "It will save me some time if I don't have to go back home before the museum."

Once inside the building, the two women come face-to-face with John Wallace, leaving for a lunch meeting.

"Hello, Amanda; Grace," he says, looking from one to the other. "Just back from a run?"

"Yes, it's a perfect day to be outside," Amanda replies.

"And you were in perfect company. Grace holds the women's record for our annual Turkey Trot."

Grace is shaking her head and grimacing. "Not anymore, John. Amanda blew my doors off — and talked the whole way. I think I hate her."

John laughs. "Well, then. You'll have to join us this year. A little competition is healthy for everyone."

"If the museum schedule permits," Amanda says, wisely.

He studies her face for a moment. "You have gray eyes," he says finally. "I didn't notice that when we met. They're quite unique."

"I'll tell my mother you noticed; they're some of her finest work."

Another laugh. "You have an answer prepared for everything, don't you?"

Amanda shrugs amiably. "All in a day's work."

Grace is tugging her sleeve. "The gym is this way, Amanda. See you later, John."

MONDAY, OCTOBER 8

"Welcome to the lab, Parsons."

"Yeah, thanks," Matt replies, taking a seat at the conference table. "Good to be here." The uncertainty in his voice elicits a smile from Anand.

"You have no idea what we do, do you?"

"Well," Matt says frankly. "Nobody does."

Now Anand laughs out loud. "Good point. And it's not exactly like we conduct interviews. But you must have impressed the hell out of John Wallace for him to move you over here after only four months. New record."

Matt shifts uneasily in his seat. "I guess so."

"All right." Anand sits back in his chair. "It's not really a big mystery what goes on here. The low profile is mostly to keep our team small. We don't need to field a bunch of queries from employees who are looking to make a quick rise in the organization. We get new members from direct referral only."

"And how many of those referrals have come from Wallace?"

Anand looks at him pointedly. "So far, only two."

"Who's the other one?" Matt looks around the room.

"Me," Anand says, his voice suddenly serious. Then he smiles. "Here's how it works. We have the folks who make the money — the revenue stream. Then, we have the folks who invest the money for a reasonable return. And then, we have us."

"And what we do is…?"

"We invest the investments, of course."

"Come again?"

"A reasonable return is fine for a company with reasonable goals," Anand explains.

"Vantage doesn't have reasonable goals?"

"Nope. Wallace and the board aren't interested in small-time stuff. We've found some instruments in the last few years that have put the

S&P to shame. Good for our clients, and even better for us. You think it's reasonable to see so many Porsches in a parking garage?"

Matt shakes his head and smiles, his ears prickling with interest now. "Not really."

"Exactly," Anand concludes, as if German sports cars are the key to everything. "But you'll have one inside of three months, if you do a good job here. You just find a couple more companies like Fox Trade, and let us reel them in."

So that's the game; Matt finds the acquisition targets and Anand and his team find the capital. But why the secrecy? Matt shakes his head slightly. Who the hell cares, as long as he does his part, right?

# # #

Anand is very troubled by the new addition to his team, but he had not been given a vote. He had simply arrived at work last Wednesday and learned of the decision. Apparently, he was to consider it cutting-edge that the company would locate an M&A buzzard in the elite finance group. He was to feel flattered that company leadership had recognized the impact of his team on the rest of the business. For him, though, it is merely one more person to whom he must now lie on a regular basis.

He down shifts his road bike and signals a left-hand turn. A quick glance over his shoulder and he twists the handlebars to take him across the two-lane road that bisects Memorial Park. The traffic is light, now, post-rush hour. In a couple of weeks, the time change will prevent him from taking his late-evening rides.

In the clear again, Anand's mind returns to work and the burden that is Matt Parsons. The timing could not be worse. John Wallace decides to get acquisition-hungry again when leveraged capital is vanishing faster than the box of doughnuts from the coffee bar each morning. Just last week one of the largest and oldest firms on Wall Street had posted a loss and attributed it to the subprime crisis, but the message still is not sinking in across the country. Anand believes nobody understands the enormous volume of subprime debt that exists. Houston exists as a bubble inside the nation; the signs of wealth are staggering even as he pedals through the park and notes the hood ornaments on the cars that pass him. He corrects himself: the signs of over-extension are staggering.

He will have to find a way to keep Matt occupied without divulging too much information about how his team functions. Maybe the kid will come up with a few good acquisition targets soon and keep himself busy. The Fox Trade deal was pretty swift, even though Vantage can't actually afford it. But that means very little to someone like Matt, who is compensated on his ability to identify deals — not to close them.

FRIDAY, OCTOBER 12

"How are things at the museum? Will you be ready next week?"

Amanda interrupts her garlic-chopping to consider the question. Margaret Wallace had shown up with a huge chip on her shoulder that Monday and had not yielded in her criticism of Amanda's process during the four days that followed. It was nothing overt — the woman was a master of passive-aggressive behavior — but it was plain enough to Amanda, who had seen it all before. And, it didn't help that Amanda shrugged it off, remaining professional and polite, just as she had explained to Grace. She could be passive-aggressive with the best of them. And it was driving Margaret insane that she did not react to anything, instead pressing on toward the goal.

Like yesterday, when Margaret had asked to review John's script for the ribbon cutting ceremony.

"Have you retained a professional writer for the speech yet?"

"No, I've written some talking points already."

A sigh, gentle but clearly exasperated. "My husband has a fleet of speech writers. I'll just ask him to identify somebody."

"That would be a huge help. You'll know exactly what he wants to say."

Back in the present, however, Amanda smiles at Matt and starts chopping again. "It's going just fine," she says mildly. "How about you? Busy week?"

"Crazy," he says, sounding completely energized by it. "This is the first time I've been home before nine in days."

"I know. Hence the feast," Amanda replies. "I hope you're hungry."

"I am." He plants himself on a bar stool. "Can I help?"

She shakes her head. "Nope. Tell me about your week. You're on a new project?"

"Yeah." He is excited again. He didn't really want to help her anyway, but he would have if she had asked. "It's huge. Potentially career-making. And I owe it all to you, my dear."

She stops chopping again. "How's that?"

"Apparently, John Wallace requested me personally."

"Don't be silly, Matt." Knife moves again but slowly. "You earned it all by yourself. You've done great things in the last few months, and you're being recognized for it. Vantage is a meritocracy."

Matt smiles crookedly at her. "You've been paying attention at the happy hours."

"I'm always paying attention, Matt." She scoops the chopped garlic up on a wide metal spatula and scrapes it into the melted butter. "Would you bring me the shrimp, please?"

He slides off the stool. "Of course. You know I love being your *sous chef*." Halfway to the counter, he stops. "Oh! I forgot. Hold on." Matt disappears into the foyer.

Amanda scowls after him and gets the shrimp herself. By the time he returns, they are ready to be flipped.

"My first paycheck since the big move." He opens it with a flourish and holds it in front of her.

"A raise, too. Very nice," she comments. Then she smiles. "And look, you're at the holding company now."

"Hm?" Matt pulls the stub away and peers at it. "Vantage Financial Services. I didn't notice that."

Amanda is not surprised. Hardly anyone she has ever met actually reads pay stubs. "It's good," she says. "You're part of the central nervous system now. Before you were in the peripheral."

Matt laughs and rolls his eyes. Amanda and her analogies. "So what's the sales force, then?"

"Autonomic," she concludes, eyes dancing. "The knee-jerk brigade."

"Well, the jerk part anyway, right?" Matt breathes deeply. "Smells great. I love your garlic shrimp, baby."

Especially when you don't have to help, she adds silently. She moves to the cabinet and gets out serving bowls for the shrimp, rice and edamame. Matt carries the edamame to the table and they sit.

"So, I'm going to New York on Sunday night." He takes a bit of the shrimp and closes his eyes, happy.

"Yeah?"

"Yeah. Due diligence on Fox Trade. Frank Riley is coming with."

"That's great." A slight frown. "Frank?"

"I'm still dotted-line to him, apparently."

"I guess that makes sense," Amanda says, pondering it even as she speaks. More sense than reporting to Anand, anyway. She had found Matt's move to the new group very peculiar. Why couldn't he do M&A research in his old department? Didn't it make more sense to keep it all together and gain some efficiencies?

"Yeah, it's good. I get to keep a foot in both worlds. Makes me more marketable to each side."

Amanda nods. It's a good point, but the nagging sense of doubt still tickles at the base of her brain. "Well, have fun in the big city."

"I'm all about work, baby. You know that."

TUESDAY, OCTOBER 16

Matt has never been so hung over in his entire life. He has no recollection of returning to his room at the Parker Meridian last night; in fact he has little recollection of the last eighteen hours at all. Once the formal meeting with Fox Trade's due diligence team had concluded on Monday evening, the entire group had gone to dinner at McCormick & Schmick's, and then ended up at some bar in the meatpacking district; Matt cannot remember the name. And after that, he has no idea. He does remember waking up at seven that morning and barely making it to the toilet before the entire contents of his stomach forced their way through his mouth and nose. The next five hours had passed in a haze of pain, nausea and delirium. He can't even be sure how he had managed to pack his things and meet Frank at the taxi circle downstairs.

He sits, now, hunched over in the back of the cab, head spinning with every lane change. Frank is staring out the window next to him; he is almost as bad off.

"I feel like shit," Matt says, for the third time since they left the hotel.

"Yeah." Frank is quiet for a minute and then laughs. "But you were funny last night, man."

Matt shakes his head and instantly regrets it. "I don't remember any of it. Where did we go after the bar?"

"Seriously? You don't remember?" Frank looks at him skeptically. "Tell me you remember some of it."

"Uh-uh. Where did we go?"

Frank digs into his pocket and retrieves a matchbook. He flips it onto Matt's lap.

Matt reads the label. "*Shit.*" A strip club. Amanda is going to kick his ass. "Amanda is going to kick my ass."

"Only if you tell her. Besides," Frank reasons. "Company business."

Matt squeezes his eyes shut. Images from the club weave in his mind. "Did we at least get what we came for?"

The purpose of the trip had been to sit down with Fox Trade and hammer out the details of the acquisition: number of employees in various departments, key transition team members, timelines and deliverables, communication strategies. Matt thinks they had covered it all in the conference room yesterday afternoon, but he cannot remember a single point of the discussion.

"Well, yeah." Frank's tone is sour. "Of course we did. It's all in your notes. You took notes."

"Oh. Yeah. I took notes." Matt does remember the notes. His eyes feel like they are on fire; he thinks his capillaries are actually sweating.

"You impressed the hell out of them, in fact," Frank adds. "That's why we had so much fun last night. They were all buying you drinks." A grin. "And lap dances."

Matt ignores this. Where are his notes? He fumbles on the seat next to him, searching for the portfolio he had grabbed off the hotel room desk that morning. He opens the cover and takes a quick peek — just long enough to see his handwriting without inducing a fresh wave of nausea. He snaps the book shut and relaxes. He will read the notes when he gets home; then it will all make sense again. For now, he can concentrate on finding his plane and then sleeping for the next three hours. Thank God for business class.

"Here," Frank is holding out his fist. "Take this. You'll feel better by the time we're in the air."

Matt opens his palm and receives a small, red tablet. "What the hell is it?"

"Hangover pill. Haven't you ever tried one?" Hands Matt a bottle of water.

"No." Matt opens the water and puts the pill on his tongue; it could be strychnine and he wouldn't care. He swallows. "Thanks."

On the plane an hour later, his head is clear and he reviews his notes, smiling at the comments he had scribbled in the margins about the willful naiveté he had observed in Fox Trade's representatives. He opens his laptop to create the formal report for hand-off to the Vantage implementation team. They should have some fun with those guys.

Transition Team Members: Legal, Accounting, HR, IT. He pauses; then adds: Communications. Let them think they play a role so they will stay off his back. Just like IT. He types in the names of the Fox Trade representatives for each role and leaves blanks for Vantage. Next, the number of Fox Trade employees, by department. He sees his note, promising all reasonable steps to ensure the preservation of jobs. And then the margin comment: *(for Vantage)*. He creates a column for post-transition numbers. Sales: zero. Legal: zero. HR: zero. IT... well, they might have a fighting chance, at least until the Vantage crew figures out their engine. Management is a bit trickier. He has to study their buy-out terms before committing to any numbers here. Sounds like a job for HR and Legal, in fact. He flips over to MS Project and assigns the task to them, smiling to himself as he considers the turf war this will ignite. By the time he gets back to the office, he will be ready to hand the whole thing over to Anand and his boys to make the rain come. He wonders if this is how rich kids feel at the mall with their parents' credit cards.

THURSDAY, OCTOBER 18

"Nervous, Mandy?"

"Me?" She looks up from the newspaper to make sure another Mandy has not joined them for breakfast. Never mind that she hates the nickname and always has.

"I know," Matt concedes. "But I thought it would have been rude not to ask."

"That's sweet, baby. Thank you."

"It would be okay if you were, you know. Normal, even." His eyes twinkle at her.

"Will you be there?"

"I will." He pushes back from the table and carries his plate and mug to the kitchen.

She is surprised. Her question was perfunctory; he usually avoids these events. "Really?" Looking over her shoulder at him, skeptically.

"Yep. Big day for you. I wouldn't miss it." He is back at her side and bends to kiss her cheek. "See you later."

"'Bye," she calls after him, still puzzled by his show of support. He typically lets her enjoy her professional moments without him, mostly because he has very little interest in what she actually does. So why, today of all days, with John Wallace present —

With John Wallace present.

Of course.

She smiles to herself. Poor Matt. For such a smart man he is politically hopeless. The smile fades into a frown as she loads the breakfast dishes into the washer and cleans the coffee press, setting aside the grounds with the morning's eggshells for the roses. She has come to accept his tendency to coat-tail; she recognizes that what is good for Matt is ultimately good for her, as well. And in a back-handed way, she supposes it's a compliment. What concerns her, though, is his inelegant manner of acting on his ambition. His coworkers will not indulge him the way she does. The smile returns as she considers that he will meet Margaret Wallace at the opening. That would probably keep him away from the museum and off her back about it forever, after today.

#

Amanda checks her watch. Two hours to go. These events are grueling from a procedural angle. It's true she never gets nervous — she plans too well for that — but she will be exhausted anyway, when it is finally over. Especially with Margaret on-hand. Amanda has never been corrected on matters of protocol so much in her career, and she has worked on projects in New York City and D.C. It is staggering, but she has taken it in stride; when the ribbon is cut and the media have gone, it will be hers. And it is at the point when the real work begins that the greatest satisfaction comes. Amanda is happy to trade all the photo ops and sound bites for that.

She keeps this thought at the front of her mind as the final pieces come together. Margaret arrives and immediately begins directing the volunteers to move signs, adjust lights, remove the covers on the microphones (too *fuzzy*). She glances at Amanda's minute-by-minute schedule and dismisses it as incomplete.

"Where is the videographer?"

Another glance at her watch. "He has five minutes yet."

"Your watch is slow," Margaret huffs and snatches her phone from the reception desk.

Amanda hears the door swing open and turns, expecting to see Dave and his camera crew but finding John instead.

"Where's my mark?"

"John? Is that you?" Margaret has finished ripping in to the videographer and comes stalking out of the office, phone still in hand. "You're late."

"Margaret, not only am I not late, but I am a full hour early." He kisses the cheek she offers. "Relax."

"Easy for you to say," she pouts. "What do you care if I look like a fool today?"

"I care deeply, dear. Deeply." He turns to face Amanda. "And how are you holding up? Today's the big day."

"It's very gratifying to be at this stage at last," she says smoothly. She feels Margaret's glare burning her cheeks.

"May I have a moment with Amanda, to review my talking points?" John's voice is perfectly smooth, as if his wife's animosity for the younger woman has escaped his notice entirely.

"Talking points? I thought you were scripted? I thought Albert had written your speech."

John ushers her gently back to the office. "He did. And I whittled it down to some talking points so I won't sound like I'm reading from a script. You know I don't like to appear over-rehearsed."

He returns to Amanda's side, an exaggerated sigh emitting from his lips and eyes cast toward the ceiling. "Nerves. She means well."

Amanda nods. "Of course. She has a lot riding on the success of this event — and the museum itself." She smirks. "So you received my talking points."

"Yes. I don't think Albert changed a word."

"Well, that's all Melissa. She headed Margaret off before she got to Albert."

"It's going to be a good day for you, I think." His voice is proud, as if her success matters to him on a personal level. "You've come quite a ways since the last time I was here."

"I saved you some plywood, though," she jokes. "I saw you eyeing it."

He laughs. "Yes, I build bird houses in my spare time. I'll bring you one for the reception desk."

"I won't hold my breath."

"You're sharp. I like that." His green eyes glint at her and she feels a bit unsteady on her feet all of a sudden. "It's good for my investment here," he adds, as if realizing the need to qualify the object of his approval.

The front door opens once more, and Margaret resurfaces from the office. "Amanda? Has the video crew shown up yet? Where are they?"

But the latest arrival is Matt. He crosses the floor quickly and stands at Amanda's side.

"This looks great. I'm blown away."

Amanda smiles at him and turns to John. "John, this is my husband Matt Parsons. Matt, John Wallace, the museum's top benefactor."

"Pleasure," John says, shaking Matt's hand.

"It's all mine," Matt replies carefully. "Amanda appreciates your support and interest. She's never had such solid backing before; I can only imagine the results she'll get with it."

Margaret huffs again as she emerges from Amanda's office and strides past them to plant herself at the front door. Amanda glances sideways at John and catches his eyes. They both smile; it will be over soon.

She turns to Matt. "You are overselling me, as usual. But thank you."

"The camera crew, Amanda," Margaret calls from her post. "Will you please call them *again*?" Margaret is the rare woman who can make the word *please* sound impolite.

"Certainly," Amanda murmurs, excusing herself from the men and entering the number into her phone. Matt frowns but recovers quickly; he may oversell, but he doesn't like to see her underappreciated, either.

"How's life in the lab?" John is speaking now. Although he had personally referred him, the two men have never met, face-to-face.

"Running at an accelerated pace, for sure." Matt grins, eyes alight.

"You're in good hands," John says easily. "You'll learn a lot from Anand, and the rest of the team will learn a lot from you, I think."

"Thanks. It's a great opportunity. I really appreciate the nod."

John smiles. "Fox Trade was a good move, and you managed it well, for your first major deal with us." He pauses and glances at the papers in his hand. "I really ought to review these one more time before we get much farther down the track," he says, referring to his talking points.

"Of course; don't let me keep you."

"I'm sure I'll be hearing from you — or about you — again soon," John says as he leaves.

The words settle uncomfortably in Matt's stomach. It's true: he's only as valuable as his latest deal. He'd better start looking for something to top Fox Trade. Soon.

John walks into Amanda's office and takes a seat on the sofa, eyes moving quickly over the talking points. They are succinct and yet meaningful; not a lot of waste here, as he has observed in everything he has seen of her so far. An indulgent smile touches his lips. He understands Harry Lexington's fervor; he has since the moment Amanda stepped into his office and handed him a detailed financial report for something that was no more than a blip on his fiscal radar screen. He closes the folder and takes out his Blackberry, which has been buzzing unrelentingly since he entered the museum. Rob, again.

can you plz tlk to mom re w/e?
What's up?
bch trp. ev1 gng but me.
Will do. Whose house?
firestones
Nice. Co-ed?
duh

John smiles; there's the problem. Margaret's sense of propriety doesn't sit well in a house filled with young men.

Duh to you. Should have kept that under your hat.
u type 2 much - lrn 2 txt
Right.

"Is that Rob?" Margaret's voice erases his smile; it usually does.

"No," he says smoothly, flicking back to the home screen. "Work. Why do you ask?"

"He wants to go to the Firestones' beach house this weekend. No adult supervision; boys and girls." She draws herself up. "I said no."

"Maggie," John begins. "He's eighteen years old."

"Exactly my point. He will ruin his life, getting some girl pregnant before he even finishes high school."

The challenge is in her voice; the rest of her thoughts unspoken and unneeded. They face each other squarely in the small office. Silence settles around them; uncomfortable, piercing silence.

A throat is cleared just beyond the door. "Excuse me," Amanda's voice precedes her into the room. "The video crew would like to run some tests with Mr. Wallace in position," she explains.

"On my way." John stands and steps lightly past his wife and into the museum proper.

The building slowly fills with members of the media, local dignitaries and the Vantage Community Affairs crew. A minor stir erupts when Marcus Jones, starting small forward for the Rockets, appears. Amanda keeps half an eye trained on her sports-star struck husband, making sure he does not overstep his bounds with the man. She spies the two of them chatting easily and allows herself to relax; she is too hard on Matt. He's not a child, after all.

At last the ribbon is cut.

"Why do I feel like I should be stuffing cake in your mouth?" John comments, as he and Amanda snip their cartoonishly large scissors and the blue satin band falls into pieces on the floor.

She shakes her head, smiling. "I have some ring dings in the office. Will that do?"

He laughs enthusiastically and puts his hand on her shoulder, giving it a friendly squeeze as the cameras click around them. Amanda laughs, too, her usual guardedness absent for once as she enters the home stretch of the morning's gauntlet. She sees Grace looking at her intently. She straightens her face and takes a few subtle steps to her left, a more respectable distance away from John. His eyes send her a befuddled apology. From the periphery of her gaze, Amanda catches Grace's approving nod.

# # #

"God, Amanda," Matt exclaims when they arrive home that evening. "That woman is horrible. How can you stand it?"

"It's no big deal," she insists. "I know it's not about me; it's all her stuff. I just ignore it and do my job."

"You should quit." Matt takes his wallet out of his pocket and puts it on the front console table, next to his keys. "I mean it. And Wallace, how does he stand her?"

"I imagine he spends a lot of time at the office," she says mildly. "It's fine. I like my job. I like the museum. Will you please not worry about this?" She stands in front of him and touches his face. "I'm a big girl."

"But Wallace," Matt continues, not hearing her at all. "He really likes you; that's clear."

She freezes. "What do you mean?"

"Nothing bad, baby. I think it's good that he likes you. He has a reputation for being a serious prick at the office, but if he likes you, that can't be anything but good for me, right?"

"Right," she agrees.

"And why didn't you tell me Marcus Jones was going to be there?" Matt is incredulous. "We play the same position."

"Sorry, baby. I had some doubt even as late as yesterday morning, so I didn't want to get your hopes up." She smiles winningly at him. "Forgive me?"

"Yeah." He smiles and shakes his head. "I still say you're a saint, to put up with his wife for what they pay you."

"Money isn't everything, baby." She smiles coyly, wanting to turn the subject from the Wallaces. "Especially not when I have you."

"Mm-hm. Come here," he says, pulling her close. "I haven't given you my official congratulations for a kick-ass opening." He kisses her forcefully. "You really did it, baby. You rock. I'm so proud."

She smiles and kisses him back. "Come show me how proud you are."

FRIDAY, OCTOBER 19

"How relieved are you to have yesterday in the rear view mirror?" Grace takes a quick sip of her iced tea and leans in closer to the table.

"You have no idea," Amanda intones, as if confessing; she understands that is what Grace wants. "It was fun, and I don't mind staging those events — they are necessary after all — but I'm just ready to get to work already."

They pause as the waiter delivers their plates. When Grace speaks again, her voice is cautious.

"John Wallace seemed to enjoy himself."

Amanda nods. "He's really into the whole museum concept."

Grace purses her lips and sighs forcefully. "I don't think that's it, not entirely."

"What?"

"I hate to rain on your parade, Amanda."

"But you're going to anyway."

"I have to. You've been in nonprofit for so long — the corporate world is different. The people are motivated by different things."

"Okay." She will argue her experience with corporate donors another time. She knows it will not be heard until Grace speaks her mind.

"John Wallace has you in his sights."

"What do you mean? He doesn't want the museum to succeed?"

"No, not that kind of sights." Grace sounds exasperated. "Romantic sights."

Amanda laughs out loud; it is the proper response. "Grace. That's outrageous. I've seen him maybe three times in my entire life, including the two minutes in the Vantage lobby that day after our run. And his wife was lording over the ceremony yesterday like she had created the entire concept of museums."

"Doesn't matter," Grace insists. "I'm speaking from experience here."

Amanda looks at her sharply.

"No, not first-hand," Grace says, raising her hands as if to push the very notion away. "But I've been around for the aftermath, and it's not pretty."

Although Grace has never interacted directly with one of JW's conquests, or even known for certain whom they are, she — along with the entire department — has felt the tremors when the liaisons eventually crumble. Besides, every rumor is based on at least a kernel of truth.

Grace leans forward and lowers her voice even more. "It's like a revolving door to his bedroom, and he doesn't stop it for anyone."

No response.

"I recognize the signs, even if his wife doesn't." Then another thought. "Or at least, if she does notice, she doesn't care anymore."

Amanda focuses on her penne for a moment. The vodka sauce is spicy, with red pepper flakes and chunks of garlic, just the way she likes it.

"I appreciate your concern," she says at last, her words careful but sincere. "But I do think it's unnecessary. He's just happy about the museum — it's his pet. It has nothing to do with me." She smiles as if she is truly conspiring with Grace. "Besides, he's old. And look at Matt; I'd be crazy."

Grace rolls her eyes in agreement and grins widely. "I know! Where did you find him — GQ mail order?"

I didn't find him; I made him, Amanda thinks. But she responds, "I'm one lucky girl, that's for sure."

"And I'll tell you a few little nuggets about John Wallace," Grace continues. Amanda winces inwardly. She has never been interested in "nuggets" about anyone.

"He dyes his hair," Grace says, ticking it off on one finger. "His eyes? Tinted contacts." Another tick. "And speaking of his eyes, lots of work done there. And I don't mean Lasik."

Amanda forces herself to smile and nod. *Tell me I can't have something, and then watch how long it takes me to get it. Whether it's good for me or not.*

#

"Thanks for taking some time today, John." Kate Wells, vice president of Human Resources, smiles brightly at him from across the table at La Griglia.

"Happy to," John replies, nodding.

"It's so hard to focus on the people thing when you're surrounded by the people all day."

John laughs. "I suppose it is. What's new in your world, then, Kate?"

She draws an almost-reluctant breath. "I'm afraid it's employee satisfaction survey time again."

John's face is still. Kate knows what he thinks of surveys; they have had this discussion exactly six times in the six years since Kate stepped into her role as the head of HR. It's not that he doesn't care about his employees' state of mind or job satisfaction; it's not that he doesn't want their feedback. The problem is that each time a survey is conducted the results go into a black hole from which they do not emerge for months. By the time they do see the light of day, the company has undergone reorganization and the feedback is obsolete.

"I know what you're thinking," Kate begins. "But my OD team wants to try something different this time."

John still has not moved. An idea out of Organizational Development is hardly compelling; they are heavy on theory and light on practical application, in his experience.

"They've been looking at implementing a balanced scorecard — "

He laughs out loud; he cannot help it. Someone has read a book, it seems. If he were inclined to do it, John is convinced he could track the sales of business books directly with the uptick in "innovative" ideas spawned by his management team.

"I'm sorry, Kate," he says, his voice still rich with laughter. "We did the whole balanced scorecard thing back in the late nineties, after the book came out. It was before your time, so you didn't know."

Kate inhales sharply through her nose and narrows her eyes at him, shaking her head. "Maybe you didn't have the right people in place to make it work then."

John smiles gently at her. "I hate to take the wind out of your sails, but I don't think so. Unless you can prove that the feedback is actually going to be used for something concrete, it's a bad investment."

Kate sighs. "I'm not giving up just yet," she insists. "I'll find a way to prove the value to you."

"I'm sure you will," he agrees, his tone indicating that the subject is closed for now.

The waiter interrupts, to deliver their meals.

As soon as he departs, Kate shifts gears. "What's your take on Amanda Parsons?"

John grins again. So this is why she had really asked him to lunch. He cuts into his steak; it is overdone. He twists in his seat, looking for the waiter. "I thought we agreed on pink in the middle," he says pleasantly, when the young man appears.

"So sorry, Mr. Wallace. I'll take care of it right away."

"Why do you ask?" He turns to face Kate once more.

"Oh, no reason. I know the museum is important to you, and I wondered if you're satisfied with how it's going."

He nods. "Very."

"And Amanda?" Kate spears a forkful of salad and pops it into her mouth. "How would you describe her?" she asks through the spinach.

"Sharp. Driven. Focused."

"That's all?" Kate regards him steadily as she takes a sip of white wine. "Not pretty? Sexy? *Unique*?"

He shakes his head. "Let's just have it, okay Kate? I'm hungry, my steak was wrong, and I've got earnings to deal with when I get back. Go ahead and tell me to keep away from her. I'll deny that I've done anything improper. You'll say you're just thinking of my own interests — after all, we don't want a harassment suit, even though she doesn't technically work for me…." He cranes his neck, looking for the waiter again. "And I'll thank you for being so circumspect. We'll agree that it doesn't have to go any farther than this table, and then we can move on."

Kate smiles at him. "You're so well-behaved when you really try."

The waiter has returned with a new steak and waits patiently for John to slice it.

"Beautiful," he says, when the juice fills the base of his plate and the pink center is exposed. The waiter leaves and John addresses Kate again. "And tell Dave Galvan and his flunky Grace they can both bite me." As the words leave his mouth, he replaces them with a chunk of meat and chews it. Very slowly; very deliberately.

MONDAY, OCTOBER 29

Matt's boredom has returned, chased with a shot of trepidation after John Wallace's parting remark at the museum opening. He has handed Fox Trade over to the transition team and is back to monitoring the virtual death row of medium-cap insurance companies. The pressure to top Fox Trade is enormous — and almost entirely self-imposed. Vantage has not been in the acquisition market in a decade; expectations are extremely low. But this means nothing to Matt. He wants action and — more importantly — credit. What he needs, though, is a different approach. He had stumbled upon Fox Trade, not because it had appeared on his list of likely targets, but by simple accident. He knows this will not happen again, but he is certain there is a better way.

A prompt on his screen tells him a new message has arrived in his Inbox. He clicks over to Outlook and sees the latest update on Fox Trade. He scans the note, seeing that Fox Trade's CEO will be traveling overseas next week, visiting the tech support team in Mumbai to soothe concerns about the hand-off. Mumbai. Sounds exciting and a little dangerous, especially for a CEO visiting a disgruntled and frightened workforce. Matt wonders what his security arrangements are like. For that matter, he wonders what John Wallace's security arrangements are like when he travels overseas. Corporate CEOs are attractive targets for kidnapping. He sits up straight in his chair. How do companies pay ransoms when their leaders get nabbed? Surely they don't open the operating account and write a big check, or go to the nearest ATM and withdraw a stack of bills.

Must be an insurance policy for it, Matt muses. *Now, that sounds like fun.*

Revitalized, he attacks his keyboard, tabbing back to the Firefox page and executing a search on corporate ransom insurance. The results fill his screen; all linking directly to firms that offer the coverage. He needs to step back a bit and learn more about the concept itself. Wikipedia. Kidnap and ransom policies are actually indemnity policies, so the insured must first pay the amount and then report it as a loss covered by the policy. It's a boutique offering, compared to what Vantage currently provides, but Matt thinks he could make a case for it. The guys in the lab would love having a few, stout premiums to plug into their system, whatever it is. And, if he can find the right firm to snatch up, he could make a place for himself at the top.

First, he has to bone up on exactly how this works. He would bet everything he owns that Amanda's father has a policy; oil executives are always going to South America and the Middle East. Hell, Amanda may still be covered by it, as well. Matt's blood is humming; he is in the perfect position to make this happen. He is an insider, for the first time in his life.

NOVEMBER 2007

TUESDAY, NOVEMBER 6

Matt makes brief eye contact with each person at the conference table before he speaks.

"K&R insurance," he says simply.

Larry Foote, head of Risk and Finance at Vantage, leans back in his chair, arms folded across his chest, a thoughtful look on his face. "I like it. Tell me more."

"I assume we carry a policy on JW, right?"

Larry hesitates. This is not common knowledge, for obvious reasons. At last, he nods. "And his immediate family."

"So that part of our due diligence is finished already; we have an intimate understanding and appreciation of the value — and necessity. The next piece is the financial fortitude to make what could be a huge payout." Matt looks at Anand, who gives a barely-perceptible nod. "The lab has that covered, and Fox Trade's proprietary software adds speed and agility to our arsenal."

"Did you run it through RAROC?"

"I did," Matt says slowly; he knows this is a test. "And then I did return on risk-adjusted capital." Matt looks at Larry sharply. "I think that's a more compelling scenario than risk-adjusted return for this project."

Larry studies him for a moment. The boy knows his shit. "And what about our market entry strategy?"

Matt slides a piece of paper across the table. Larry reviews it and smiles, finally. "Really? That many members of our board travel to South America on a regular basis?"

Matt is nodding as Larry speaks; a triumphant glint lights his eyes. "It's like a gift from the commercial gods." His face shifts subtly. "I'm not suggesting we build this completely from the ground-up, of course. I've got my eye on a few players who are in serious trouble right now."

Larry looks at Anand. "This is your idea?"

Anand shakes his head. "It's all Parsons. I guess JW knew what he was doing. Again." He smiles. "I think maybe I should be worried about my job." And the job of everyone else at the table, for that matter. Last week, the Fed had made a multi-billion-dollar infusion into the nation's money supply for banks to borrow from each other. He would love to see the machine they use to keep printing up that money. But he maintains his smile and his temperament. As far as anyone else knows, Vantage is coasting on its savvy and conservative investment strategy.

Matt laughs, because he is supposed to. But Anand has no reason to worry; it's not Anand's job he is eyeing. He faces Larry again. "So, what do you say? How do we pitch it to JW?"

Larry ponders the question for a moment. The standard PowerPoint dog-and-pony has never been JW's style, regardless of how addicted the rest of his organization seems to have become. But Matt may not know that. *Let's see how he does.*

"Kidnap and Ransom, huh?" A pause. "I can get you about thirty minutes, max. I'll put it to you to figure out how best to use it."

Matt smiles. "That's great, Larry. Thanks." He never assumed Larry would make it easy for Matt to replace him as head of Risk, after all.

# # #

"Pull his policy," Amanda says, as she places the bowl of soup in front of Matt and joins him at the table.

"Yeah?"

"Yeah. All you really need is the summary page, in fact." She takes a sip. "Tastes funny."

"No, it's good," he says. "Lemony. But I was thinking a PowerPoint with the cost-benefit, ROI and then one-three-five year projections."

"Oh, no." She puts down her soup spoon. "That's overkill. That's what you do for the people one or two levels down from him."

"But he'll want to know I've thought it through."

"All he wants to know is that *you* know. You made it past Larry. If the idea weren't compelling, you wouldn't be meeting John. Who else will be there?"

"Larry and Anand."

"Okay. Anand is your wing man. He can load up his folder with all the details, but you should travel light. Larry is your vote of confidence. I can't eat this." She pushes the bowl away. "I don't know what I did."

"Maybe you're coming down with something; it's good." His face becomes suddenly animated. "Hey! Are you pregnant?"

Amanda sighs, frustrated. *This, again?* "No, Matt. I just had my period last week."

"Oh." He sounds disappointed. "You did? I missed that."

"I wonder how…."

"I'm sorry, baby. I'm gone way too much." His voice is conciliatory.

"It's okay," she says gently. "And it's exactly why we're not having a baby any time soon. Anyway, pull John's policy. He's probably never even seen it."

"How can I get it, though?" Matt is frustrated. It's not as if someone is just going to hand it over.

"I'll call Melissa; she'll help, as long as I tell her what it's for."

Matt ponders her advice. "Just the summary page?"

Amanda nods. "Anand can hold the rest. But John won't even want to see it." She rises from the table and takes her bowl to the kitchen. "Either way," she concludes with half a shrug.

"Hey," Matt calls after her. "You're doing the Turkey Trot, right?"

Amanda shrugs. "I don't know. Why? Does it matter?"

"Yeah it matters," he snaps. "You don't skip something the CEO has invited you to do."

Amanda looks at him coolly. "So you're worried about my funding?"

"I'm worried about *our* funding if you insult him by not showing up."

They regard each other over the bar. A curious sensation is rising up Amanda's spine; she thinks it may be anxiety, which she rarely feels. Matt is treating her position at the museum as a piece of his machine, rather than something she can call her own. And she finds it personally unsettling to be around John; his presence is too stimulating. Too dangerous for someone like her, who is drawn to intellect and power like a moth to the flame.

But she merely shrugs again. "Sure, I'll run it."

"And make sure he sees you out there," Matt adds, bending his head to his soup once more.

Amanda empties her bowl down the drain; she does not ask if Matt wants any of it.

MONDAY, NOVEMBER 12

Matt enters the conference room on the fiftieth floor confidently, although his gut has been tied in knots since midnight.

"Matt, nice to see you again," John says, coming in just after him.

"You, too, John."

Handshakes are exchanged and the two men sit, as Larry and Anand join them.

"How's Amanda?"

"She's great, thanks for asking." *I knew it*, Matt thinks, mentally patting himself on the back for insisting she join the run later this morning. "The museum had a solid first month."

"Good. I'm not surprised at all." John smiles pleasantly. "So. What do you have for me?"

Matt slides a single sheet of paper across the table.

"What's this?"

"The summary page of the Kidnap and Ransom policy Vantage holds on you." Amanda had warned him not to use abbreviations, no matter how high up the chain his audience.

"Oh, yes. And why are you showing it to me? Do you have a better offer?"

Larry and Anand laugh dutifully. Matt smiles and touches his Mont Blanc to a highlighted figure mid-way down the page.

"This is the annual premium for that policy."

"Okay." John sounds hesitant, but game.

"Imagine that figure multiplied by 100 and then fed into the lab for a return."

"Okay." From hesitant to interested. "And we can do this?"

"We can." Matt nods and stops speaking. John will either bite or pass on this alone.

John nods once. "I like it. Larry?"

Larry nods.

"Who sells it? Not our current sales force; this isn't their market."

"No. It's yours."

"I suppose it is," John agrees. "I suppose it is."

#

The report from the starter's gun echoes off the glass-curtained office towers. Amanda and Grace and approximately three-hundred Vantage employees set out together in the cool afternoon air. The atmosphere is light and festive; the pace is easy.

"Big plans for Thanksgiving?"

Amanda shakes her head. "Dinner with my family. Matt's folks are in Indiana; we'll see them at Christmas. You?"

"My folks, in Dallas." Grace shudders.

"Oh," Amanda observes. "Turkey and trauma, then."

"Yep. I wouldn't expect you to understand, Ice Queen."

"Ouch." Amanda grins. "I guess, right?"

"Case in point. Off you go, chatty. I know I'm holding you back. See you on the flip-side."

"I'm not that fast," Amanda protests, but she picks up her pace and pulls ahead, waving over her shoulder as she goes. This is her favorite part of Houston, right along the bayou that had given the city life. Not far from where she grew up and in the shadow of skyscraper where her father still influences the scope of oil exploration and production for the entire nation. A slight smile as she revels in the fact that in her homecoming she is no longer measured against his name, in spite of her concern when Matt had shared his news back in May. She runs alone in the crowd for at least a quarter mile, passing people she does not know, until a familiar figure comes into view. A storm of butterflies takes flight in her stomach and she silently scolds herself before pushing a little harder to catch up with him.

"Nice day for a trot," she says, at his side.

"Unless you're a turkey, of course." John's voice is even; he breathes easily through his mouth as he runs.

"Funny."

"Not really. I think I try too hard with you. You're kind of a tough room."

"So I've heard," she admits.

"I met with your husband this morning," he says casually.

"Yes, he mentioned that today was a big day for him. How did it go?"

John looks at her from the corners of his eyes. He had detected more than a touch of Amanda's influence in the morning's meeting.

"Very well," he says simply. "He's sharp. You two make a formidable team."

"Thank you," she says, nodding. "But he's the brains of the operation. I just know how to ask people for money."

"An important skill, in any line of work," John notes. "How far back did you leave Grace?"

Amanda shrugs. "I'm not sure. I haven't passed another woman in a while, though."

He laughs. "No, I don't expect you will, at this point."

Amanda focuses on the path ahead. Four men to beat. She maintains her pace. "So who holds the men's record, then?"

A smile plays at his lips before he answers. "I do, of course."

"Of course." She gestures up the path with her head. "Don't let me keep you."

"Not at all," he insists. "It doesn't look good for the boss to win every year, does it?"

Amanda glances down the trail; the finish line is in sight. Her eyes slide smoothly to John's face; he is peering at her, as well, one eyebrow raised in a silent challenge. She flexes her fingers and takes a deep breath. In unison, they launch into a full-on sprint for the final fifty yards. They are neck-and-neck until the line, when John pulls up and drops his hand to his right hamstring. Amanda crosses the marker lightly and trots back to his side, bending at the waist to see if he is okay.

"What happened?"

John lifts his head and grins, speaking softly. "A true gentleman always lets the lady finish first."

He stands up straight and takes her arm, limping toward the photographer with a sheepish look. "Come on, get a picture with me. It's tradition."

Amanda's heart is pounding in her ears, and she is glad there is a reasonable excuse for her face to be flush. She could not possibly have mistaken his innuendo. But rather than justifiably insulted, she is excited by his words.

WEDNESDAY, NOVEMBER 14

Matt rubs his eyes. He has been looking at the monitor for too long today; he can feel the tell-tale twitch in his left eyelid. But he is following the movements of three small insurance firms in the throes of failure. One of the three had shown signs of rallying that morning, but he knows it was just the "dead cat bounce" that so often heralds the end of the end. He turns his attention to the printed, one-page summary of each firm on his desk, reminding himself of the specifics so he will be prepared on very little notice.

The Ithaca Group is an almost eighty-year-old company that got its start in the personal protection business, guarding the assets and leaders of Wall Street banks after the Great Depression had made them targets of both fiscal and physical threats. Based in Ithaca, New York, the company had expanded insurance coverage when World War II had restored confidence and value to the banking system and its management. In the last six months, the company has lost thirty percent of its value, as clients have sought ways to bundle K&R coverage with other risk management policies.

Next, Yates & Co., a St. Louis firm that had gotten cross-wise with the Missouri Attorney General's office over failure to pay state income taxes for a period of nearly ten years. Matt isn't as interested in Yates; there would be an awful lot of bad sentiment to manage and scandal doesn't make for an ideal acquisition target when there are other options. Still, the right price could make him learn to love this deal.

And finally, the dead cat. Kohl & Lesley out of San Francisco. This is the real gem, a firm dating back to the Gold Rush era, when it provided the precursor to K&R insurance for the lucky few who had found their fortunes in the Badlands of South Dakota. According to the company's Web site, Ezra Kohl had set up shop right next to the first banks in every major mining town in the Northwest. As sobering as some might find it that a firm with such rich history is about to vanish from the landscape, Matt cares only about the opportunity it creates for Vantage. And for him.

He looks back at the screen, certain that whatever he chooses will meet with little resistance. He has proven himself with Fox Trade; proven not only his ability to locate strong candidates for a take-over, but also his complete focus on maximizing the value for Vantage. He feels no compunction at all about the glad-handing reassurances he has made to Fox Trade's leadership about the security of their jobs and the integrity of their company. He doubts they actually believe him, anyway, which makes them just as guilty as he is when they pass the information along to their employees.

By the end of the day, he will have made his decision. Then it will be up to Anand and the others to make it happen. They are expert at striking these deals, bending the rules just enough to avoid scrutiny while making sure everything serves the interests of Vantage. If Matt had had access to them at the beginning of Fox Trade, it would have saved the company millions. That mistake won't be repeated.

His cell phone buzzes at his hip. He glances at the display before flipping it open. Amanda. "Hey, baby. What's up?"

"Just reminding you we have dinner with my mom and Bill tonight."

"*Fuck.*"

"Matt."

"Sorry," he grumbles. "I'm just kind of tied up today, and I can't guarantee that I'll get out of here in time. Can I meet you there?"

She does not answer immediately; a very bad sign for Matt and he knows it. When she does speak, her voice is pleasant — also bad. "That's fine, honey. Just meet us there as soon as you can."

"Okay." This is really going to cost him. Good thing Christmas isn't far off. "I love you."

"Me, too." She ends the call.

# # #

"Where's Matt?" Ann leans forward to kiss her daughter as she enters the house.

"Tied up at work," Amanda explains, hugging her tightly. "Good to see you."

"You, too. Hungry?"

"I could eat." They are in the living room now, where Amanda's brother is sipping from a high ball glass as he and their step-father rehash the day's financial news.

"I'm telling you, Bill, there's a recession looming."

Bill is shaking his head. "You don't know what you're talking about. Kids; you want to blame Bush for every problem in the world." He looks up. "Hey, speaking of, here's another one."

"Switzerland," Amanda claims, hands up defensively as she crosses the room to kiss Bill's cheek. "Nice to see you, Bill." She turns and hugs her older brother. "And you Ed."

"Drink, Amanda?" Edward walks to the bar, hands ready for her instructions.

"Whatever you're having is fine, I'm sure."

He smiles; this means whatever he mixes, she will pretend to drink. "Done. No Matt?"

"Work. He'll be along." She takes the glass and her first, artificial sip. "Thanks."

"So, was Fox Trade really his deal?"

Amanda nods. "All his," she confirms.

Edward whistles. "Nice. How'd he do it?"

Amanda shrugs. "I don't get involved. Don't want to step on his toes, you know."

A very skeptical look from her brother. Involvement is part of the Griffin DNA. "Right. Switzerland."

Their mother has returned to call them to the table. "Amanda," she says, as they enter the dining room. "I visited the museum last Tuesday, but it was closed."

"Mom," Amanda says gently. "We're closed every Tuesday. Why didn't you call me first?"

"I wanted it to be a surprise."

"Then you should have checked the Web site."

"Why would a museum like yours have a Web site?"

"So people will know when it's open, for one thing," Edward opines as he takes his seat.

"Edward, don't be fresh."

"Don't worry, Mom," Amanda soothes. "I'll leave a tri-fold with you; it has the hours and all sorts of other information." She sits across the table from her brother and frowns at him. He is too hard on Ann. If she doesn't like the Internet, she doesn't like it.

"Does it have a photo of you? I'm sure that would be a big draw." Ann smiles at her daughter.

"Mom." Amanda shakes her head. Her mother is stuck in 1955, even though she is technically a child of the sixties. Terminally sweet and gentle to a fault. It can't have been easy for her during Ted's ascendancy to greatness during the early years of their marriage. Amanda is not surprised they hadn't made it. Bill is a much better match, successful in business but of a milder temperament than her father. He is able to dote on Ann without treating her like a child in the process. She studies her mother over the rim of her water glass. At sixty she is striking, wearing her silver hair at shoulder-length, her blue eyes as clear and sharp as ever. A lifetime of wide-brimmed hats and good moisturizer had paid off in lustrous skin that Amanda knows she has already squandered for herself. Ann catches her daughter's pleasant scrutiny and smiles in return.

The men have begun discussing politics and the economy again. Amanda believes her brother is right, this time. The country is spending billions of dollars a month on a war and doing nothing tangible to fund it. At home, the push to create homeowners out of every family has kept interest rates so low that the dollar can barely stand up against foreign currency, while the cost of gasoline enters the stratosphere. And citizens follow like lemmings, over-spending on houses and cars and anything else they perceive as a need. But it is an argument that has no legs in the neo-conservative Memorial home of her mother. She will have to wait until Thanksgiving dinner with her father to find a compatible point of view. His brand of conservatism has to do with fiscal policy, rather than moral agenda-setting.

Amanda sneaks a look at her watch. Seven-thirty already and Matt has not even called. She pushes aside the unpleasant thoughts of government and her husband and resolves to enjoy the evening on its merits, alone. She will deal with Matt later. As for the economy, she suspects everyone will have to deal with that much sooner than they think.

TUESDAY, NOVEMBER 20

"So, tell me about Fox Trade and what that means to Vantage." Mike O'Malley from *Bottom Line* magazine places the digital voice recorder on the table between himself and John.

"The Street loves this deal," John begins. "Both companies saw a nice pop in the stock after we announced."

"Yeah, it's definitely gotten some positive attention on the Street," Mike agrees. His voice is expectant. He had been drenched in an unexpected downpour as he crossed the streets at surface level to get from his hotel to the Vantage Tower. There had better be something more than a regurgitation of press release sound bites in it for him.

"And the tool-set we've acquired will bolster our development of new products, help us enter new markets." John spreads his hands as if it's obvious. "It keeps us on target with our growth strategy — in fact it will help accelerate that strategy and drive shareholder value right along with it."

Mike pushes the pause button on his recorder. "That's essentially what you've said in your last two major press releases," he says. "Can't you give me something more? We're working on a feature article here, John."

John sighs. "We're not there yet, Mike. If I tip my hand now, we could leave ourselves exposed to regulatory issues, shareholder issues…." His voice trails. "You know how this works."

"Yeah," Mike agrees testily. "I know how this works."

Dave Galvan, John's vice president of PR, has been silent thus far; but he speaks up as the tone shifts. "Mike, come on. What do you want him to do? Screw the whole deal for your story? We've gone out of our way to give you access to John, here, two days before Thanksgiving. We could just as easily have put you in the same pool as the rest of the media. Would you prefer that?"

Now Mike sighs. "Of course not." Dave Galvan is a royal pain in the ass to deal with when he *isn't* pissed off. Mike refuses to speculate on how much worse it could be. "Maybe a crumb about something else?"

John glances at Dave, who shrugs and nods. "I can tell you that we're close to a big announcement on Fox Trade," he tells Mike. "A new product offering that has huge implications for our bottom line."

Mike grins appreciatively as John slips in the reference to his publication's name. "All right; all right." He looks at Dave. "So, what do you have for me?"

Dave stands and gestures toward the door with his hand. "An inside peek into our executive development program for recent MBA graduates."

Mike groans; they've snookered him. Now it will be a recruitment piece for Vantage. But he can play along for a little while. He stands and heads to the door with Dave.

"And an exclusive when you're ready with the other?" He looks back at John, face filled with hope.

"Absolutely," both men promise.

Outside John's office, Dave hands Mike O'Malley over to a media relations associate and steps back in.

"Got a minute, JW?"

John looks at him, eyes unreadable. "Yeah. What is it?"

Dave closes the door behind him and walks to John's desk. "May I?" John nods.

"We need to talk about something, and I know you're not going to like it." He pauses, trying to gauge John's reaction so far.

"Go ahead, Dave." He has not moved.

"You threw the Turkey Trot so you could run next to Amanda Parsons. And then," Dave looks disgusted, "you let her beat you at the finish."

John shakes his head. "I had an off day, that's all. My hamstring's been bothering me for weeks." A firm look. "Call my orthopaedist."

"John." He switches to the CEO's full name for impact. "Everyone was talking about it. You can't do things so…obviously like that. You have a reputation already."

"A twenty-year-old reputation," John interjects. "Ancient history."

"Whatever you say."

"Did it ever occur to you that some women make up stories about sleeping with the CEO because they think it will get them someplace?"

"Did it ever occur to *you* that some women who are stalked by the CEO of their husband's company file lawsuits?"

John still has not moved. He sits like a statue in front of his computer monitor, its light casting a sallow haze over his face in the storm-darkened room. John rarely turns on the lights inside his office; the glare makes his head hurt.

"Noted." His voice is crisp and he moves at last, turning his head back to the screen and dismissing Dave with the word.

THURSDAY, NOVEMBER 22

Amanda and Matt sit in the car for a moment outside her father's home in River Oaks. Matt is breathing deeply and rubbing his temples with his fingertips. His eyes are closed.

"You'll be fine, you know," Amanda tells him, in her most encouraging voice.

"I always run out of things to say to him," Matt protests, although he knows his hold on her patience is tenuous, after the no-show at her mother's house last week. He was surprised the neighbors hadn't summoned the police. The aftermath was worth it, though. Amanda is pretty amazing in the sack when she's fired up.

"Not this year, baby. You have Fox Trade." She touches his knee. "He's very impressed by what you've accomplished. He told me so, himself." True, it was via response to her e-mail; but praise is praise.

Matt opens his eyes and looks past Amanda, at the front of the mammoth home. This is the real deal, not a brick monster crammed into a lot that was meant for a bungalow. "Someday," he tells her. "Someday we'll be in a place like this."

Amanda shakes her head. "I've been in a place like this," she reminds him. "It's not all good."

"How can you say that?" He turns on her. "You have no idea what it's like to go without."

She sighs. *Turkey and trauma.* "There's a price for everything. You may not have grown up in a big house, with all the trappings, but you had two parents who worked hard and loved each other — and you." It sounds trite, even to her ears, but that doesn't make it any less true.

"Yeah." He gives a half-hearted smile. "Poor little rich girl. I know."

She rolls her eyes. "Just look at how uncomfortable you are every time we come here. You think that's a good thing?"

"It is for him." Matt jerks his head toward the house. "Let's go in. Someone has probably seen us sitting out here and thinks we're smoking pot or having sex or something else that I don't want to have to deny to your dad."

"Right." She opens her car door and steps onto the motor court. "Because I'm sure he's completely unaware that we have sex."

"Eew, Amanda." Matt shivers at the thought of her father even considering what Matt does with her. Maybe it's better they don't have kids; it gives him plausible deniability, anyway.

"God, he's going to want to play basketball, isn't he?" Matt's Yale undergraduate education had been funded by a basketball scholarship; possibly the only thing that makes him tolerable to Amanda's father. He is literally moaning as they climb the steps to the front door.

Amanda pushes the door open and steps into the foyer confidently. "Dad? We're here."

Ted Griffin strides around the corner, arms outstretched for his daughter's hug. "Hey, sweetheart. You look healthy."

Matt stifles a groan. *Healthy.* The man is a nut. It's a wonder Amanda isn't even more neurotic about fitness, with Jack LaLanne for a father.

"And Matt." Ted has broken away from Amanda and is walking briskly toward his son-in-law. He grips one hand and claps Matt on the shoulder with the other. "How's the world's newest acquisition mogul? Warren Buffet called; he's nervous."

There it is. That way of complimenting and insulting in the very same sentence. Letting Matt know that he is nothing, after all, no matter what he has accomplished. Not good enough to play with the big boys, and certainly not good enough for Ted Griffin's daughter.

"So tell me about Fox Trade," Ted continues. "How is Vantage going to put that to use?"

"Dad," Amanda interrupts, coming to stand at his side and placing her hand on his arm. "You know Matt can't tell you that. It's confidential. Let's go get a drink. Is Lisa here?"

"Oh, she's in the kitchen. No staff on Thanksgiving. You know. So," he says, as they walk together, "Tell me how much Vantage has given the museum. I might want to double it. That John Wallace is one smug son of a bitch." He laughs in appreciation; from him, this is high praise indeed. "Better keep your eye on him."

Amanda guides her father easily into the drawing room for cocktails, bending his ear with news of the museum and asking about her step-mother and half-siblings. Matt draws a shaky breath, settles his nerves and follows them. It's going to take an awful lot of Scotch to get through the day. Good thing he's come to the right place.

DECEMBER 2007

MONDAY, DECEMBER 3

"Hey, Matt. Got a minute?"

Matt looks up from his monitor, somewhat shamefaced, and sees Frank Riley leaning over his cubicle wall. He has been perusing ski vacations. The Ithaca acquisition will be announced before the end of the week, cementing Matt's position as an impact player at Vantage. Two deals in three months. He can afford to take a little breather once the dust settles. And maybe once he gets Amanda away from the museum for a few days, he can open her mind to the prospect of a baby and semi-retirement.

"Sure. What's up?"

"We have to hold off for a bit on Ithaca." Frank's eyes are apologetic.

"Why?" Matt stands up; he cannot stop himself in time.

"We're getting some negative buzz from analysts about the Fox Trade deal."

Matt sits down again, falling heavily into his chair. Negative buzz? The Street had loved that deal when it was announced. "What the hell happened?"

"They're questioning our ability to fund it," Frank explains. "If we make a lot of noise about another acquisition right now, investors are going to be nervous."

"But we need Ithaca to do K&R," Matt complains. His voice sounds whiny, even to his own ears. "What does this mean for K&R?"

Frank pauses before answering, studying the young man's face. He has a reputation for failing to control his emotions; Frank had seen it a few times when he was still officially in M&A. The team has thus far played it off as youthful enthusiasm, but the boy really should watch it. After a moment, he sees Matt relax.

"We have to wait on that, too." Frank stops again, watching Matt's eyes. When he is satisfied that the drama is over, he continues. "Not for long; we'll get it done early next year. And in the meantime, we keep talking to Ithaca. We'll find a way to keep them afloat until the time is right for us to make a public move."

Matt is nodding, although Frank knows he hates what he's hearing. "I understand. I do. It's just a surprise, that's all."

"Yeah, sometimes even a good move has to wait," Frank says. "And it's still a good move, Matt. It's no reflection on you. Not at all."

"Right. I know that. Thanks." Matt's tone is clipped. He tries to keep the disappointment out of his voice but can't. How is he going to tell Amanda? She'll think he failed. And her father; thank God she had stopped Matt from telling him about Ithaca at Thanksgiving. What a disaster *that* would have been, now.

"You okay?" Frank is looking at him curiously.

"Oh, yeah. I'm fine. Sorry. I was thinking about something else."

"The next big deal, no doubt." Frank smiles. "Some of us are heading to the Tavern after work. Why don't you come along?"

"Yeah, I might do that," Matt replies. A few drinks will take away some of the sting. As Frank walks away, though, Matt's mind is a mess. Ithaca was to have been his golden ticket. Anything could happen between now and January; he knows how things work. He'll have to find another way to stay in the spotlight. He is not content to be a cog in the gear that makes Vantage turn. He wants to be at the switch.

SATURDAY, DECEMBER 8

"There's John Wallace. Go dance with him."

"Matt. I can't just walk up to the CEO of your company and ask him to dance."

"Sure you can. He likes you; you're working on his pet project, outside of the office." He speaks to her as if she has managed to forget how she spends the bulk of her days, as well as the funding source for that activity.

"I'm not worried about whether he likes me or not." Her voice impatient, as it frequently is when Matt's tunnel vision takes hold. "If you want me to dance with him, you have to take me out there and let him cut in. It's not right for me to be that aggressive; it's not good for you."

"Okay, okay. You're right." He smiles at her; the hang-dog smile he had used in college to win her over. She softens a bit and lets him guide her onto the floor.

The song is brisk but fluid, with a four-count, and Matt leads Amanda in a fox trot. They skirt the edge of the parquet veneer, angling to catch John's eye. It takes less than a quarter turn around the floor.

"May I?" He is at Matt's shoulder, and the question is for him, but John's gaze is fixed on Amanda.

"Of course," Matt responds. "I'll be at the bar; I see Jim Curtis from M&A."

John grasps Amanda's fingers and steps in easily to the space left by Matt. The fingertips of his right hand rest lightly on her spine and she tries not to acknowledge the effect this has on her skin. So this is why Matt had pushed for a backless dress. She has not seen John since the Turkey Trot, but she has caught herself replaying his comment at the finish line during some extremely awkward moments with Matt. Moments made even more awkward by the fact that Matt apparently is not aware of that particular entry in the gentleman's code.

"You look lovely."

She smiles, she hopes graciously. "Thank you. It's fun to get dressed up now and then."

John nods. "It's nice to see someone dispensing with the basic black," he adds, referring to the silver hue of her dress.

"Well, dare to be different," she replies. "I probably took those after-school specials a little too seriously when I was a kid."

He laughs and then looks at her curiously. "I'd say you turned out just fine."

"You don't know me very well yet," she counters. "You might change your mind."

"I hope I get the chance."

The song is over but another one begins immediately. A Big Band number.

"Do you have another dance in you? I know it's not your era."

Amanda smiles ironically. "Oh, but it's yours? I can manage."

He propels her easily around the floor, even twirling her a few times when the music calls for it. She feels herself laughing and tries to stop, knowing they are attracting too much attention. At last the song ends, although she would have been happy to continue. The next song is slow. Amanda and John stand facing each other in the center of the floor.

"That was pretty good," he compliments. "Lessons?"

"I made Matt take ballroom dancing with me when he was in B school. I thought it would come in handy some day."

He is smiling at her thoughtfully. "And so it did."

The air between them is restless, as if the molecules themselves cannot decide where it is safe to land.

"Thank you for the dances," she says at last.

"It was my pleasure." The tenor of his voice creeps into her ear like mist and settles there, twisting around itself as it crawls into her brain. She finds it suddenly difficult to breathe and steps back a pace, finally breaking contact with him.

"Have you come to reclaim her?" John is speaking past her shoulder now, as Matt makes his way toward them.

"I thought I might, if you don't mind," Matt says, slipping a proprietary arm around her waist and tucking his hand inside the shimmer of her dress.

"Not at all. As long as you'll give me a call option on another dance, sometime."

Finance humor. Amanda smiles and rolls her eyes to demonstrate that she has gotten it. "Of course," she says. "Did you have an expiration date in mind?"

He rewards her swift up-take with a slight bow and takes his leave.

"So, how was it?"

"I need a drink," she confesses.

"That bad?"

"He's pretty intense." She shakes her head. "But it wasn't bad at all. He's very friendly; it's just a little unnerving to spend time with him like that, with everyone watching. I worried the whole time about what I was saying."

"Mandy, that's not like you," Matt protests. "Just be yourself."

"I was. Let's hope he likes sassy."

Matt looks at her frankly. "I've heard things. I don't think you need to worry. In fact, if anything, I'm the one who should worry."

"Right." She hopes she has given the word just enough bite to close the subject for a while. Matt is not usually so insightful. He *should* be worried; her knees are wobbly. "Drink, Matt. I want a drink."

"Sorry." He actually sounds sorry. "Cosmo?"

"No, too sweet. Dirty martini."

When Matt brings her drink she sips it slowly, letting the taste settle on her tongue. Her latest meeting with John Wallace has been just as tense as all the others. She understands that it is part of his job to keep people slightly ill-at-ease, to convey subtly that he has the upper hand. But it intrigues her that he takes this approach to aspects of his life beyond business; she wonders how his wife manages it. Then she realizes; his wife doesn't manage it, she avoids it. She escapes to the foundation every day and buries herself in philanthropic work. Is this what she has coming, as well, once Matt's ambitions are finally met?

"You okay, Mandy?"

"I feel a little flushed. I'm going to the ladies room." She hands him her glass. "I'll be fine; just give me a minute."

FRIDAY, DECEMBER 25

The leather-bound box creaks open on its hinges and Amanda ducks her head to peek inside before the contents are revealed.

"Oh, wow," she breathes. "It's so pretty, Matt." She captures the three-stone diamond drop with her fingertips and wrests it from the stiff backing. She holds it up for everyone to see.

"Well done, son." Matt's father squints for a better look. He smiles and nods at his son, pride glowing in his eyes.

"Oh, my, yes," adds his mother. Amanda passes the chain to her.

"I was looking for a stone that matched your eyes," Matt teases.

"I'm glad you didn't go for rubies, then." Amanda stands up to retrieve his gift from its hiding place behind the television. He is notorious for trying to guess — and his track record is too good for her to risk it.

He tears into the silver wrapping and exposes a high-speed digital camera. "Nice!" He whistles. "This is the best one out there right now."

Amanda smiles at him as Joan helps with the clasp of her necklace. "Only the best for you, baby. And there's more; lots of accessories. I didn't wrap them because — "

But he is already on his feet, looking for them behind the television.

" — I knew you'd want to set it up right away."

"Always was an impatient boy," George is saying as Matt begins opening the rest of the components.

Matt ignores him as he sets up the tripod and fiddles with the telephoto lens. Amanda clears her throat. "Matt, your parents haven't opened their gifts from us yet."

He looks at her as if he has forgotten that she is in the room — never mind his parents. "Oh, sorry." He sounds grumpy, but he puts the lens gently on an end table and sits down again.

Amanda, fulfilling her turn as Santa this year, returns to the tree and picks up an oblong box. She hands it to George.

"Heavy," he comments, pulling away the paper. He squints again, this time in confusion, as he tries to read the label.

"It's Laphroaig," Matt tells him, pronouncing it *luh-FRAYG*. "The finest single-malt whisky in the world."

"Well, thank you. I'm impressed." But he looks more confused than anything else. Whisky is whisky, isn't it?

Matt nods. He should be impressed. He may not get it right now, but he will later, when he tries it. And when he tells his buddies back in Gary.

"Okay, Joan," Amanda says. "Your turn." She extends a small box to her mother-in-law.

"What pretty wrapping." Joan looks slightly worried as she carefully opens the paper. What if she doesn't know what hers is, either? But the risk is minimal; every woman on the planet — even ones who live in Gary, Indiana — knows a pair of diamond stud earrings when she sees it.

"Matthew!" Her tone is both grateful and scolding.

Matt laughs. "Come on," he insists. "You have to like them."

"It's too much," Joan protests, even as she pulls the back off one and slides the post into her ear. The stones are not large; Joan would have refused them if they had been.

"No, it isn't," Matt replies. "Mandy?"

Amanda shakes her head. "It's not too much at all," she confirms as Joan secures the other earring in its place. "They look lovely on you."

Matt stands up. "And, just one more thing," he says, walking toward the coat closet in the foyer.

Joan and George look sharply at each other, and then at Amanda. She shrugs. She was not in on this one.

Matt returns with two boxes individually wrapped and tied together. One small; the other much bigger. He hands the bundle to his father, because he knows his mother will simply refuse to open it. George grumbles unconvincingly and opens the gift.

"Is this one of those iPod things?"

Matt laughs out loud. "You might be the last person on the face of the earth who would have to ask. Yes, it's 'one of those iPod things,' and the other is a docking station — a Bose — so you can listen to your music in the house, too." He gestures with his hand, as if to help the explanation. "You know, like we used to with the old hi-fi."

George puts the items on the coffee table and looks at his son. His face is bemused. He has no idea what a Bose is, but it must be top quality, if Matt likes it. "This is really nice, Matt. It makes me proud to see you doing so well and thinking of your mother and me."

Matt shifts on his feet; his father's words have made him uncomfortable. They're just gifts, after all.

"You're welcome," he manages, after a brief and awkward silence.

MONDAY, DECEMBER 28

Vantage PLC Reports Second Quarter FY2008 Results
Beats the Street Again

HOUSTON, Dec. 31, 2007 — Vantage Property, Life and Casualty (NSE: VPLC) today reported adjusted earnings of $1.75 per share for the second quarter of FY2008, compared to $1.45 adjusted earnings per share (EPS) earned in the same period last year. Adjusted earnings exclude the impact of special items. On a Generally Accepted Accounting Principles (GAAP) basis, the company reported a net gain of $2.27 per share in the second quarter of its fiscal year 2008, compared to earnings of $1.05 per share in the same period last year.

"We are pleased to report the increase in EPS for our shareholders and other stakeholders," said John A. Wallace III, president and chief executive officer of Vantage. "This is a strong vote of confidence in our new undertakings and our continued stability. Our growth strategies have been well received in the market and by our customer base, and we will press on with our plans to expand."

Details regarding specific operational units are available on the company's Web site and will also be discussed in an analyst conference call on Wednesday, January 2, 2008 at 10 a.m. Central Standard Time.

Vantage PLC is a North American leader in insurance and financial services, operating across the United States, as well as in Canada and Mexico. Vantage services commercial, institutional and individual customers via widespread property-casualty and life insurance networks. Vantage is listed on the National Stock Exchange, with the ticker symbol VPLC.

This press release contains forward-looking statements concerning future economic performance and events. It is possible that Vantage PLC's actual results and financial condition may differ from the anticipated results and financial condition indicated in these projections and statements. Vantage PLC is not under any obligation to update or alter its projections and other statements as a result of new information or future events.

JANUARY 2008

WEDNESDAY, JANUARY 2

"Hey, Amanda. It's Grace."

"Hey, Grace. What's new?"

"Just wanted to let you know the printer delivered your gala invitations here by mistake."

Amanda sighs. "Just one more thing, right?"

"Yeah. I'll have them couriered to you this afternoon."

"No need," Amanda says. "I'll come get them. I need a change of scenery anyway. Are you free for lunch?"

"Sorry, not today. Something is up. Everyone here is antsy."

"Okay. I'll come anyway and just grab the invitations." Maybe she would drop in on Matt; they could grab a Starbucks.

When Amanda arrives on the Public Affairs floor, she sees firsthand what Grace meant. It's quiet, but awkwardly so. Nobody appears to be working, instead they are speaking in hushed tones, as if someone has died. Grace frantically waves Amanda over to her desk and pulls up a chair for her. Now is not the time to draw attention to oneself, apparently.

"What happened?" Amanda sits uneasily.

Grace whispers, "JW has been holed up in Dave's office for the last two hours. Some Wall Street analyst started making noise about our Fox Trade acquisition on the analyst call and suggested he's going to downgrade us. Says we don't have the cash to do the deal and wants to know how we're funding it. Says we're paying a premium to keep other companies from bidding, but we can't really afford it. I don't understand it. But JW was pissed. When the call ended, he called the guy at his office and reamed him."

Amanda's mind quickly processes the significance of this. If Wall Street thinks Vantage is overpaying for Fox Trade, they have worries about liquidity. Acquisitions have become rare for companies like Vantage; the cash simply hasn't been available since the dot-com bubble burst a few years back. And interest rates on commercial paper aren't quite low enough yet. Everyone is still too nervous with the subprime mess — everyone outside of Houston, that is. So far, oil prices have kept the city mostly above the fray. So, where *is* the money coming from?

"Does the analyst have holdings in Vantage?"

Grace gapes at her. "That's what JW wanted to know. He accused him of short-selling."

Amanda winces. Short-selling; betting that the value will drop. At least John hadn't accused him outright and in public; the consequences of that approach are still fresh in everyone's mind. She feels a slow burn beginning in her stomach. "He can't take pot-shots at the company's liquidity if he's short-selling," she asserts. "That's unethical."

"Well, whatever," Grace says, perplexed by Amanda's clinical analysis. "Everyone is mad at John because of what happened on — "

Sudden commotion down the hall prevents Grace from finishing her sentence, and Amanda is relieved. She has grown weary of the glib and unenlightened references to the past. John Wallace storms out of Dave's office, still barking at him, and Dave rushes to keep pace with John's long legs. John looks up in mid-stride and sees Amanda seated at Grace's desk. The picture throws him off balance for a moment, and he stops short, sending Dave several paces ahead all by himself. His eyes grab hers and hold them briefly but intently. As Dave corrects his position, John starts walking again, leaving Dave to catch up once more. He passes Amanda without a second glance.

The entire incident has lasted no more than fifteen seconds; but its uneasy aftermath lingers, making everyone feel as if they have witnessed something they were not intended to see. Amanda turns slowly to face Grace again. She picks up the box of invitations.

"I'll let you get back to work," she says, standing. Her voice is carefully devoid of emotion. "Good luck."

Grace nods. "Yeah, thanks."

# # #

"I want to cancel my appearance in Chicago."

"Not a good idea, JW," Dave cautions. "Not after this morning. You need to be the very picture of transparency for a while. We'll send McAllister with you; everybody loves him." Steve McAllister, chief operations officer for Vantage, and everybody's favorite guy. *Why not,* John thinks, *he gets to be the cool one.*

A growling sound escapes John's throat; it is accentuated by the hiss and pop of flames in the fireplace in his study. "The asshole is short-selling my company's stock and calling our liquidity into question — hurting my employees and my shareholders — and I'm supposed to just ignore it?" He likes Steve well enough, but this issue is beyond what simple optics can address.

"Look, I know you're upset, and I understand why. It's laudable, even," Dave agrees. "But to the Street, that just looks defensive. And defensive is suspicious. You've set yourself up for a lot of comparisons that are going to be difficult to overcome."

"What kind of fucked up world is it when a man can't defend himself or his company against an attack?"

"Our world."

John moves to the bar and pours himself another drink. He has no response for this, and Dave is getting on his nerves.

"Amanda Parsons was at the office today," Dave ventures.

"I saw her. Are you going to lecture me about that, too? Again?"

"No. Just wanted to tell you I thought you handled it well."

"Yeah. You're welcome." John sits back down and takes a gulp of his drink.

Dave sighs. "Do I *need* to lecture you about this? *Again*?"

"No."

"How about man-to-man, then. I'm not PR Dave. I'm Dave the Dude."

John shoots him an angry glare.

"She's dangerous, John."

"She's different," he counters. "Crazy smart. Different smart. I like that."

"Exactly. She's too smart. That's why she's dangerous for you." Dave sits next to him and sighs. "Can't you just go find a cocktail waitress, like Stan does?"

"Stan thinks with his dick."

"Oh, I'm sorry," Dave patronizes. "So this need you have to bang Amanda Parsons, that's more like a message from God, then?"

"Something like that," John mutters, looking over the rim of his glass into the fire.

# # #

Anand chews on another antacid tablet as he logs in to the Vantage message board. As expected, VCPL had taken a hit after Chris Morton's comments on the analyst call. He has already shifted the proceeds from his short-selling back over to the lab's portfolio. Now, he presses <enter> and waits for the system to acknowledge him. Time to see what the rest of the investing community has to say.

Welcome, *shimano227*.

Anand scans the thumbnail of each post, newest to oldest, in the list. People are talking, all right.

The short sellers are happy:

I told u this would happen before 2 long. nobody listened. who's laughing now?

John Wallace, that's who. Bet he's shorting his own stock.

um, that's illegal and pretty stupid, you idiot.

And slander, o btw.

Hey, shimano, where you at? Counting your cash?

thank you, chris morton. now i can finally get my new boat.

And a few optimistic, long-term holders:

Everybody take it easy. Stocks go up and down. That's why we diversify, right?

Exactly. Too many inexperienced investors out there. Nobody understands how to hold a stock anymore. Nobody wants to learn how the company operates.

The rest is mixed:

I think this is the beginning of VPLC's swan song. The end is near.

2q earnings were good. I'll ride it out until March.

Anand hesitates for a moment, fingers poised above the keys, and then he types:

you guys haven't seen anything yet.

THURSDAY, JANUARY 3

Matt does not arrive home until almost four a.m. He flops onto the bed, fully dressed.

"Hey," Amanda mumbles. "How are you?"

"Ugh," is all he can manage for a moment. "I just spent fourteen hours mining and massaging data to prove our cash position is stable. My brain hurts. *So* not my job description. But they couldn't entrust it to anyone but the guys in the lab. Whatever."

"Did you get it?"

"Yeah," he says. "We got it."

"That's good." She leans over and kisses his cheek. "Lucky for them you're such a genius."

"Yeah," he grumbles. "If you knew how many times I was called an idiot today, you'd see things differently."

"That's just stress talking. Nobody thinks you're an idiot."

He opens his arms so she can snuggle closer. "I know *you* don't. My biggest fan."

She nibbles at his ear and tugs his shirttails out from his chinos.

"I'm wiped out, baby. I'm sorry. Rain check?"

"Of course." She kisses him once more and rolls over to go back to sleep.

Matt lies awake for a long time, puzzling over the mountain of data he had spent the night arranging. Most of it was straightforward, but each time he thought he had sorted it out, three companies in the tech fund kept causing trouble. When he had finally succeeded in separating the three from the fund, he had found the same reference in a footnote on each: Prometheus.

Two hours later, as he pours Amanda a cup of coffee before he leaves for work, he puts the question to her. She will know. "Does the name Prometheus mean anything to you? I know it's something I learned in school, but I can't remember."

"Sure," she tells him. "In Greek mythology Prometheus stole fire from the gods and gave it to humans."

"What happened when they caught him?"

"He was sentenced to spend eternity with an eagle eating out his liver every day, only to have it grow back each night."

"That's pretty gruesome, Mandy. Why do you remember stuff like that?" He bends to kiss her good-bye.

She shrugs. "If I could dump it out and learn to count cards in its place, I would."

"Right. See you tonight. I'm going to be late for a meeting." He trots to his car and races to the office for his Fox Trade transition meeting with Stan Firestone.

WEDNESDAY, JANUARY 9

"Butterflies?" Steve McAllister takes a seat opposite the aisle from John on the Vantage corporate jet. They are set to take off for Chicago in fifteen minutes.

John laughs. "Not in years. It's all same ol', same ol', right?"

Steve nods. "Yeah. It's good you're going, though," he asserts. "The industry needs to see your face, needs to see you standing at the podium and moving past the bullshit."

A shrug. "That's the idea, anyway. Thanks for coming along. How's the family?"

Steve smiles warmly. "They're great. Callie's self-portrait was selected for the Rodeo art competition."

"Good for her."

"Yep, fifth year running. How about your boys? Still haven't convinced Jack to join the fold?"

John laughs out loud. "He won't budge. It's all right, though. He has his own life in California; he loves the technology game." John's face becomes wistful; he was never given the option, himself. And he was partially to blame. He had seen Vantage as his birthright, rather than something he would have to earn, or work to maintain.

"I think it's great that you've let him seek his own path," Steve says. "At some point, it will lead back to you."

"So I've heard. He's a good boy." A pause. "A good man, I should say."

"Have you told him about the Fox Trade engine? That might be pretty tempting, to a tech head."

"Yeah, I've considered it. We'll see." John's voice is brisk but not unfriendly; Steve recognizes this means the subject is closed.

"So what's the game plan for tomorrow?"

"What they want from us is a shot of confidence. The whole industry is worried — hell the whole country is worried." John shakes his head. "I'm of two minds on it, to be honest. On the one hand, there are signs of a recession looming. On the other hand, if we keep panicking, we're going to end up in one, no matter what the signs are now."

"We surprised the hell out of everyone with Fox Trade. And just wait until they hear about Ithaca," Steve comments.

"Exactly. So, again the two minds. One, everyone is excited that an old codger like Vantage can figure out how to fund an acquisition, especially of a sexy, technology-driven business. But, two, how the hell did an old codger like Vantage figure out how to fund that same acquisition?"

Steve's eyebrows shoot up. "Are you going to open the vault?"

"No," John quickly dispels that notion. "But the fact that I *say* we can fund it should be enough for this crowd. I'll touch on it, sure. Investment management, outside-the-box thinking, the usual."

"And when they ask about Morton?" The analyst from the earnings conference call. Steve looks almost apologetic for raising the subject.

"I think that's why you're with me, in all candor, Steve. Dave doesn't want me anywhere near that discussion."

Steve is nodding. "Got it. I'll do the Mid-West farm boy thing."

"That's the stuff."

"Hey, I visited the museum last week."

"Is that right?" John's voice is carefully light. "What did you think?"

"Well done. And the curator, well, she's formidable."

John laughs. If any single word could describe Amanda that was it. "Did she know who you were?"

"I introduced myself. Got a private tour out of it." Steve smiles. "She knows her subject matter."

"Yeah." John looks out the window; they are moving at last.

Steve is quiet for a few minutes as the plane lifts into the air. "John," he ventures.

John turns to face him again. "Yeah?"

"Be careful, there, okay?" Steve is leaning across the aisle and gripping John's wrist as he speaks.

"Okay." John nods and Steve removes his hand.

The two men study each other. Steve understands better than anyone else that John's life is far from charmed, and he also understands why. His mother had suffered from depression; the damage it had done to the family was unimaginable to anyone on the outside. He has heard the rumors about John and the museum curator; unlike most people though, he believes they are still rumors. But the look on John's face when Steve had mentioned the museum suggested there was more than a kernel of truth to the stories. He had seen the same keen edge in Amanda's eyes when he introduced himself to her; and he knew it was not for him. The gossip would not likely remain idle for much longer.

THURSDAY, JANUARY 10

Matt sets the weight on the shoulder press to eighty pounds and takes a seat. He is taking a late lunch break to get away from his desk, although lunch had consisted simply of a protein shake he downed before heading to the Vantage gym. He sets his shoulders and back and pushes up. Twelve reps at this weight.

As he counts up, his mind turns back to Prometheus. He is beginning to understand the arrangement. It seems Stan Firestone has a unique incentive package tied to his contract with Vantage. The golden handcuffs that keep him from taking his expertise to a company with a more exciting product or at least a more aggressive growth strategy.

Twelve. Matt reaches over and increases the weight to one-hundred pounds. Ten reps.

He has learned that Vantage owns minority stakes in the three technology firms bundled into Prometheus. The firms are technology consulting shops, incorporated off-shore as tax shelters. Nothing illegal about that, although it stinks for companies that try to keep their operations in the States and employ U.S. citizens. But Matt's appreciation for moral outrage has never been quite as developed as his appreciation for profit and loss. And if the firms do well, Vantage does well. Which means Matt does well. It works for him.

Ten. Weight increases to one-twenty.

Stan sits on the board of each firm and contributes a bit of gray-haired technology oversight; an asset to shareholders who might otherwise balk at the fact that nobody on the management team is over the age of forty. Still nothing illegal; executives sit on other companies' boards all the time. It's an ego thing.

Eight. Weight increases to one-forty.

The arrangement is also the chain on Stan's handcuffs. He is rewarded when these three firms turn a profit. Still okay, although some might find it a little malodorous. But Stan is not depriving Vantage of his services by supporting the other companies; and the relationship is duly — if somewhat vaguely — reported to Vantage shareholders in the 10Q.

Six. Matt leans back against the stiff cushion. He has met Stan a couple of times, all related to the Fox Trade transition. He's smooth. A little too smooth to be the CTO at an insurance firm. Ivy League educated, like Matt. Ambitious, like Matt. And Matt would bet that Stan is willing to bend the rules for that ambition. Like Matt.

He stands up and wipes down the vinyl. Time to work his back now, although his mind has already left the gym. It's at his desk, reviewing the numbers for Prometheus and the peculiarity he had noticed during the liquidity project. Something hadn't matched up, and now he knows why. Stan Firestone is skimming profits from Vantage's investment. That's embezzlement. And *that* is illegal.

FRIDAY, JANUARY 11

"Did you talk to your guy at the SEC?" Chris Morton speaks into the silent room, shattering the stillness.

"I did. He agrees there could be something fishy about the last two filings." Debra Wilcox sighs heavily and turns on her side to face him. "I just don't get why nobody cares where their money is coming from."

"It's not as if they're the only company in the world that uses footnotes to gloss over things," Chris reminds her. "It's their 'competitive advantage,' right? And as long as the shareholders are getting a good return, who cares?" He smiles ironically at this, considering his personal role in diminishing that return back in January.

Debra rolls her eyes. Her colleagues at Justice have another term for it: Fraud. "I had to practically beg him to open an investigation," she mutters, pushing his hand off her arm. The stroking motion has become a source of agitation.

Chris chuckles. "Why are you so bent on bringing Vantage down?"

"John Wallace is so smug. He could stand a little humility."

"Careful, Deb." Her vendetta could very well come back to bite her; vindictiveness has been known to do that in the past. "I know you think people remember the last time with the Anti-Trust; but really you're the only one who does."

"It's not about that," she insists. And it isn't; not entirely. It is about what John Wallace had done to her family. "I'll be fine. Did you call the reporter yet?"

"Yeah, he's out until next week. I'll get the three of us together soon."

"Okay." She swings her legs over the side of the bed and sits up. "Are you ready? I need to get out of here. I'm meeting Doug for dinner with the boys."

"You go on ahead," he says. "I'm going to hang out for a while. I need some sleep before I go home." The smile hangs in his voice. Chris doesn't care where she is going or what she claims to be sacrificing in order to spend time with him. He knows that he is merely a convenience for her. Just as she is for him.

# # #

Debra feels her teeth grinding as she sits on the subway car after leaving Chris. It's none of his business why she is so bent on bringing Vantage down. He should question his own motives before judging hers. His are purely financial; hers are personal. And that doesn't mean hers are any less valid. She recognizes the danger in the situation she has created for herself, but she has done it deliberately. It was the only way. Debra will not be at peace until John Wallace suffers the same kind of humiliation and loss that her own father had been dealt when Vantage devoured his firm ten years before and had cast him aside as an industry dinosaur. She steps off the train at her stop and walks the four blocks to meet her husband and sons.

THURSDAY, JANUARY 17

"Larry Foote is here to see you, John."

"Sure, send him in," John replies into the intercom on his phone.

"Hey, JW." Larry pulls the door closed behind him as he enters John's office.

"Larry. What's new?"

"Chris Morton is making noise again."

"What is it this time?" John closes his eyes. "Is he in the market for a vacation home in Tuscany?" John figures that Morton had cleared something in the high five figures from the dip in Vantage stock after the call.

"Last year's Annual Report. He wants to know what 'Other Investment Activities' are and why they account for such a huge difference in adjusted EPS versus EPS."

"What a pain in the ass," John mutters, opening his eyes now. "What do you want to tell him?"

"As little as humanly possible."

"Yeah. Such as?"

"We can make a run at the standard response; these are investments related to our growth strategy, our internal funding source for the aggressive stance we've taken in the acquisition market."

John is nodding. "Sounds reasonable to me. Think it will do?"

Larry hesitates. "Can you get Dave up here? I think he has a piece of this, too."

John hits his phone. Dave answers on the first ring. "Yeah, JW?"

"Dave, come on up for a bit. Larry and I are talking strategy and messaging here."

"On my way, JW."

John faces Larry again. "What's this about?"

"I think you need to do another interview with Mike O'Malley."

John groans. "I hate that guy. He's a prick."

"Granted. But it's good to have him in our pocket right now. Everyone is under extra scrutiny, with subprime lenders imploding all over the map, and then us buying Fox Trade and Ithaca. We need to keep him sweet."

"Keep who sweet?" Dave has entered the room.

"Record time," John comments.

"Took the stairs." He is puffing from the exertion.

"Still haven't quit smoking, I see."

"I'm working on it. Give me a few years."

John shakes his head. "May be all you have left."

"Smart ass. Keep who sweet?" He repeats the question.

"Mike O'Malley."

"That prick? Why?" Dave takes a seat next to Larry.

"Chris Morton is poking around last year's AR," Larry explains. "He wants us to open up our investment activity."

"He can go to hell and kiss my ass on the way," John exclaims. "It's none of his goddamned business how we invest our money. He thinks I'm going to open up our competitive advantage and let everyone have a peek?"

"And this is what you want to tell O'Malley?" Dave is smirking.

John sighs and relaxes. "I'm a little tense. I'll get over it."

Larry speaks again. "We're thinking of a two-pronged approach here. Give Morton the standard line about aggressive growth, and then follow that with an exclusive for O'Malley on what that growth might look like over the next couple of quarters."

Dave is nodding. "I like it," he says. "The picture of transparency, without giving anything away. I'll set it up for tomorrow afternoon."

"Good," John says, thinking it is anything but good.

"Shouldn't we loop Greta into this? IR should be included," Dave suggests.

"She's out of town," Larry replies absently. "I'll bring her up to speed. Next week."

John glances at him; he had not realized those two were back on, again. And people think he's the one with a morality problem. "That works," he says simply.

FRIDAY, JANUARY 18

The only activity John enjoys less than giving interviews is conducting them over the phone, but it seems that is to be the latest punishment for his public vilification of Chris Morton. It bothers him when he isn't able to see the reporter's reaction to his words.

"Thanks for your time, John." Mike O'Malley sounds tinny over the speaker phone in the conference room. He must be on his cell. And perhaps in a cave.

"Glad you could fit me into your schedule. I have Steve McAllister and Dave Galvan with me, as well."

Dave nods approvingly at John's conciliatory tone. John glares at him. Steve stifles a smirk behind a cough.

"So, let's talk Fox Trade, then."

"Okay," John begins. "The initial idea was to apply the technology to our financial services activities, for the benefit of our clientele. We also saw it as an opportunity to manage our internal investment activities and shorten our cycle for capital growth."

"But now?"

"We're adding a product line that will mesh nicely with that plan and may accelerate the third objective of the acquisition."

John and Steve nod at each other; as far as anyone on the outside knows, Ithaca had been planned right alongside Fox Trade. No need for the rest of the world to know it was all happenstance, initiated by a junior associate with an Internet fixation. This interview will set the table nicely for the Ithaca announcement, after the shareholder meeting next month.

"Okay, hold on. First, what was the third objective of the acquisition?"

Dave rolls his eyes. *He bit.*

"That's not something I can share yet."

Arrogant son of a bitch, Mike thinks. "And when might you be able to share?"

"End of next quarter, for sure," John promises. "Another exclusive, of course."

Mike sighs. "Okay. So tell me about the new product line, then."

"Kidnap and Ransom insurance."

"Really?" Mike is surprised. This is a specialty offering with relatively small returns for a company the size of Vantage. They must have something really big cooking for the end of next quarter.

"Really."

"Huh. Well, let's talk K&R for a while. I'm sure you have some boilerplate you'd love to see in print."

John laughs. "We'd never give you boilerplate, Mike. But I will hand it over to Steve and Dave to share the particulars. You'll run it past us before going to press, so I can approve my quotes, right?"

"As always, John. Thanks for the time."

"My pleasure," John says, rising from his seat.

TUESDAY, JANUARY 22

"What the hell?" Matt snaps as he is pelted in the head with a barrage of Nerf balls.

"Sorry, dude," Carlo apologizes, approaching his desk. "We didn't think you'd mind a couple of balls in your face." Thomas grins behind him.

"Clever. Just not a good time." Matt's sour mood is evident in his tone.

"What's up?"

"Is Anand here today?"

"Nah," Carlo laughs. "That's why the Nerf wars. What's up?"

"Problem with Fox Trade. The FTC wants more detail about our financing."

"So hand it over to Lawson-Kent." Carlo is referring to the third-party auditor for Vantage.

Matt shrugs. "I want to figure it out myself," he insists.

"You can figure it out for yourself," Carlo agrees. "But then you and your ass are all alone if something goes wrong. Give it to the outside guys. Mitigate your own personal risk, dude."

"Hmmm." Matt ponders the advice. "Probably a good idea."

Carlo nods enthusiastically. "Good man. What's their issue, anyway?"

"They don't like our footnotes on Q1 and Q2 earnings."

"That's all? Lawson can make that go away in an instant." Carlo rolls his eyes. "It's always something with the footnotes, like nobody else in the world uses them. After what happened on Smith Street, a company would be nuts to hide anything even remotely questionable down there."

"Yeah…." Matt is growing uncomfortable with the shift their discussion has taken. "I'll call someone at Lawson."

"Now you're making sense. CYA." Carlo stands up and heads to the coffee room.

"Hey," Matt calls after him. "Foote was looking for you."

"Yeah?" Carlo takes a half step back toward Matt's desk, eyes eager. What does the CFO want with him?

"Yeah, says you left some teabags in his office?"

"Damn, Parsons!" Carlo laughs vigorously. "And Thomas was afraid you wouldn't fit in around here."

WEDNESDAY, JANUARY 23

"Hey, Stan. Mind if I join you?" Matt takes a seat in the barstool next to Stan Firestone. Nighttime in New York City in January is intolerable to them; they have chosen to stay and drink at the hotel bar while the rest of the team heads to ESPN Fan Zone to place bets on the NBA action for the night. Tomorrow they meet again with Fox Trade and try to assuage the concerns that were raised by Chris Morton on the analyst call. Stan's presence is a nod to his role at Vantage and his involvement with bleeding-edge projects outside of the firm; Fox Trade will be satisfied that they have the ear of someone who truly understands how a technology-driven organization operates.

"Not at all," Stan says. "What are you drinking?" He flags down the bar tender.

"Glenlivet, neat."

"No, I've got it," Stan interjects when he sees Matt reaching for his wallet. "It's on my tab."

"Thanks."

"So are you ready for tomorrow?"

"Yeah," Matt replies after a healthy swallow of his drink. "This is the big time, huh?"

"Yup. We'll get it sorted out. Morton has been making noise for the last few quarters; it's only now that anyone has started paying attention, because of Fox Trade."

"Anand told me. But we have nothing to hide, right, so there's nothing to fear." His tone is slightly paradoxical, as if he is not quite sure he believes it. Or, Stan thinks, as if he knows it is not true.

"That's right," Stan agrees cautiously. "Of course any notion of impropriety would be devastating for the company and the shareholders. We all remember what happened a few years back."

Matt looks at him, unfazed. "I know John would be disappointed if someone was less than honest. With him or with an analyst."

"JW is a dying breed," Stan offers. "He's a man of integrity. He's every bit as tough as his reputation, but he's honest. He'd be beside himself if there were even the whiff of professional misconduct."

Matt is nodding, biding his time.

"And I wonder who would bear the brunt of his ire," Stan continues. "The person who committed the offense or the one who knew and didn't report it."

"Tough call." Matt lifts his hand for another drink. "Top you off, Stan? This round is on me."

Stan studies him evenly. Either this kid knows his wife is probably screwing the CEO at this very moment and is okay with it, or he's an absolute idiot. His presence in the lab would seem to rule out the idiot theory. Stan wonders if he may have even offered up his wife like a lamb to the slaughter. He is bold; that much is certain.

"Thanks, I'm ready for another."

When the drinks arrive, Stan faces Matt and speaks bluntly. "What are we talking about here?"

"I'm talking about Prometheus, Stan. What are you talking about?"

"The same."

They sit in silence for a few minutes and then Stan speaks again. "What do you want?"

"It's not just about what I want," Matt asserts. "It's about what I can do in exchange for what I want."

"Go on."

"I can get you a bigger return," he continues. "Some of the stuff we're doing in the lab…it would be mind-boggling to anyone else."

"But not to you."

"Nope." Matt sits up straighter. "I *get* it."

"Give me a proposal when we get back," Stan says. "And we'll talk. I'm sure we can reach an agreement."

FEBRUARY 2008

THURSDAY, FEBRUARY 7

Amanda approaches the gate in front of the Wallaces' home and rolls down her window to push the button for access.

"Yes?" The voice is familiar. Surely he is not answering his own security phone.

"Amanda Parsons here to see Mrs. Wallace."

"Just a moment please." Now the voice sounds amused and she is almost certain that it is John. *CEO humor*, she thinks.

The gate swings open slowly on its enormous hinges and Amanda inches her SUV through the gap. *Get in, get the invitations, get out.* She repeats it to herself the entire way from car to door, and even as she stands waiting for someone to let her in. With any luck, it will be a member of the household staff, invitations in-hand, and she will have only to accept them and leave. When she finally glimpses a form approaching through the beveled glass, however, her stomach sinks like a rock. John Wallace himself. She has avoided situations in which they might be together since last month; even the memory of the look in his eyes at that meeting sends a bolt of electricity through her body.

"Amanda," he says formally as he opens the door. "How nice to see you again. Please come in."

Amanda draws a long, stabilizing breath and crosses the threshold, casting her eyes furtively for any sign of Margaret.

"Is Mrs. Wallace here?"

"Margaret?" He frowns slightly. "No, she's in Napa for a long weekend. Was she expecting you?" He has led her into a small sitting room crammed with English Traditional furniture, Oriental rugs and an abundance of hunting scenes.

"Yes. At least I thought she was," Amanda ventures. "I'm here to pick up some invitations for the museum gala. She wanted to include personal notes in a few." At John's unspoken direction, she has taken a seat in a wing-backed chair.

"I see," John replies, seating himself across from her in a matching chair. "That's next month, isn't it?"

Amanda nods, mildly surprised that he bothers to keep up with the minutiae. "Four weeks from Saturday, in fact." If the rest of the invitations do not hit tomorrow's mail, Margaret will be furious — no matter if she was the reason. But Amanda smiles and says, "I'm sure she finished them."

John is looking at her thoughtfully. Studying her, she realizes. She meets his gaze directly, muffling the alarm bells in her head. A smile begins to pull at his lips; she believes she has passed some kind of test.

"Let's go have a look in her office, shall we?" He stands, and Amanda follows suit, walking next to him as he crosses the wood floors with his long, easy strides.

Margaret Wallace's office resembles a spread from *Martha Stewart Living*. Amanda is not surprised. Her desk is so organized it seems impossible that work has ever taken place at it, but right in the middle of the blotter, in a tidy stack bound four-square with a black, organza ribbon, stand the dove-gray envelopes for the gala.

Silent relief clears Amanda's mind, and she allows herself a smile.

"Find what you need?"

"Yes," she says. "May I?"

John waves a hand toward the stack and Amanda reaches for it, crossing her arm in front of him on the way. As she draws her hand back, prize secure in her fingers, he shifts his weight slightly and her arm brushes his chest.

"Excuse me." Amanda jerks her hand and drops the invitations. She moves to pick them up, but he stops her, hand on her wrist.

"It's my fault," he insists. "Let me." He stoops to the floor and retrieves the bundle. "At least they were tied together," he remarks as he holds them in front of her. His other hand is still on her wrist.

"Yes. Thank you." She takes them with her free hand and moves to break their contact, but his fingers flex gently around her.

"I wanted to apologize for the other day," he says. "When I saw you at the office. I was rude."

The other day? *Last month*, Amanda corrects silently. But she shakes her head quickly and says, "No need. You were working; it wasn't a good time." And besides, he was anything *but* rude. Only a fool would have missed the charge in the air between them.

He smiles at this, as if she has made a joke. "No, it wasn't a good time," he agrees. "I was in a terrible mood. But that's no excuse."

"Please don't worry about that. I'm a grown-up." She tries an ironic smile but it does not feel right on her face. "And nonprofit work has given me a thick skin. I get told 'no' all the time."

He is still squeezing her wrist. "You're very nice to let me off the hook so easily. But," he continues, "When I said that was no excuse, what I meant is that it wasn't the reason."

"Oh?" Trying to keep her voice light; nearly impossible with his skin on hers.

"I was told by a few members of my PR team that I was too friendly with you at the holiday party."

Amanda frowns mentally at this. She had told Matt not to push it so hard. She shakes her head again, face blank. "That was probably my fault," she insists. "I'd had so much fun with you at the ribbon cutting and then the race. I was too familiar at the party."

That measuring look again and she feels his thumb moving in small circles against the underside of her wrist. "Quite the diplomat, aren't you?"

"On-the-job training." Her voice is growing distant and she fights to sound definitive. "The nonprofit thing again."

"The truth is…." He pauses, as if groping for the right words. Something she is certain he does not often have to do. "The truth is I have given them reason to worry. When I saw you that day last month—" *so he does remember when it was* "—I could have tripped over my own feet to get to you." He stops again and then finishes, simply, "I was so excited that you were there."

She does not move, does not blink, does not even allow herself to swallow, though her throat is tightening like the coils of a python.

"And I wondered if perhaps I was right in thinking that you felt something similar," he continues. "Because it seems to me we do have some sort of connection, and I like it."

She feels her head nodding slowly, just one time down and then back up.

"And then I wondered what you might want to do about that."

Amanda steels herself for a silent minute before answering. "I think it would be extremely unwise to do anything about that," she says carefully. "I imagine it would end badly for everyone concerned."

It is almost as if she has rehearsed this response; and he realizes that in fact she has. And because of this, instead of dropping her wrist and stepping back — which he had been fully prepared to do — he leans in and presses his lips against hers, snaking his free arm around her back and smiling when she yields immediately and returns the kiss. He releases her wrist and she winds both arms around his neck, clinging to him in the middle of his wife's office until that thought strikes her at the same moment she feels his body react against hers, and she lets go suddenly and pushes herself away.

"I'm sorry," he laughs quietly, not sorry at all. "I told you; I get excited when you're around."

She has brought her hands up to her face. Cold relief against the blistering skin of her cheeks. "Yes, well. I'm glad you don't exaggerate." Takes another step back, increasing the distance between them. The invitations have fallen to the floor again. This time he does not stop her when she bends to recover them.

He laughs out loud now, noting the deliberateness of her movements. "So I can't change your mind? Still don't want to do anything about it?"

She shakes her head. "I never said I didn't want to; I said we shouldn't."

His face shifts to seriousness. "I understand." He is the CEO again; brisk and authoritative. "Well, you have your invitations. Can I offer you a drink? I know Matt is out of town." Mischievous again.

"I promise to be good, if you stay. I do enjoy your company, whatever form it takes."

"I think I'd better turn that down, too," she says cautiously. "And besides, I have a lot of work to do for the gala. I'll be at the museum all tonight and tomorrow, since you've sent Matt on a mission." As she utters the words they take on a significance she had not intended. She looks at him suspiciously.

He shakes his head, smiling again. "I'm not quite that calculating," he says easily.

"Why not?"

"Honestly," he speaks quietly, "I don't think I need to be."

# # #

Matt runs the numbers through Fox Trade's simulation one more time. The result is even better than what he had expected when he approached Stan in New York. He takes the tech fund that contains Stan's three interests and unbundles the twenty companies it comprises. Next, he invests them via Fox Trade into the high-return derivatives market. Before he bundles them back together, he skims the returns from the three off-shore companies over to Prometheus; when everything is put back together on the other side, Vantage still reaps a decent return. And because the companies are bundled back into his tech fund, the portfolio effect distributes the gains across all the players. The best part is that even if someone notices the fund once he pulls the trigger, it won't matter. Why wouldn't that fund be eligible for some higher returns? Hell, he would probably get another bonus for taking the initiative on it. That's how meritocracies work, after all. Still, he'd better make sure he has a clean exit strategy for the first couple of months. He can't be sure what impact the move will have on the lab's portion of earnings.

He tries to focus his attention on tomorrow's business. A friendly visit with Ithaca's M&A team, to keep them on the line until things settle down with the shareholders and Vantage can move forward.

It starts with an office meeting on Friday and then some skiing on Saturday with his counterpart. Matt cannot believe this counts as a business trip, but whatever. He's not going to complain if Vantage wants to send him to Stowe and bankroll a weekend of black diamond slopes and black label whisky. He wishes Amanda had been able to join him; she loves to ski and it's been a couple of years since they've gone. Their last few trips have been to tropical destinations. If he had known how soon they would be living in a mosquito-infested swamp, he might have proposed different vacation plans for them.

Rising from his desk, he grabs the remote and turns on the TV. There isn't much else he can do to prepare for tomorrow. The meeting is a junket and everyone on both sides of the table knows it. He's in town to make some friends; nothing more. Besides, the Knicks are playing and one of his college teammates is an assistant coach now. He flops onto the bed and settles in for the next three quarters. When the game is over, he returns to his laptop and the Fox Trade simulation. He still has plenty of work to do on this before he pitches it to Stan next week.

MONDAY, FEBRUARY 11

John arrives at the museum just before closing on Monday. Amanda is not surprised to see him; he is not surprised by this.

"How was business today?" He leans on the counter of the reception desk, nonchalant.

"It was good," she replies, as if she had been expecting him all afternoon; as if he visits at closing on a regular basis. "A couple of school groups; even some home-school kids."

"So," he picks a brochure out of the Lucite stand. "You still feel good about the location? We shouldn't have put you in the Museum District?"

"Oh, no." She frowns. "This is much better, from a historical standpoint. The proximity to the bayou, to the city's birthplace."

"More foot-traffic over there."

"I'd miss my neighbors." She points in the direction of the 420 shop.

He smiles; she has won the point. "And how are *you* today?"

Amanda busies herself, packing papers and her Mac book into her bag. "I'm good."

"Get those invitations in the mail?"

She nods. "We should start receiving RVSPs on the Web site late this week."

"Ah, technology," he says. "I can't remember, will there be dancing at the gala?"

Another nod. "Wouldn't be a real gala without dancing, right? Why?"

"I might want to exercise my option."

She walks toward him, peering at her watch. "I need to lock up; excuse me for a minute, please."

He watches her back as she moves to the door and turns the deadbolt in its chamber, then pulls the shade closed. She is wearing a skirt, like almost every other time he has seen her. He likes that; it's a throw-back to an era when women were comfortable being women.

And she is smart enough to recognize the advantage it gives her over her peers, without detracting one whit from her intellectual appeal.

"Do you leave through the back?" His tone is somewhat bothered. She was joking about the neighbors, but it is a dangerous area.

"No, I go out front and walk around. But I always lock up as soon as I close, so I can finish what I'm doing."

She is standing in front of him. He looks at her, mild confusion on his face — an unfamiliar condition for him, certainly. He glances at her bag, fully packed now.

"And what do you have to finish tonight?"

"A dance, apparently."

He shakes his head. "I was speaking of the gala."

"I won't be able to dance with you at the gala," she explains. "Especially not after tonight."

"And why is that?"

She meets his gaze directly, just as she had at his home four nights before. "I think you know why," she says slowly.

He sighs and lifts his hand to her face, brushing the backs of his fingers against her cheek. She closes her eyes and tilts her head upward, leaning into him.

"I thought about you all weekend," he says, his mouth against her ear.

She nods. "Me, too." Her voice is tinged with resignation, as if she had no other choice but to think about him all weekend.

"Where can we go; where can I take you to make you comfortable?"

Amanda shakes her head. "I don't know. Why not here?"

He kisses her, and it is exactly as she remembered it. She had tried for days both to store it in her mind and to forget it, although she had been fairly certain neither course would matter. Fairly certain there would be another chance.

"You mean, on the reception desk?" His voice is amused and confident.

"I thought maybe my office; the sofa." Her mouth is moving across his face, seeking his lips again.

"I think we can do better than that." He breaks their embrace. "Come on. You can lock up from the back door, yes?"

"Yes. Where are we going?" Her eyes are narrowed, voice uncertain.

"I'm sorry," he says. "Did you want to stay here? Was the spontaneity important?"

A serious look. "I don't do anything on spontaneity."

He laughs at this. "I'm not at all surprised. Come on," he repeats. "I have a loft downtown, near the ball park. You can ride along or follow me."

# # #

The contrast between John's loft and his sprawling Tanglewood home could not be more pronounced. Whereas the house is crammed with Country French, Tuscan and English Traditional vignettes, the loft is a study in straightforward, urban design. Art glass pendants hang over the low, stainless steel bar and sink. Every piece of wooden furniture is black; every piece of upholstery is white. The only relief to this color scheme is the pendants and the hemp-colored Sisal rugs that cover the scored-concrete floors.

"Like it?"

Amanda nods slowly, taking it all in. "Love it," she says, her voice cool with appraisal. "And that's a great view of the ball park and downtown."

He stands behind her, looking out the window. "During the season, my sons and I sometimes go up to the roof and watch the games." His hands are on her shoulders. "May I take your coat?"

She shrugs her arms and lets him pull the coat away. He drapes it over a bar stool and returns to her side.

"Are you okay?"

"Yes, I'm fine." She looks at him intently. She has no idea what to expect, now that she is here, beyond the simple mechanics of what they are about to do. Although as she studies his face, she considers the possibility that the mechanics may not be so simple with him, after all.

"How about some wine? I'm thinking you're red."

She nods. "I am."

"I think you'll like this," he says, walking to the kitchen to open a bottle. "Sit; relax," he urges as the cork pops out. "This isn't a command performance."

Amanda takes a seat on the sofa, facing the skyline. "It's not such a bad city," she observes. "In the dark, anyway."

He joins her with the wine. "It has its moments. Where did you grow up?"

"Right here," she says. "You didn't know that?"

He shakes his head. "No, I never checked your résumé. Why don't you bring me up to speed?"

"Okay." She takes a sip of wine. "Very nice," she says. "I grew up in Houston, went to St. Agnes."

"That explains a lot," he notes, smiling at her.

"I suppose it does," she agrees. "Then college at Trinity, grad school at Columbia, spent some time in Chicago, New York, D.C. and then back here."

"Columbia?" He is clearly surprised. "What kind of degree?"

She smirks. "MBA," she confirms.

"What the hell are you doing at the museum? Why aren't you working for me?"

"No, thanks. Nonprofit deserves sharp minds, too."

He is looking at her blankly. Not a good enough answer, apparently. She draws a long breath and continues, "I graduated from Columbia in May of 2002. Not much of a market for MBA-types then." She refuses to make the Smith Street reference; he can provide the context for himself.

"Okay…."

"And it occurred to me that corporate giving was about to take a nose-dive, too, so I started talking to nonprofits, telling them that they needed someone like me to find new sources of funding."

"God, no wonder I like you so much," he mutters. "You are a shameless opportunist." He laughs and leans in to kiss her.

"That's something I've wondered about, actually," she tells him, when he pulls his head back. "Why me?"

"Well," he says softly. "You're just so damned…cool." Lips connect again. "I've never seen anything like it, how poised you are. Just so neutral all the time, no matter what's going on around you. You'd be invisible if you weren't so incredibly intense."

"I see."

"But I have a theory," he whispers. "I suppose you're familiar with the term 'market neutral,' Miss Columbia…."

She nods, taking a nip out of his lower lip and eliciting a smile for her effort. "You think I'm straddling the line between long and short positions?"

"Yeah, and I want to see what kind of volatility erupts when I tip the balance." He takes her wine glass and puts it, along with his, on the end table.

"Are you planning to tip it in favor of short…or long?" Weaving her fingers into his hair; colored or not, she could not possibly care less at this moment.

"I think I may be in heaven right now," he says, leaning her back on the cushions. "Keep talking dirty finance to me."

He moves his fingers swiftly from button to button on her blouse; pushing the silk aside and letting it drop from her narrow frame like a feather from a bird. She reaches behind her back and unhooks the black lace bra but he stops her when she tries to remove it.

"A little impatient, are we?" he murmurs into her neck. His tongue dips into the hollow like a cat drinking from its bowl and he breathes slowly and deeply, in and out, feeling her tense and relax beneath him with each breath.

Amanda settles for addressing the buttons on his shirt, shoving it down his arms and then tugging the undershirt over his head. She tries to sit up and bring skin to skin but again, he stops her, smiling at her haste. *Ah, youth.* His hands move on her, creeping beneath the black lace, up from her rib cage, letting his fingers whisper lightly over the curves, and only then does he allow her to push aside the scrap of fabric. His lips between her breasts, moving down the line of her stomach and stopping just above her navel. Her once crisp skirt now a crumpled, twisted mess between them and he does not protest as she slips it over her legs and onto the floor. As he drags his mouth back up her ribs he feels her hands at his belt and smiles as she pushes away the dress pants, engaging her feet in the process when she runs out of reach with her arms. His mouth at her breast now, teeth nibbling and tongue teasing and lips pulling, and she sighs, half in pleasure and half — he thinks — in relief that he is finally getting on with it.

"Come on," he whispers, lifting his head reluctantly. He pulls her to her feet and then onto the bed, where they kneel at the center, facing each other, flesh against flesh at last. John runs his hands along her back, delighting in her very texture, his nose buried in her neck and hair. Her scent at this moment a dizzying combination of perfume and raw excitement. As his senses grow more acute and his thoughts less lucid, he is aware of her hand pulling at him, his boxer briefs dispatched while he was distracted by her smell. And now she has him clasped tight between her legs, dragging herself back and forth along him, the lace boy-shorts creating a sensation that shackles his resolve to prolong the experience. His legs quiver and he drops his eyes between their bodies, finding that her hand is inside her own shorts, fingers stretching the lace as they move in time with the thrust of her hips against him. He looks around the room, as if to make certain this is actually happening; that she is actually doing what his brain tells him she is doing.

"Oh." It is the only word he can manage.

"Well," she breathes into his ear. "It's really about damned time you joined me for this. I've been ready since November."

It is enough, finally. In one swift movement, he has Amanda on her back and the shorts flung behind them, landing in the kitchen sink for all he knows or cares. Her fingers in his mouth for a taste that will have to suffice for now and he is inside her at last, so deep he thinks he may drown but then he pulls back almost to the point of withdrawal and dives again. And again and again, until she captures him with her legs around his waist and keeps him close as they breathe and moan and finally shout into each other's mouths and then everything is stillness and silence again, but for the lazy tracing of her fingers through the film of sweat growing cold now on his back.

# # #

Matt's sniper falls from the tower just as his platoon leader hurls a grenade into the burned-out building. The building crumbles, killing everyone inside and racking up a ridiculous point total.

"Get back, motherfucker!" Matt pumps his fist in the air and shouts at the ceiling. He spins around and then, overcome by sudden self-consciousness, glances around to make sure Amanda hasn't come in. No sign of her. She hates it when he drops the f-bomb.

He puts down the Wii controller and strolls to the kitchen for some water. As he breaks the seal on a new bottle of Evian, he notices the time on the microwave clock. Midnight and Amanda still isn't home. She must be sleeping at the museum again. He will leave her alone; she sets the building alarm and works until she collapses. If he goes to visit her, he'll trip the alarm and cause a scene. Matt opens the fridge and pulls out the left-over pasta from last night. He grabs a fork and eats it cold, out of the container. His mind has wandered back to Amanda. He worries when she pulls these all-nighters; she used to do the same thing in school, staying at the library until she fell asleep in a study carrel. Matt had lost track of the times he had gone to retrieve her, bleary-eyed and starving the next morning. But at least she was in a safe place, then. As for now, he doesn't like the location of the museum at all. He walks to the foyer and picks his cell phone up from the console table. A text message wouldn't be too intrusive. If she's asleep, she can ignore it.

Hey, u awake?

He pushes the send button and takes the phone with him into the den. He waits a few minutes for a reply, drinking his water and watching the phone. She must be asleep. Settling back into his game chair, Matt pushes the *A* button on the controller and moves on to the next level in Medal of Honor; plenty more Nazis to kill. And now he has to find a new sniper, too. *Pussy.*

TUESDAY, FEBRUARY 12

Amanda awakens with a jolt at three a.m. He is still asleep beside her and she studies him quietly. Six months, she realizes. She has known him for six months and seen him perhaps as many times during that span. But she had known at their first meeting that this was likely. And she believes he had known, as well.

He opens his eyes and smiles at her. Runs his hand along her side under the covers.

"Exquisite," he murmurs, moving until he can feel all of her skin against his. He nuzzles her neck. "How long have you been awake?"

"Not long. It was nice to watch you at peace. I don't think many people get to see that." Her voice is thoughtful and she feels him smile against her throat.

"I'm at peace whenever you're around," he claims.

"I thought you were excited whenever I'm around."

"That, too. The emotions are not mutually exclusive."

She is quiet for a moment, enjoying the velvet of his lips against her skin. Eventually, she sighs. "I think it's time for me to go, before the sun comes up."

"Why? Are you a vampire?"

"No, but I may turn into a pumpkin."

He looks up at her. "Now, see, I knew you had a sense of humor. First the ring dings and now this. You should use it more often."

"Only when I'm at peace," she teases.

A laugh. "Okay. And when might I see you at peace again?"

She stiffens beneath him. "Again?"

"Well, yes." He has risen up on his elbows. "Unless you'd rather not."

"It's not that," she assures him quickly. "I just didn't expect — "

He rolls onto his back. "What have you heard?" His voice is suddenly tired.

"What do you think I've heard?"

"An endless stream of women. I'm insatiable. A shark. No moral compass. Blah, blah, blah." He waves a hand in the air with each *blah*.

She waits to be sure he has finished. "A revolving door that you don't stop for anyone."

He turns back over and takes her face between his hands. "Do you remember the day we met?"

"Of course."

He does not say anything else, waiting for her to catch up.

"You held the revolving door for me." She closes her eyes. "But that was an actual door —"

"Doesn't matter. Still counts."

Eyes open, lit with suspicion. "So, what is this, then? What do you want?"

He is still holding her face. "You." As if it is the most obvious fact the world has ever seen. "I want you."

"For how long?" As soon as the words are out, she regrets them. For once her famous filter has not worked. She squeezes her eyes shut briefly and then opens them again, fearful that she has blown it with him and, more importantly, alarmed by this fear.

"I don't know," he confesses. "Can you live with that for a while?"

"You want me to be your… mistress?"

He makes a face. "I don't like that word." He strokes her cheeks. "Do we have to call it anything?"

"I guess not." She pauses. "This is new to me. I thought this would be the only time — also new to me, incidentally. I spent all weekend preparing myself for a one-night thing."

He can picture it: Amanda at her laptop, making a cost-benefit analysis for a fling. His thumbs move across her lips and then he kisses her again. His lips leave her face and travel downward, past her neck and to her breasts.

"I can live with a little uncertainty," she decides, when he lifts his head. "With some conditions."

"You process very quickly." His tone amused. "What are your conditions?"

"No e-mail; no letters." She thinks for a moment and adds, "No phone calls, either. And no gifts."

"No phone calls? How do I come near you? Carrier pigeon?"

"You can call me," she relents. "But only at the museum."

"Cell phone."

"No. No precedent for that. And for God's sake, no text messages."

He whistles. "You're tough."

"And I thought this was all because I'm so damned cool."

"Ha!" He shakes his head. Does she always have a retort? "It's true. Well, that and it was all I could do not to bend you over your conference table that first day."

"Are we in agreement?" It is not time to play again. Not yet. She looks intently at him; she does not believe he is wearing contacts, at all. And at this range, she can detect the fine lines at the corners of his eyes and on his forehead, too. Is anything she has heard about him true? She cannot imagine being the target of such petty speculation.

He sighs. "Okay."

She relaxes again. "Okay."

John studies her face and smiles. "You are completely unreadable," he concludes.

"You can thank me for that later." She shifts beneath him, opening herself up to him again, now that their terms are settled.

THURSDAY, FEBRUARY 14

"What's this?" Matt's voice trails after Karen as she drops an envelope on his desk and moves briskly down the aisle.

"Little sumpin-sumpin, I guess," she calls over her shoulder, winking at him.

Matt slides his finger under the flap to open it and extracts a check. A really big check. A note is stuck to the back.

Matt, great job on Fox Trade and the liquidity issue. Get something nice for yourself and something nicer for your wife. Never forget, they make it all happen. – JW

"Holy shit," he whispers. *So this is what it feels like to be an idiot.* He could get used to it.

Moments later an e-mail from Melissa Kemper appears in his inbox.

Matt, JW asked me to forward some suggestions for an appropriate gift for your wife. Please see the following. – MK

The one link in the message takes him to www.patek.com and the most intricate watch he has ever seen. Case set with 34 diamonds, approximately 0.66 carats. Crown set with one diamond, approximately 0.05 carat. There is no pricing information on the site. Matt swallows hard and navigates the pages to find authorized retailers in Houston. Tiffany & Co., in the Galleria. Of course.

"Taking an early lunch," he calls to Karen, grabbing his coat from the stand by the window.

"A little Valentine's Day shopping?"

Valentine's Day. "Yep," he says.

He had totally forgotten. That wasn't like him at all. And Amanda has been working like a dog at the museum all week, getting ready for the gala. Matt doesn't understand how she can put up with that insufferable woman. He is still seething from her treatment of Amanda at the opening. He mentally thanks God for John Wallace and his assistant. She is incredibly thorough.

"You're wife is a lucky woman," the Tiffany associate tells him. "And you have excellent taste. She'll be thrilled." She hands the signature egg-shell blue bag to him, keeping the receipt separate.

"Thanks," Matt says, palming the receipt and stuffing it into his coat pocket. He still cannot bring himself to look at the numbers; he has to get to the bank and deposit the check before he vomits all over this nice, grandmotherly woman on the other side of the case.

Even as he punches the numbers into his bank's ATM terminal, he finds it almost impossible to believe. He has enough left over for… for a new set of golf clubs and probably some lessons at Hermann Park, as well. His stomach grumbles as he watches the envelope feed into the metal box.

Dinner, he thinks. *Dammit*. He needs to make reservations somewhere, and fast. Anxiety rises in his chest and pulls at the hairs on his neck. He'll never get in anyplace this late on Valentine's Day.

At the thought, his Blackberry buzzes. Melissa again. What the hell?

Matt, Also wanted to let you know I have a table for you and Amanda at Mark's for 8 p.m. Enjoy. – MK

He sighs with relief, although the whole thing is starting to creep him out a little bit. Karen must have called Melissa; she can read him so easily. He'll worry about the creepiness factor later. For now, he auto-dials Amanda to wow her with their dinner destination.

"Hey, shorty," he says when she answers.

"What's up, babe?"

"Happy Valentine's Day."

"Oh, you remembered." For a minute, her voice carries that little-girl quality she had effused when they met. He wonders when she changed, and then shrugs. It's not important now.

"I have dinner reservations at Mark's tonight."

"Seriously? It's really hard to get in there on Valentine's Day."

"I know. Just a little secret I've been keeping," he says playfully. "Want to meet me at the house around six, so we can have a pre-party?"

"I do," she says. "See you then."

# # #

When the wine has been poured, Matt reaches into his coat pocket and retrieves the Tiffany bag.

"No way," Amanda says. "Are you proposing again?"

He smiles at her. He loves her the most when she is like this — relaxed and slightly mischievous. She hasn't been this way in months. Since he started at Vantage, he realizes suddenly, with an internal frown. He'll have to slow things down at work for a while. Their interlude at home before dinner had reminded him that there is more to life than one-page deal summaries. And this is the first time she hasn't snapped at him for something he has said or done in ages.

"Open it." His voice is eager.

"Whoa, Matt." She looks at him, fear on her face. So soon after Christmas? "This is crazy. Patek-Philippe? How did you afford it?"

He grins at her. "Courtesy of a big, fat bonus from JW himself. A reward for the all-nighter I had to pull last month; and Fox Trade, I guess."

He has started referring to John as JW; it grates on Amanda.

"Wow," she says. "It's gorgeous," she croons, putting it on. "Thank you." She laughs. "There is no way I can give you my gift now. You'll have to wait a couple of days for the dazzle factor of this to wear off."

"I can do that," he agrees. "I'm so happy you like it."

"It's a little too big for me," she comments. "I'll take it in and have some links removed."

"Sure," he concurs. "I'll put the receipt in your purse tomorrow. Don't look at it." He laughs. "I know I haven't."

"I promise," she agrees. "And then I'll give you my gift over the weekend."

Matt's face falls slightly. "Oh, man. I'm sorry, Mandy. I totally forgot to tell you."

"What?"

"I'm headed back to New York this weekend. One more round of hand-holding with Fox Trade before the shareholders' meeting next week."

Hand-holding. Amanda sighs. He means plying their management team with drinks and strippers to keep them quiet until the vote on the acquisition is final. If it were serious business, he'd go during the week, after all. It amazes her that the Fox Trade leadership is simple enough to be placated with a visit from someone as junior as Matt. It should be John and Steve flying up to make assurances at this stage — if a personal visit is even necessary. The trip is a boondoggle.

"It's okay, Matt," she mollifies. "I understand. Next week is fine." She smiles at him; she hopes brightly enough.

FRIDAY, FEBRUARY 15

"Anybody home?"

Amanda has just locked the front door; he has entered through the alley. Evidently, he has a key.

"Just me," she says, walking quickly but fluidly toward her office to meet him. He catches her as she crosses the doorway and kisses her eagerly. They have not seen each other or even communicated since he had dropped her back at the museum in the pre-dawn shadows on Tuesday. She leans into him briefly but then shoves him away, aiming for her conference table, which is littered with a colorful array of miniature sticky notes and several tabloid-sized table diagrams.

"Wow. You're mad at me for something; I can't imagine what." He grins. "But I think I like it."

She glares at him and holds up her left wrist.

"Oh, the watch." He moves to her side for a closer look and his brows draw together in a frown when he sees the Rolex emblem. "That's not the one I wanted."

"No. And I didn't want one at all, so I guess we're even." The scowl on her face should be unattractive but isn't. "A Patek-Philippe? What were you thinking?"

"I was *thinking* that the Seiko you got for high school graduation needed an upgrade."

"How many women my age, in my line of work, do you see wearing a Patek-Philippe watch?" She sputters the words. Matt had been heartbroken the night before when he had noticed. She had explained that it was not smart for either of them, politically, for her to have a watch that Margaret Wallace might wear. It was level-jumping. He had grudgingly seen the reason in her argument.

"Zero," John says firmly. "That's why I picked it. You are nothing like any other woman your age — or in your line of work."

She shakes her head. "I said no gifts. That includes laundering them through Matt."

A look of admiration for her analogy. "How many people ever get to see you angry, Amanda?"

Her shoulders square. "Zero," she says with a lift of her chin. And she has *never* worn a Seiko. But she will address that later.

"You like me." He seems blissful as he closes the distance she has imposed between them.

She is shaking her head again. "You are such a little boy."

He kisses her again and this time she returns it, breaking away more gently and then sitting at her table. She is clearly distracted.

"All right," he concedes the moment. "What is this?" Sweeps a hand over the collection of paper.

"Gala seating chart. I've spent all afternoon on it."

He scans the sticky notes and frowns. "You have the Arthurs at the same table as the McMillans. You might want to reconsider that."

She peers up at him. "Indeed?" Her voice is mildly challenging; he thinks it is defensive.

He sits next to her. "Yes, indeed. Tom Arthur and Natalie McMillan have been sleeping together for the last six months."

Amanda sighs the way a mother might as she prepares to indulge her child. "I know. I did it on purpose. I had to give Margaret something to correct." She points to another table and continues, "I also put Mark Hoffman and Ari Lerner together, and they've been feuding for months about a business deal that went awry. And, just to be sure, I seated Leticia Murdoch next to Sandra Carson. Given the likelihood that they will wear the same designer 'original,' Margaret may actually stroke out when she sees that."

"Damn, woman," he says. "You're absolutely Machiavellian."

"Flattery." She wags her finger at him. "You're still in trouble for the watch."

"So, you have this pretty well wrapped up, then?" He has moved his hand across the table and captured her fingers. "You have some time for me?"

"Some." She likes the effect a little attitude has on him. "Why?"

"I'm on my own this weekend. Margaret is in Atlanta with the boys. Visiting Emory."

"I know," Amanda says matter-of-factly. "Melissa sends me her schedule every Monday."

"Melissa," John says evenly. "Very thorough."

"That's what I've heard." She stands and shoves the diagrams into a folder. "I caught the bus to work today. No car to take home. And Matt is in New York again — all weekend, in fact. Very thorough."

SUNDAY, FEBRUARY 17

"This is almost double the return I've been getting." Stan pushes the paper back to Matt, skepticism dripping from his eyes and his words. They are seated at a small table in a corner of the President's Club at La Guardia.

"Exactly," Matt says, not touching the page.

"Explain it to me again," Stan suggests. "Because I don't see how it's possible."

"It's complicated," Matt assures him. "Don't worry if it doesn't make sense right away."

"It looks like all the money is moving in a giant circle," Stan says, tetchily. "That much is clear."

Matt smiles gently. "It has to do with the velocity at which I'm able to move things around using Fox Trade. And pulling the pieces apart helps mask the trail. Each transaction becomes just one of hundreds in the entire portfolio. Nobody is going to look at one of these and say, 'That's not right,' when there are others achieving the same result."

Stan is quiet for a minute. This is Matt's third attempt to explain what he is proposing and the most reasonable so far. The young man seems to get ahead of himself and forget that he is communicating with people who may not share his level of financial intellect.

"Okay," Stan says at last. "We can give it a try. What are the instruments called again?"

"Credit default swaps," Matt reminds him. "They were developed to function like insurance policies on all the mortgage-backed derivatives the major lenders created in the last several years. So it's like a built-in hedge."

Stan doesn't think that sounds quite right, but he is at a loss to argue the point. And the kid does know his stuff. Everyone at Vantage is beginning to talk about him — and not just because of his wife and John Wallace. It staggers Stan that the only one who doesn't seem to know about that is Matt, himself, given that it has probably been going on for at least four months now. He opens his mouth to say something about it, just as First Class boarding is called for their flight over the club's PA system.

# # #

Amanda soaks in the claw-foot tub, fingers brushing against the mark John has left on her, his lips and teeth and tongue insistent against her skin.

Stop; I'll have to hide it or explain it later.

You'd hide it?

Yes, of course I would.

I like the idea of that. Maybe I'll just cover you in them every day, so he can't touch you at all.

Is that what you want?

Yes. Yes, it's what I want.

For how long, she wonders now, sinking lower into the water until it covers her head. As she resurfaces for air, she finds Matt standing at the side of the tub.

"Hey," he greets her. "I'm back."

"How was your trip?"

He is pulling his sweater over his head. "Why don't you move over, and I'll tell you all about it?"

She laughs but shakes her head. "Sorry, baby. I was just getting out. I'm all pruned up and the water is cold." She reaches for the towel and drapes it in front of her as she stands. "Long run today."

"Oh, okay." He sounds disappointed but quickly recovers. He knows it can't be fun for her with him gone so much. "Where did you run?"

"To the park."

She must mean *at* the park. "Memorial?"

"No, Discovery Green, then to Minute Maid, then back."

"Holy cats, Amanda. How many miles is that?" He is shaking his head. She's over-training again; he blames himself. He really has to knock off the travel for a while, at least on weekends. And it's way too soon after the marathon, although he knows she was disappointed with her time.

"A lot," she agrees, wrapping herself in the towel. "My whole body hurts. So, did you get things settled with Fox Trade this time?"

"Yeah," he replies. "It's going to be fine. That's my baby," he adds.

"I know. Is take-out okay for dinner? I'm too tired to cook."

"Of course. I'll even pick it up. Your call."

She has moved to the mirror and picked up a comb. The towel shifts downward and Matt's face wrinkles with concern.

"What happened?"

Amanda looks at her side. "Wore the wrong bra."

He crosses the slate floor and touches the purple mark below her breast; bends and presses his lips to it. "Poor baby," he murmurs against her skin. She winces. "Still hurts?"

"Yeah."

He frowns and hitches the towel up for her. "You're cold. How about Auntie Chang's?"

"Sounds great," she replies. "Let's eat there, in fact. I'd like to get out of the house, if that's okay with you."

"Sure. Whenever you're ready." His feelings are obviously wounded as he turns and leaves so she can dress. She studies him from the mirror, his body retreating down the hall. She wonders why he isn't enough for her as she closes her eyes and pulls the comb through her wet hair.

TUESDAY, FEBRUARY 26

"Are you ready to call to order?"

The secretary speaks in hushed but urgent tones, shaking John into sudden and disappointed awareness of his surroundings. He had left Amanda at his loft, dozing in a patch of winter sunlight on the bed. The museum is closed on Tuesdays; Melissa has blocked the day each week on his calendar but the shareholders' meeting had been on the books since last year.

"Thank you, yes," he replies, if a bit late for the comfort of his companions at the dais. "Call to order the Vantage PLC Annual Meeting of Shareholders."

Leigh Chambers nods and begins her official record of the meeting. "Is there a motion on the floor to dispense with the reading of the roll call of stockholders present?"

Her arm trailing over the edge of the low platform, fingertips grazing the floor.

A gesture from the audience. "I so move."

She is prone on the mattress and he pulls the sheet away to expose her back.

"Second," emerges a voice from the back of the room.

Trails his nose lightly along her spine, from top to bottom; she stirs. Eyes nearly colorless in the stark, eastern light. Writhing like a serpent as he moves his lips across her back; advance and retreat, advance and retreat.

"All in favor?" Hands in the air. "Opposed?" The room is still.

Don't you have a meeting or something? I'll wait for you; don't worry. On her back now and her hands on his tie, reeling him in for a lingering farewell.

"Motion carries," Leigh notes. "Proxies have been presented and filed with me; we have a majority of shareholders represented by combination of attendance and proxy."

I should be back before two. Stay right there.

Leigh continues speaking; reading a copy of the notice of today's meeting and confirming that it was mailed with ample time for participation of all shareholders. John's thoughts shift now to Fox Trade and the real reason he is present: the vote. He thinks they have quelled the liquidity concerns raised by Chris Morton in recent weeks, but the proof will be in the outcome. His face pulls into the merest of frowns as he ponders the impact of a strong objection to the acquisition. Between his father and himself, they have enough votes to approve the transaction themselves. The entire proceeding is simply to keep them legal and create some goodwill.

They have moved on to the reading of last year's minutes. John is bored and his mind travels back to Amanda. *Will she really wait?* Now Leigh is swearing in the election inspectors; John turns his head to acknowledge them. They have no new directors on the slate today; nothing but Fox Trade. The meeting is sparsely attended; this should bode well for an approval. At last he hears Leigh winding down the procedural requirements and sits forward in his seat. She will wait for him, he is certain.

"Is there a motion to call for a vote regarding the intent of Vantage PLC to purchase Fox Trade LLC?"

"So moved."

"Second."

"The motion is made and seconded; all in favor?"

John scans the room. This one is not unanimous. He groans mentally. Someone wants to *talk* about it.

"Opposed?"

Some twenty hands stretch toward the ceiling. John glances down the platform and catches Greta's eye. Greta responds with a barely visible shake of her head and an upturned hand. It is John's moment to shine; he is well-known for his willingness to hear from shareholders. The fact that this group did not request time on the agenda is frustrating, but they will make no formal complaint. Bad PR to gripe about your shareholders.

John clears his throat. "How can I help you?" He speaks softly into the microphone in front of him, not troubling to dip his head closer to it.

In the audience, a man stands and approaches the microphone in the aisle. "I have some concerns about the funding for this acquisition, Mr. Wallace, and I'd like to give you the opportunity to alleviate them."

"Certainly," John says agreeably. "I know it's been a trying year for a lot of big names in our industry, as well as the financial sector in general. But I want each of you to rest assured that Vantage has entered into this acquisition thoughtfully and with the best interests of our company, our shareholders and indeed the overall health of our industry."

"I'm sure you have," the man replies. "But I'd feel a whole lot better if I knew exactly *how* the company was paying for it. In short, will we see a decrease in our dividends because of this deal?"

John keeps his face still, but he wants to laugh. *A decrease in dividends?* What a stupid question. *Jesus.* He works very hard not to look down the table at the faces of the officers and directors who are present. To do so would risk a chorus of eye-rolling that would derail the entire meeting.

But he smiles. "Certainly there will be an impact," he explains. "But the long-term goal is to create growth in the share price that will outstrip any dividends we might have otherwise paid."

"Well, Mr. Wallace, I'm just not sure I can support that."

So sell your shares. All two-hundred of them. "I understand, and I'm sorry you feel that way. But for the first time in several years, we are looking at a growth trajectory, versus the status quo. We believe this acquisition will actually enable us to fund future growth — organically. That is, we will be less likely to seek leverage for future ventures."

"I see," the man replies, pondering John's words.

John looks at him expectantly. He looks to be retired and probably counts on the dividends as part of his fixed income. John appreciates his apprehension, but if he would seek advice from someone with real knowledge about the transaction and investments in general, he would see the benefit.

"I thank you for your time, then, Mr. Wallace." He looks back toward his seat, to see if anyone else in his cadre has lingering questions. When nobody speaks, he returns to his seat.

"You're most welcome," John replies, his voice cordial. He looks at Leigh and nods.

"May I have another motion to call for a vote regarding the intent of Vantage PLC to purchase Fox Trade LLC?"

"So moved."

"Second."

"The motion is made and seconded; all in favor?"

And the vote proceeds. John wonders, as the ballots are collected, if there will be exactly twenty *nays*. He lets his mind go numb once again as the meeting returns to simple procedure. Minutes are read, reports are approved. John stares straight ahead and tries not to glance at his watch while the seconds pass as though made of lead.

WEDNESDAY, FEBRUARY 27

"You've let yourself become completely distracted by that girl. You're paying lip-service to shareholders, the market — not to mention employees."

"I don't know what you're talking about."

"This." Dave drops a copy of the *Wall Street Journal* on the table. He points to an article mid-way down the front page. "*Although optimistic about the company's growth strategy, Vantage CEO John Wallace was alternately distracted and intense at the shareholder meeting. Market analysts speculate this has to do with recent inquiries into the company's liquidity and long-term stability in an increasingly volatile capital market.*"

John does not respond; he seems intent on reading the entire article.

"I'm torn, JW. On the one hand, I'm glad the media and the market don't realize your brain is stuck in your pants right now. On the other hand, you've planted a seed in the marketplace that's going to be tough to manage. I know you're accustomed to getting what you want, but there will be major consequences for this."

"Getting what I want?" John looks up from the paper at last. "When exactly do I get what I want? All I do is worry about what everybody else wants. The market, the shareholders — *not to mention employees*," he says in a sarcastic echo of Dave's own comment. "I wake up each morning and wonder, 'What'll it be today? A lawsuit? An SEC investigation? A rogue analyst lining his own pockets with my company's dwindling market cap? Or — your personal obsession — maybe a female employee who claims I looked at her for too long on the elevator six months ago?'"

"So you're not even denying it anymore. This thing with Amanda Parsons."

"I never have. There's no reason to."

Dave studies him critically. John is adept at evasion, a quality that Dave usually appreciates in him but now finds maddening. "No reason because there is nothing to deny, or no reason because you just don't care?"

A venomous look. "Honestly, Dave, I've never known a man so interested in the extra-curricular activity of my dick. Kind of makes me wonder."

Dave's face flushes with anger at John's suggestion. He opens his mouth to respond, but John does not give him an opening.

"More importantly, though, I wonder about your competence. If you think this is about me getting what I want, maybe I need someone else running Public Affairs for me. Someone who knows more than fuck-all about what my job is so he can represent me without my constant input."

Dave fumes silently until he is certain John has finished his rant. Then he stands. "We'll leak a story about your father's health and pin the distraction on that."

John nods; his face stony. "Now you're doing your job, Dave. Next time, lead with the solution. I'm not interested in your problems."

MARCH 2008

TUESDAY, MARCH 4

Amanda stares out the window at the buildings, dressed in pink by the early light. Her eyes fixed on a point far in the distance; if he asks her to identify it, she will have nothing to say. She feels him shift, restless, beside her.

"I'm sorry," he says quietly, to the ceiling.

She does not respond.

"I didn't mean to say it."

"You didn't mean to say it, or you didn't mean it?" Still watching the horizon as the dawn continues its steady crawl toward her.

John sighs; it is always semantics with her. "The former."

Now she turns to face him. "Then we have a problem."

"Well, yeah. For one thing, my timing sucks." It is a regular feature of his facts-of-life talk — advanced theory — with his sons that under no circumstances are they to pledge their love during sex. Women hate it. And Amanda had proven the point; turning to stone beneath him, her face rendered a harlequin of ardor and dismay.

She shakes her head. "Least of my worries. This can't be about that."

His hand moves to touch her shoulder; she balks slightly at the intended contact, causing his brows to draw together with concern. Seeing his face, she relaxes and accepts the caress.

"I know," he confirms. "But there it is. I've told you before, you mess me up. I don't think properly around you."

"That's not love," she says, touching his face, in spite of her frustration with him and his rash declaration. "That's heat and infatuation and ... and sex. Not love." But her voice is gentle; she will forgive him.

He looks at her, relieved to see her face softening. He could argue his point, but he knows it is useless. "Okay."

"So, don't say it again, unless — " She appears startled and halts suddenly.

"Unless what?" He is surprised, too. And hopeful.

Amanda shakes her head. "I don't know; I didn't mean to say that."

He laughs a little, at this. "Must be something in the water. Will you stay, then?"

She nods. "I'll stay."

He opens his arms, inviting her back in. She slides across the bed and rests against him, raising her head to receive the kiss he is offering. Her eyes probe his face.

Unless you're going to do something about it.

John nods, as if he has heard her unspoken challenge.

SATURDAY, MARCH 8

"You look amazing, Mandy." Matt squeezes her knee on the car seat.

"Thanks, baby." She rests her head on his shoulder. "The limo was an impressive touch. You think of everything lately."

"Yeah, I'm on my game. What can I say?" But he isn't; not at all. The limo was arranged by Melissa. It seems as though anything regarding Amanda's comfort is addressed by JW's assistant before Matt can even consider it. What puzzles him, though, is that the two women don't appear to be close. Probably all museum-related.

"I talked to the Realtor today," he ventures; he knows this is a touchy subject, although he does not understand why. He has noticed that almost everything is a touchy subject with Amanda, lately.

"Did you?" Her voice is light.

"I did, and she found a perfect tear-down for us in West U. It's near the elementary school, which could come in handy someday...."

Amanda lifts her head. "I'm not ready yet, Matt. We have so much going on. In six months or a year, things will have settled down. It will be a better time to make a change." The edge to her voice cuts the happy atmosphere around them into shreds.

"Or," Matt plunges ahead uncharacteristically. "We could get the lot now and get started with construction so that in six months we're totally settled. And the housing market, well, I think it's a good time to sell. Houston's bound to catch up with the rest of the country at some point. If we don't do it now, we may be stuck where we are for a long time. And if we buy a tear-down, we can still bide our time and start building when rates decline. We could rent for a while. The construction industry is going to take a hit."

She looks at him, assessing this new argument. If he is applying logic rather than emotion, he will get much farther with her. Still, his timing is terrible. He knows she is focused on the gala; he's trying to catch her while she is distracted.

"I really don't want to get into this right now," she says, keeping her voice even.

She feels him shift and sits up, away from him.

"You never want to talk about it," he snaps. "It's all your agenda; your timeline. You decide when we move, when we start a family. I just get to work my ass off to support your project plan."

Amanda inhales deeply. He is always so emotional. Does he act like this when he doesn't get his way at work, too? She looks at him, her face calm. "If you wanted to start a family, we could have done it before I took the job at the museum. We discussed this then. We agreed on The Heights because it's close to downtown and we didn't want a freeway commute. If you want to change things up, that's fine, but don't pretend you never had a vote."

His face draws into a worried knot. "I'm sorry, baby. This is your big night. I shouldn't have brought it up."

"It's okay, Matt." She places her hand on his arm. "Just let me focus on the night, please. We'll talk about it more; later."

They have arrived at the Hilton Americas. A bell man helps Amanda out of the car, smiling appreciatively at the way her light green dress clings and drapes. She smirks at him and shakes her head. Matt and Amanda ride up the escalator to the mezzanine level. She is quiet; he is restless. Once they are inside, she will dispatch him to the bar and he will be happy.

When Amanda had left the finishing touches in the capable hands of volunteers two hours earlier, she had been confident that the remaining pieces would come together without issue. She was right. The centerpieces are perfect; pipe and drape hangs just right behind the stage; lighting has been tested; the final sound-check is underway at the podium. She spies Grace across the ballroom and waves at her. Grace's husband Tony is at the bar already; he sees Matt and orders another scotch.

"Showtime," she says to Matt.

"I know; I know," he says sullenly. She had bested him in the car; his feelings will be hurt all night, she knows. "I'll see you when the lights go down. Save me a dance, I guess."

"I will," she promises.

Grace is shaking her head when Amanda approaches. "Nothing quite like being upstaged by Ken and Barbie at every major function," she laments in good humor.

"Right." Amanda grasps her hand in greeting. "It looks fantastic. When did you get here?"

"Oh, not long ago. Your crew did a great job."

Amanda is nodding. "They did. Did you bring the scripts?"

"Yep. Five copies; and Michelle is working with the light and sound guys on the cues. I don't think there's much left for you to do except worry." A quick look. "And I know you never do that, so I guess that leaves exactly nothing."

"Why worry?" Amanda says. "It doesn't fix anything. There's Margaret," she says, looking toward the door.

"Yeah." Grace has seen her, as well. "Good thing about tonight, there will plenty of attention to go around for her, too."

Amanda smiles. "You've been practicing."

And there is plenty of attention for Margaret, especially when she takes the podium to kick off the event. Amanda has deferred this honor to her. She does not like speaking in front of crowds so it was an easy crumb to throw; although she had appeared duly distressed when Margaret had seemingly squeezed the offer from her.

"And I am particularly delighted to tell you all," Margaret is saying as Amanda fights to pay attention. "That as of five p.m. today, the gala has raised one-hundred-eighty-five-thousand dollars for the museum."

Applause fills the ballroom. Even Amanda is impressed; it's a huge figure for a small museum. She suspects John has padded it liberally with his contribution. She will thank him later.

When at last the speeches have concluded, the house lights are dimmed for dancing and Amanda relaxes. Her eyes scan the room, searching for Matt to fulfill her promise to give him the first dance. As she skims over the couples already on the floor, she feels a lead weight settle in her stomach. She cannot look away, as if a car wreck has just taken place in front of her. John and Margaret on the dance floor. Margaret leans against his chest and he touches his cheek to the top of her head, briefly. Amanda forces herself to turn and continue her search for Matt. She finds him talking to Stan Firestone, an odd couple for a social setting, to be sure. He smiles when he sees her coming.

"Sorry, Stan. I promised the woman of the hour I'd save her a dance."

"You'd be a fool not to," Stan says, waving them away.

"What's that all about?"

"What; Stan?" Matt's voice is careful, she notes. "Nothing. Just shop talk. Fox Trade."

She nods. That's reasonable. "No more work for you tonight. I've cleared my dance card. And," she pauses, her mind flashing to the image of John and Margaret. "You can call the Realtor back. I'll go look at the lot."

"You will?" The delight in his voice sends foreboding waves up her spine, but she is committed.

She nods. "I'll *look*," she emphasizes. "We can take it from there."

Matt beams as he spins her onto the floor. He has no idea what has changed her mind, and he could not possibly care less. The notion that it was the sight of her lover dancing with his own wife will not occur to him until months later, when it is too late for all of them to turn back.

MONDAY, MARCH 10

Stan lifts the oversized wedge of pizza to his face and takes a greasy bite. "So, what do you have for me," he utters around a mouthful of pepperoni, cheese and crust.

Matt labors to conceal his distaste for both Stan's meal choice and his manners. He stabs a piece of romaine with his fork and pushes it around the salad bowl, gathering feta cheese and some artichoke heart before answering.

"It's looking good," he replies. "That segment of the market is high-performing." He stuffs the bite into his mouth and chews it self-consciously, Stan's scrutiny like a heat lamp on his face.

Stan rolls his eyes. The kid lays it on pretty thick with the finance jargon; as if all Stan knows how to do is fix printers and project manage operating system upgrades. "And you'll be able to pull it out before earnings, right? Nobody will notice?"

"It'll be fine," Matt assures him, although he has no way of knowing this. He has endured two earnings cycles in the lab and seen nothing unusual from his colleagues either time. They run the same report as any other operating division, just on a different set of data. He can work Prometheus back into the primary investment portfolio so there won't be gap on that side of the house — or a bulge on his side, for that matter.

"Okay." Stan chews another bite. "You don't like pizza?" Inclines his head toward Matt's salad.

"Oh, sure. I like it. Had it for breakfast, that's all."

Stan laughs. He has never met anyone more full of shit than Matt Parsons. It's probably his favorite thing about the young man, in fact. And it's also probably why Matt is so blind to everything else around him; he's too worried about being exposed, himself. Stan almost feels sorry for him. Almost. He had been wondering for months how he could get his fund into the lab. But given that nobody was supposed to know what those guys were doing, he couldn't exactly ask. The fact that Parsons had dropped it on him as some sort of bribe was the greatest irony Stan had ever experienced, first hand.

Back at the office thirty minutes later, Matt runs a sample report from the lab's portfolio, just to make sure he knows what he is doing. He has over-stated his comfort level with the team's investment practices for Stan's benefit. But there is no need to worry him with the details, as long as everything turns out in the end. Matt can't imagine anything that would cause a problem with something so small, compared to the overall collection. It would come off as no more than a simple error, as far as he could tell.

"What's up?" Anand has appeared at his cubicle wall.

"Oh, just a little self-study," Matt replies, his voice casual. He has practiced this, taking a page from Amanda's play book. He is flying solo on this one, which makes him nervous, but he thinks he can draw enough from everything she has already taught him about steering people down the path of his own choosing. Answer only the question that has been asked; avoid over-communicating at all costs. It will only look defensive and suspicious.

Anand grins. "Looking to branch out of M&A?"

"God, yes." Matt's bland tone is sincere. "How many more little companies can I track before I lose my mind?"

"Well," Anand speaks slowly. "I hope quite a few."

Matt's spine tingles with alarm; he has pushed it too far. He studies Anand's face for a few seconds. "Yeah, there's always someone looking to be bought, right?"

"Right." Another smile. "But, hey, if you want to learn about our system, that's cool, too. I'll show you the basics; it's not rocket science."

Matt nods. "Sure. I'd appreciate that. Maybe next week sometime."

"Good. I'll send you an invite. We'll block out about thirty minutes; that's all it should take." He lifts his empty coffee mug in a salute and leaves.

As Anand walks down the hall to the coffee bar, Matt forces himself to relax. Had he set off some kind of system alarm, or was it just good timing on Anand's part? Either way, he'll gain some cover next week when he learns the ropes. There is a significant benefit to appearing clueless sometimes.

# # #

Amanda hears John enter the museum but does not leave her desk. She knows it is him because she heard the Porsche snarl into the back lot, just outside her wall. As she listens, he locks the front door and pulls the shade.

He pokes his head into her office and says, hesitantly, "Hey."

"Hey," she replies, not looking up from her laptop screen.

His face is worried. She usually meets him halfway between the front door and her office. He enters the room cautiously and sits in the chair in front of her desk.

"Talk about it?"

She raises her head but closes her eyes for minute, fingers hovering over the keyboard. He sits quietly, watching her breathe, anxiety rising in his own chest as he fears the worst from what she is going to say. He is not ready; not yet.

At last she opens her eyes and gives him a token smile. "Did you enjoy the gala?"

He nods, still cautious. "Of course. It was your night. How could I not have enjoyed that?"

Amanda shakes her head, blinking. "What?"

He shrugs. "Watching you in your element, talking to the guests, working that room. It was much better than the opening or the museum board meetings, where you've been restricted by time or personalities." *Or Margaret*, they both add silently.

She lifts her hands from the keyboard now and plants her elbows on the desk, lacing her fingers and leaning forward. "*That's* what you took away from it?"

He still cannot pinpoint the quality of her voice. She is not angry; not tired. And certainly not happy to see him. As he words his next question, it strikes him at last: she is sad.

"What did you take away from it?"

A long silence settles between them.

"That you are not mine," she says at last.

His shoulders sag and he closes his eyes. He opens them and says simply, "I'm sorry, Amanda."

"I just wasn't prepared for how difficult it was going to be to see the two of you together like that; and I'm always prepared." She straightens her back. "And so then I realized it may be time…."

"No." His voice is sharp. "It's not time."

He stands and comes around her desk, sitting atop it and taking her hands. "It's not time," he repeats. "I almost didn't go on Saturday, because I thought it would be awkward for you — and for me. But I had to be there, so I made the best of it."

"I understand all that," she insists. "I'm not giving you an ultimatum or saying that you shouldn't be affectionate with your wife. I'm just saying that it was uncomfortable. And I felt… I felt… guilty."

John is already shaking his head as she fumbles for the word. "Don't. You know one side of the story, so don't feel guilty about what you perceive you are doing to her." He looks at the wall. "And God only knows what people have told you about me, beyond the revolving door comment."

"Are you saying it's not true?"

He turns his head back to her; his face almost tortured. "Not entirely true, anyway," he mutters.

Another quiet minute passes.

When John speaks again, his voice is gentle. "Margaret is a very unhappy woman," he explains. "She always has been. In fact, that's what drew me to her in the beginning — a wounded bird; and I had hurt my first wife so badly. And… I thought I could help her and maybe redeem myself a little bit." He is looking at the wall again.

Amanda waits patiently for him to continue. She did not know he had been married before Margaret.

"But that was wrong. I was wrong. She never stopped being unhappy. Therapy, motherhood, philanthropy. Nothing made a difference." He shrugs; eyes back on her face now. "We can't be responsible for anyone else's happiness," he concludes.

"That's one hell of a way to learn a lesson."

He stands now and walks around the desk. Pulls Amanda to her feet and looks her in the eye. "It was. Are you better, now?"

Amanda nods. "I'm okay."

"How many people ever get to see you sad?"

Her lips curve briefly at this. "Zero," she confirms.

He nods confidently. "I knew you liked me." Squeezes her hands and lets her stand quietly for a few minutes, until he believes she has recovered her composure. As happy as he is to be allowed behind the curtain, he does not want to push it.

Before long, her mask is back in place. "Ready?"

"Yes." A full smile, now. "I need to make a stop on the way. West U; I have to take a look at a lot."

"Oh, moving already?" John's voice is curious. "How long have you been in The Heights?"

Amanda shakes her head. "Not long enough to move. Matt is fired up about doing it now, for some reason. Claims the sellers' market in Houston is winding down and we should make a move now."

John's face is inquisitive. "Really?"

"Yeah." Amanda notes the tone of his voice. "Is he right?"

John shrugs. "He could be; lots of creative mortgages out there in the last few years — interest-only loans — to say nothing of what investment firms are doing with those mortgages." He frowns slightly. "Maybe I need to rein in the boys in the lab; I think they've been dabbling in that market."

He raises his hand to her back and guides her to the rear door, speaking almost to himself as they walk. "That would be a mess. It would make what happened on Smith Street look like an afternoon in the park."

#

The "tear-down" on University is a beautiful 1940s cottage, complete with front sun porch and arched entry. Amanda looks with disbelief from it to the Realtor's report in her hand.

She turns to John. "This is kind of heart-breaking, don't you think? To knock this down and put up a big brick monster?"

"You mean, a *McMansion*."

She is shaking her head. "I can't do it." For once, she is being emotional. "It's just not right to destroy history like this."

"Oh," he says, understanding it now. "I hear you. What are they asking?"

Her eyes drop once again to the sheet; the price had seemed outrageous when she thought the current home was on the verge of being condemned. It was worse now that she realized they would be razing a perfectly livable structure.

"Four-hundred-twenty-five-thousand."

John laughs out loud. "And your estimated cost to build?"

"Another seven-fifty, according to Matt."

John is smirking at her now. "Welcome to the big time, baby. What does the Realtor think you'll get for the place in The Heights?"

Amanda breathes deeply. "Five-twenty-five." Before he can ask, she continues, "We paid four-ninety for it last May and refinished the floors, replaced some dated fixtures, spruced up the yard…mostly cosmetic stuff. It's absurd," she concludes. "We owe three-eighty-something." Her voice is incredulous. "We can't do this."

John is grinning at her. "I know you don't need my advice on financial decision-making," he begins, "But this may be a battle better left unwaged. Matt is surrounded by people with cache addresses. He's looking to fit in."

"I know," she concedes, slumping back into her seat. "And after the watch, I guess I shouldn't kill his buzz again so soon." And she understands that this is as much for his parents as it is for him — and her, she supposes.

"Hey," John says, as if the thought has only just occurred to him. "Saturday night wasn't easy for me, either."

"What?" She is still distracted by the house. "Oh." Puts down the report and takes his hand. "Yeah, I didn't think about that. I'm sorry. Were you sad, too?"

He nods. "I was." His voice is thoughtful. "I was very sad."

She squeezes his hand. "We can go now," she says softly. "I don't want to look at this anymore."

MONDAY, MARCH 17

"What's the mileage on it again?" Matt asks the question although he is standing right beside the window sticker. He wants to know if the salesman knows.

"Just a hair over thirty-thousand." Doesn't bat an eyelash. "It's low for the age, but not for the car."

Matt nods; this is not an everyday ride. He looks at the sticker again. Twenty-three-five. Not great, but not terrible. He steps back and surveys the car once more. A 1991 Porsche Carrera 2; black with tan interior. Gorgeous. Larry had given him the good news about Ithaca that morning; the announcement is finally coming.

"Okay, let's go inside and see what we can do."

"Excellent." The salesman points the way with his arm, inviting Matt to precede him. Matt slips his brain into professional mode, now. He can get excited about the car again when it's his. But he can't wait to see the look on Amanda's face when he picks her up at work in it. He checks the time: eleven-thirty. He can wrap this up and stop by the museum on his way back to Vantage Tower.

# # #

"How many more do you have to do?"

"Three."

John groans. He is stretched out on the sofa in Amanda's office, tie undone and loose around his shoulders, shirt open at the neck, coat hanging on the back of a chair. Amanda is seated at her desk, handwriting the last of the thank-you notes for the gala. The museum is closed for lunch.

"I'm on the volunteers, now," she adds, as if it makes a difference. She looks at him, catching an ironic twist to his lips. "What's so funny?"

"I was just thinking about the first time I came here with you." He turns to look at her. "And how glad I am that we were renovating a conference room at my building."

She shakes her head and returns to the thank-you note at her hand.

"I was trying to trip you up that day, you know."

"Is that right?" Her voice is mild, but he detects the current underneath.

"And I thought I had you, when we walked in and this place was a disaster."

"Well," she says, sliding the completed note into its envelope and moving it to the pile at her left. "You didn't know."

He chuckles, drawing a sharp look from her.

"Of course I knew," he confesses. "I'd been inside a couple of days before."

"Big, fat liar." Her voice featureless.

"But not in a mean-spirited way," he insists. "I had to see if everyone was right about you. Even Margaret was impressed. And Margaret is never impressed." And then, as if an afterthought, "She's too heavily medicated, to tell the truth."

Amanda stares at him for a moment, her face a cipher, and then returns to her task. John closes his eyes again.

"Go on," she urges. She has finished another note; he hears the cardstock slide across the blotter and into its sheath.

"Well, I couldn't break you. You sailed inside, acted like it was nothing at all that the floor was covered with lumber and plywood and plastic sheeting; wires and duct work hanging from the ceiling. It was beautiful." He stops and sighs, then laughs. "That was when I knew."

Now he sits up; she is pushing the last note onto the pile. She puts down her pen and creates several stacks with the cards, hands moving swiftly as he watches.

"When did you know?"

She pushes back from her desk and stands; walks to his side, kicking off her shoes. "Around the same time."

"Don't you have to lick all those envelopes now?"

"Mm-mm," she says, sitting next to him. "I have some students coming to do it, along with some other things. They'll be here as soon as I open up after lunch." A peek at her watch. "In about fifteen minutes, actually."

"You can be so mean."

"Don't you forget it. Besides," she scolds, but gently. "I thought you enjoyed my company, no matter what form it takes." She rests her hand against his cheek; tucks her toes inside the hem of his trousers.

"True," he admits, leaning forward until their noses touch.

"And a little self-restraint can be a good thing."

He snorts. "Overrated." He draws his head back and studies her, wondering what it would be like to have her all to himself. Would she ever be completely open, or is the black box around her mind welded shut?

"I have to meet Matt for dinner right after work," she says, for once misreading his contemplative gaze. "I can't show up for that smelling like you."

"Where are you meeting him?"

"Star Pizza. Why? Afraid we'll run into you?" A delightfully vicious look. "Or were you planning to have the Health Department close it down before we arrive?"

He laughs. "But, seriously, what do you *really* think of me?"

She tilts her head slightly, as if considering the challenge he has issued. "I think you have another secret," she concludes.

John shakes his head. "I don't know what you mean. A secret about what?"

"About me." She leans back into him, stopping when their noses touch again. "Some other form of mischief you committed, trying to be clever."

He tries to steal a kiss but she grabs the sides of his tie and stops him. "Spill it."

He shrugs. "Nothing to spill." But his smile tells her she is right.

She drops the silk and begins to pluck at the buttons on his shirt. "Tell me."

"You're a terrible negotiator," he observes. "What's my incentive?"

Her eyes flash silver at him as she glances first at her watch, and then at his face. She continues, tugging the shirt down his arms. "Cufflinks," she orders, and he opens them, shrugging the shirt from his arms. Her hand at his belt, now, pulling at the buckle and then moving to the button of his trousers.

"Hey, I thought you had students coming to do the envelopes."

She shrugs, sliding the zipper down. "Just practicing my negotiating skills." She props herself up on her knees and swings a leg over him, hovering just above his lap.

"Seriously. Amanda. This is not good." Anxiety oozes from his words; his eyes dart around the office.

"Mm-hm." Hitches her skirt up her thighs. "So you have a decision to make, then." Looks him squarely in the eye.

In spite of his discomfort, she hears the low rumble of a laugh begin deep in his chest.

"I take it back," he capitulates. "You are an excellent negotiator."

"Tell me." She sits on him now, rocking slightly as she settles.

"One consideration," he manages to whisper. "If you render your opposition completely senseless, they won't be of much use to you."

"You'll do just fine," she assures him, patting his chest. "Tell me."

"Okay, okay." He laughs again, head resting on the back of the sofa. "The gala invitations. I knew you were coming to get them. They were on the foyer table, and I moved them." He lifts his head and looks at her. "Now, I can't believe I'm saying this, but get off."

A close-lipped smile; eyes narrowed. "Why? Are you expecting someone?"

His bottom lip drops. "No student volunteers?"

Amanda shakes her head; her face artificially guileless.

"Star Pizza?"

"*Please.*" She dismisses it with a wave of her hand a twist of her torso that makes him swallow and catch his breath.

"Evil." *She* should have been the Parsons dealing with Fox Trade and Ithaca. Probably would have saved him a million dollars without even opening her mouth.

"Incarnate," she confirms, pushing him back into the cushions of the cast-off Vantage sofa and sliding down until her knees rest on the floor between his feet.

John sighs as he reaches behind his neck to pull the tie away and drops it on the cushion next to him.

# # #

An unfamiliar car greets Amanda in the driveway when she arrives home that evening.

Oh, Matt. What did you do?

She enters the house gingerly, almost afraid to learn the truth. He is seated at the bar, reading a magazine and drinking a Shiner from the bottle. She stops and looks at him for a moment, waiting. A slow smile begins across his face, although his eyes remain glued to the page.

"Okay," she says. "Let's have it."

He grins, now, and launches himself from the stool, digging into his pocket for the key. He tosses it to her and she snatches it out of the air, shaking her head even as she smiles.

"So I guess Ithaca is back on."

"Oh, yeah. It's on, baby." He crosses the room and stands in front of her. "Wanna go for a spin?"

"Of course I do." She hands the key back to him. "When did you do this?"

"Over lunch. Hey — " he cuts himself short. "I stopped by the museum. It was locked up. Your car was there, though." He guides her out of the house.

A chill runs along her spine. "I had lunch with my mom; she picked me up."

"Yeah, I figured. I almost called to find you, but I didn't want to share my news with anyone else." Holds the door open for her. "In you go. If you're really good, I'll let you drive home."

Amanda smiles at this, in spite of the way her conscience is hemorrhaging. "I'll do my best," she promises, buckling the seatbelt around her and resting her hand on his thigh. "But if you can wait until later, I'll make it worth your while."

Matt races out of the drive and heads to Allen Parkway. Great curves over there. As he speeds off, Amanda swallows the wave of nausea that has worked its way up her throat.

TUESDAY, MARCH 18

Vantage PLC Announces Acquisition of The Ithaca Group
Deal to open new investment and growth opportunities.

HOUSTON, March 18, 2008 – Vantage Property, Life and Casualty (NSE: VPLC) today announced it has reached an agreement to acquire privately held Ithaca Group for a purchase price of $18 million.

President and CEO John Wallace cited the move as confirmation of the firm's aggressive new growth strategy. "This move adds a sharp new tool to our set and will provide the flexibility we are seeking to further broaden our earnings and dividend targets," he said.

Vantage shares declined $.07 on the announcement.

Vantage PLC is a North American leader in insurance and financial services, operating across the United States, as well as in Canada and Mexico. Vantage services commercial, institutional and individual customers via widespread property-casualty and life insurance networks. Vantage is listed on the National Stock Exchange, with the ticker symbol VPLC.

This press release contains forward-looking statements concerning future economic performance and events. It is possible that Vantage PLC's actual results and financial condition may differ from the anticipated results and financial condition indicated in these projections and statements. Vantage PLC is not under any obligation to update or alter its projections and other statements as a result of new information or future events.

MONDAY, MARCH 24

Fat raindrops fall on the car, spattering as they hit the sunroof and then fanning out in shapes almost like snowflakes. Amanda watches them through the open visor. John sits at the wheel, head back and eyes closed. He is playing a CD from the movie *Once*.

"Thanks for coming with me," he says. "I needed to get out of there."

She reaches across the gearshift and takes his hand. "Of course."

"The age of the rock star CEO," he says wearily. "It sucks. I have work to do, and a make-up artist is in my office, strapping a paper bib around my neck and slathering me with foundation while some guy with a camera is scarfing down an Egg McMuffin. It *reeked*."

"You were on Squawk Box."

"You watched it?"

She smiles. "Mm-hm."

He groans. "Don't. Please."

"Why not? You looked good." Squeezes his hand. "Sounded good. Smart."

"Yeah?" He laughs. "I have no idea what I said. And then, when it was over, I sat and watched the stock price for an hour, certain it would tank. Wasted my whole damned morning." He opens his eyes and looks pointedly at her. "Seriously, I wish you wouldn't watch that. It's not necessary."

"Do you think I don't understand it?" She bristles, slightly.

"I'm certain you understand it perfectly," he insists. "You're brilliant; wasting your time in nonprofit, I've told you that. No," he pauses. "That's not it. I wish you wouldn't watch it because you are the only person who doesn't constantly ask me about it. I like that."

She smiles now. "Oh."

"And," he continues, as if seeing her for the first time, although they have been sitting silently in the car for half an hour now. "I like your skirt, too. How much time do you have?" He slides his hand up her thigh.

"I left a volunteer in charge; I have to get back." Her smile turns sly. "Why?"

"I want to go someplace where I can be inside you," he whispers against her neck, hand creeping higher.

She laughs. "You're not supposed to talk like that."

"Why? Because I'm too old?"

Shakes her head. "No, because you're...you. Mr. CEO."

"It makes you uncomfortable?" His hand has disappeared under the fabric.

"Yes."

"Good. You need to be shaken up. You're kind of a goody-goody, aren't you, St. Agnes girl?"

She swallows at the pressure of his fingers. "If that makes this more fun for you, sure."

He watches as she turns her head to the side, eyes closed. Her lips are parted and her hands grip the sides of her seat as she moves against his hand. Brow wrinkled, eyes squeezed shut tightly now. His eyes drop briefly from her face to the uneven rise and fall of her chest and then back to her face as she shudders and relaxes. He catches her chin in his hand and kisses her, lingering on her mouth until she laughs and gently pushes him away.

"Did you see this movie?" He nods at the CD player as he starts the engine.

"I did," she says, sleepy-voiced. "*They* had a lot of self-restraint."

"I still say that's overrated." Squeezes her knee and laughs. "I should get you back before you turn into a pumpkin, I guess."

He smiles at her drowsy expression and shifts the car into first. He hesitates for a moment and then says softly, "It's like witnessing the birth of the sun, watching you like that."

"Please," she says, covering his hand with hers. "You can be so sappy." She turns her head to the window in dismissal, but he can see the smile pulling at her cheek.

He releases the clutch and starts driving, holding her hand on the gear shift. The silver Cayman snakes down the ramp of the parking garage, passing a small group of men off for an early lunch.

"Hey, was that Wallace's car?"

Matt turns to see. "Yeah, I think so. What was he doing up there?"

Carlo grins. "You mean 'who,' not 'what.'"

"Yeah, he wasn't alone, and the windows were totally fogged up," Thomas adds.

"Wonder who it was, this time?" Carlo muses.

"Maybe your mom," Thomas says to Matt.

"Maybe your dad," Matt counters.

"Maybe your wife."

"Dude!" Carlo interjects. "*Uncool.*"

But Matt laughs. "She *would* do anything for my career, you know."

Thomas and Carlo hesitate only a few seconds before exchanging high fives. "Takin' one for the team!"

All three men laugh. Then Matt says, "But I'm pretty sure it was your dad."

More laughter echoes in the concrete garage as they duck into Carlo's BMW and drive away.

# # #

John stops his car a few doors down from the museum. The rain has ceased and the sun is making a show of fighting through the gray.

"I'm leaving for Baltimore this afternoon," he says, as she opens the door.

"You certainly know how to make an exit."

"Always leave them wanting more." And with a cunning smile he is gone.

Amanda shakes her head and rubs her arms vigorously to erase the lethargy his attention has induced and enters the museum to find Margaret seated at the reception desk.

"Good afternoon." Her voice is frosty, but Amanda does not put much stock in it. Her voice is always frosty.

"Good afternoon," she replies. "Were we scheduled today?"

"No." Margaret stands and walks around the desk, clutching something in her diamond-bedecked hand. "I was passing by and had something for you."

She hands Amanda a pamphlet: National Nonprofit Leadership Conference, Baltimore, Maryland. Marriott Waterfront.

Amanda's face is steady as her brain races back to the smile John had given her as he drove away.

"I received this a while back but forgot about it until yesterday. I expect you to attend. We can't rest on the laurels of one successful gala."

"Of course not," Amanda says, infusing her words with just the right level of eagerness and admiration for Margaret's heads-up move.

"Good." A stern look for Amanda's enthusiasm, tempered as it may have been. It's only Baltimore, after all. "The foundation will cover your expenses, which means this is a working trip. Talk to Melissa about your itinerary."

"Melissa?"

"Yes." Margaret is exasperated by the young woman's sluggish brain. "My husband's secretary. She's coordinating the trip. It starts tomorrow morning; you'll have to leave tonight. Will that be a problem?"

Not for me, no. "Of course not."

#

"Melissa; this is Amanda Parsons. Margaret Wallace asked me to contact you about some flight arrangements?"

"Of course, Amanda. Would it be too much trouble for you to stop by and pick up your itinerary and a couple of other things? Some of it I can't fax or e-mail." Melissa's tone is even and practiced. Amanda is suspicious.

"No trouble at all. I can swing through town on my way home." Downtown is not close to being on the way back to The Heights, and Melissa knows this, but Amanda recognizes the necessity of the words she uses with her.

She pauses in her office to check in with Michelle, the volunteer on duty for the afternoon.

"Did Margaret talk to you about covering for the rest of the week?"

Michelle nods. "She did. Sounds like a lot of fun. You deserve a break."

"We'll see," Amanda says, uncharacteristically cryptic. She gathers her laptop and some files and calls to Michelle on her way out the door, "Call my cell if anything comes up."

When she arrives on the executive floor of Vantage, John's office door is open; the room is dark. He has already left, then. Amanda faces Melissa confidently. Her Coach purse and matching tote are perched upon her desk; she has been waiting for Amanda's arrival so that she can go home.

"I have your itinerary right here," she says, pushing a manila folder across the top of her desk. "And then Mrs. Wallace asked me to give you a foundation credit card for meals and lodging. If you'll just sign here to indicate that you received it."

"How did she get this in my name?" Amanda is alarmed. She had not signed an application.

"Oh, they worked it out. Don't worry."

Amanda signs the receipt. "Okay." She flips the folder open and frowns slightly at the gate information. "Where is this?"

Melissa smiles gently at her. "That's just off JFK Boulevard. You'll be flying on the corporate jet, since we were already sending it up for Mr. Wallace." The subtlest flicker of her eyes, so slight Amanda might have imagined it. "Efficiency at its best, don't you think?"

"Yes, it certainly is."

"I know you'll need to pack, so you can take your car home and a driver will pick you up in about forty-five minutes. Will that be enough time?"

Amanda nods. "Plenty of time. Thank you, Melissa. You're a lifesaver, as usual."

Melissa draws a breath, as if she has something else to say; but then she closes her mouth and settles for another smile. "Have a good trip."

"I'm sure I will; there's always a lot of good information at these conferences. Good synergy with so many brains in the room." She tucks the folder under her arm and leaves. Melissa watches her; eyes narrowed with concern.

As soon as Amanda is seated in her car, she calls Matt.

"Hey, honey, what's going on?" Her tone is brisk; she knows he is probably treading water.

"The usual. What's up?"

"I have to go to Baltimore tonight," she says. "A little bombshell from Margaret. I think it's actually some sort of reward for the gala. Anyway, I'm leaving in about forty-five minutes, so I won't get to see you."

"Damn," Matt says. "Wish I could come, too, but I just had a pile of work dumped on me."

Imagine that.

"That sucks," Amanda agrees. "I'll bring you an Orioles cap."

"Yeah, thanks. And go to the aquarium. I hear it's awesome. Watch the dolphin show, if you have time." His voice is distracted now, as his thoughts have clearly shifted back to work.

"Will do. See you on Friday night."

# # #

John is already seated when she boards the small plane. She shakes her head as she steps down the aisle and sits across from him.

"And you told me you didn't need to be calculating."

"That's right."

"Then what do you call this?" She sweeps her hand around the cabin.

"I call this fun." He grins. "It's fun to mess with your head; you keep it so locked down."

"Does this conference even exist, or did you make the brochure in Photoshop?"

John laughs. "Yeah, and then I used the special off-set printer I keep hidden in the garage to run a few hundred copies. It's next to the router I use for the bird houses." Now a serious look. "You don't trust me at all, do you?"

Amanda looks at him sharply. "Trust is not exactly the basis of this…relationship."

His shoulders sag a bit with her words. "No, I guess it isn't," he muses.

"And what if we see someone we know?"

"God, you're a buzz-kill. Sit, please." When she takes her seat, he continues. "Have you ever seen anyone you know — unexpectedly, that is — when traveling on business?"

She stares firmly at him for a moment, and then shakes her head grudgingly. "How long have you had this planned?"

Now he laughs again. "She's been sitting on the conference pamphlet since January, at least. Just waiting to see how you were going to do. But me, I've been planning it for a couple of weeks. Since the gala; I knew she'd send you after that." His face becomes serious. "This is a huge coup for you, by the way. You should be proud. As close as you will ever get to a compliment or a thank you from her."

"That's almost funny." Another glare. "Almost."

"Yes, almost. She's a little…controlling."

"I'm sure you would know better than I." She will not take the bait. She might be sleeping with the woman's husband and traveling all the way to Baltimore for an assignation with him, but she will not verbally insult her.

John sighs. "She's not my first wife, you know."

Amanda nods. "You mentioned."

"I married when I was in college. Stupid."

"What was *she* like?"

"Very sweet; very young. Not my type at all." A wicked grin at Amanda. "What a mess we made." His voice has become indulgent. "My oldest son, Jack, he's hers. Divorce is awful. Especially with kids, no matter how young or old they are."

"I've heard," she says quietly.

He looks at her sadly. "Your parents?"

"Yep." She smiles ironically. "My dad and his secretary."

"Oh." He is quiet for a moment. "This is kind of messy for you, then."

"Kind of." She clears her throat and forces her face to brighten. "Can we talk about something else now? Tell me what we're going to do in Baltimore."

"Yes. It's is a great city; so much history and so well maintained, even with all the new development at the harbor." He is genuinely appreciative of this feat. "And there are a lot of small museums you might find interesting," he says.

"Um, I'm going for a conference?" Her tone is mildly sarcastic.

He casts his eyes toward the ceiling. "Such a buzz-kill." He leans across the aisle and takes her hand. "Screw the conference. You'll get more out of visiting these places and seeing how they operate; and how much better you already are."

"Someday," she declares slowly. "You will be rid of this need to continually stroke my ego. What will you do then?"

"I'll find something else, I'm sure."

She sighs, frustrated, and pointedly disregards his innuendo. "That is not what I meant." Her voice is pragmatic.

"Never happen," he asserts.

Amanda sends him a warning with her eyes. Never is an awfully long time, after all.

"And so that's it; this trip is field research? It's all about the museum."

A sheepish smile, now, and John shakes his head. "No, it's not about the museum; not at all. I just wanted to have you to myself for a few days. I wanted to take you on a date; to take you to dinner. Is that okay?"

She is quiet, regarding their hands joined across the aisle. The stones from her wedding ring digging into her skin under the pressure of his fingers. Amanda raises her eyes to John's face and finds him watching her intently, trying to read her, even though he never has.

"It's okay," she whispers, finally. Wishing she could tell him just how okay it is.

#

Houston

"Accounting is looking for a blessing on our part of the 10-Q," Thomas says to Anand, leaning on his desk.

"Just a little bit longer," Anand says. "I'm seeing something strange, but I think it's an anomaly. Did you move anything this week?"

"No. Why? What's up?" Thomas takes a seat next to Anand.

"We ran all the forecast models last week, anticipating a few different scenarios in the market and how our stuff might impact on earnings. But the results I'm getting today; I've never seen our models so far off. It's like someone took a chunk out of our portfolio, but I can't see where."

"Is it the K&R stuff?"

"Nah," Anand dismisses. "No worries; we've accounted for that, too."

On the other side of the cubicle wall, Matt shifts in his seat. Anand had never made good on his promise to show Matt how the system works; Matt had gone in anyway and pulled Prometheus out, just in time for earnings.

"Want me to have a look? Maybe fresh eyes," Thomas offers.

"That's okay." Anand rubs his face. "I'll look at it again tomorrow. Larry can wait a little while. I've probably been staring at it too long tonight. I'm going to get a beer." He stands up and sees Matt still at his desk. "Hey. Shouldn't you be heading home to the wife?"

"No, she left town this afternoon. Baltimore."

"Really? Baltimore?"

Anand's voice sounds strange, but Matt doesn't know how, exactly. "Yeah, some nonprofit thing, I guess."

"Huh. Well, hey, why don't you come out with us, then?"

"I might. Where you headed? I'll catch up; couple more things to do here."

"All right, man. We're at the Tavern."

When Anand and Thomas are gone, Matt takes out his cell phone and calls Stan. "I need to move Prometheus back into the lab," he says. "There's an issue; we got noticed."

He listens quietly as Stan rips him a new one. "I know, but it's necessary. It'll be fine."

# # #

New York

"O'Malley here."

"Mike, my name is Chris Morton. I was wondering if you might have some free time to talk about Vantage PLC."

"Morton... Morton. You're with Swaims-McDermott?"

"Yeah."

Mike grins. "Oh, I have time to talk Vantage. What would you like to know?"

"Well," Chris draws a deep breath. "I've been reading your latest article — much better than the recruitment piece, by the way — "

" — yeah, thanks," Mike mutters.

"And something is nagging at me about the Fox Trade stuff, but I can't quite touch it yet."

Mike nods, although they are speaking on the phone. "I know. I felt the same way the whole interview. And what's really strange is that I don't even think Wallace knows he's not telling us everything."

"Huh," Chris says. "Maybe we could get together in person, you could bring your notes?"

"Sure," Mike agrees. "I can meet you in an hour at Ray's on Madison, near Fifty-First."

"See you then."

# # #

Houston

"We need to re-run the numbers for the 10-Q."

The accounting analyst looks up from his game of Brick Breaker to see Larry Foote standing at his desk.

"What's up?" He asks the question, as he loads the software to run the report.

"Armageddon," Larry says. "Check out the Bloomberg terminal." He jerks his head toward his shoulder, to the screen hanging from the ceiling. "National Trust Co. just filed Chapter 11. Shouldn't be a problem for us, but the market is reacting badly. Well," he mutters, "It's reacting. Which is almost always bad." He sighs. "So we need to check our portfolio. No surprises on Monday, right?"

"Sure. I'll bring it to you in a few, okay?"

Larry raps his knuckles on the top of cubicle wall, tapping out a lively, unconcerned rhythm. "Yep." He walks back to his office, rubbing the back of his neck with anxiety.

Five minutes later, the analyst is standing at Larry's door. "We have a surprise," he says. He hands Larry the report.

"What the hell," Larry says. "Here." He stands up. "Run it again on my machine."

The analyst sits at Larry's desk and runs the report again, generating a slightly worse result. Larry studies the screen. "What the hell," he repeats.

"It's a twenty-five cent drop in adjusted EPS," the analyst says, unnecessarily.

"I can see that," Larry's voice is mild but his pulse is racing. He rubs his eyes and mutters something under his breath. "Can you give me a few minutes?"

As the young man leaves his office, Larry calls Anand's cell phone. He answers on the second ring. Larry hears the sounds of a restaurant or bar in the background.

"Larry?" Anxiety evident in his voice. A call from the CFO three days before earnings is never a good thing.

"Yeah. I need you to come in right now."

# # #

New York

Chris Morton has not come alone to the meeting, Mike notes, when the man enters the restaurant. A tall, attractive woman has joined him. Mike rises from his seat to greet her.

"Debra Wilcox," she says, taking his hand. "Federal prosecutor."

Mike lifts an eyebrow as he introduces himself, "Mike O'Malley, *Bottom Line Magazine*."

"I hope you don't mind," Chris says, as they join Mike at his table.

Mike does not respond.

"We've been watching Vantage for a couple of years," Debra explains. "Thought we had them a while back on an Anti-Trust violation, but it didn't hold."

Mike shifts in his seat. She sounds disappointed — isn't it a good thing when a crime is not being committed?

"And now?"

"The SEC is interested in some of the company's investment activity and how it's reported to shareholders."

"Aren't you jumping the gun a bit, getting involved so early?"

"You think I have a personal stake in this?"

Mike shrugs. "Thought crossed my mind."

"Well, I don't." Her voice is flippant.

Mike is growing more uncomfortable with each sentence Debra utters. The thought of an exclusive about shenanigans at one of the country's most venerated firms is appealing to him — but only if it's true. He decides he can play along for a while. His reporter's intuition is twitching, and it has little to do with Vantage. The woman across the table is hiding something, and he wants to know what it is.

"Okay," he says. "Tell me more."

#

Baltimore

"This feels a little awkward, coming back to your room together."

"What do you mean?"

"It's just so... normal."

"And that makes you feel awkward?"

She nods and shrugs. "Because it's not normal. We're not normal. We don't go on dates."

He thinks for a few seconds. "Would it help if I mauled you as soon as we walked in the door?"

She laughs. "Maybe."

But as the door closes behind them, John's Blackberry comes to life. He lifts a hand in apology and answers it.

"Why the hell haven't you been answering your phone?" It is Dave, and he is clearly on-edge.

"No bars. What's up?"

"You need to get back here, now. We have a problem with our 10-Q."

"What do you mean? I reviewed Q3 earnings before I left."

"Q3 earnings are only part of the problem," Dave says slowly. "Q1 and Q2 are the bigger concern."

John's blood runs cold. "You're not making sense. Are you saying we have to restate? What the fuck happened?"

Amanda steps away and sheds her coat, draping it over the desk chair. She walks into the bedroom to give John some privacy.

"Get back to Houston. Now, John. I sent you an e-mail with the details. Review it on the plane and get your ass down here. She'll keep. You can go fuck her at your loft this weekend after we get — "

John ends the call without waiting for Dave to finish. Finds the number for the hangar at BWI and dials it. As he enters the bedroom in search of Amanda, he is already finishing the call. She is standing at the window, her dress and shoes leading a trail to the picture she creates with the lights from the harbor behind her. He walks to her side and faces her sadly.

"I have to go back." He looks out the window, over her head. "I'm sorry."

"What's wrong?" Her hand moving to his shoulder.

"I'm not sure yet. Earnings trouble." His eyes are steely; face like stone. He still does not look at her.

"When?"

"Right now. I'm so sorry."

"I understand." She touches his face and he looks at her at last. Bends his head for a kiss and fights the temptation to relax against her when her arms encircle his back. He steps away, only a few paces, and draws his finger from her neck to her stomach.

"I'll come see you on Monday." One more kiss and he is gone, his promise hanging in the air.

But all that she had tasted on his lips was good-bye.

MONDAY, MARCH 31

Vantage PLC Reports Third Quarter FY2008 Results
Restates Earnings for Q1 and Q2 FY2008

HOUSTON, March 31, 2008 – Vantage Property, Life and Casualty (NSE: VPLC) today reported adjusted earnings of $1.27 per share for the second quarter of FY2008, compared to $1.39 adjusted earnings per share (EPS) earned in the same period last year. Adjusted earnings exclude the impact of special items. On a Generally Accepted Accounting Principles (GAAP) basis, the company reported a net loss of $1.07 per share in the second quarter of its fiscal year 2008, compared to earnings of $1.15 per share in the same period last year.

Additionally, Vantage restated its earnings for the first two quarters of FY2008, as follows:

Q1 adjusted EPS of $.87 and GAAP basis of $1.02.

Q2 adjusted EPS of $1.42 and GAAP basis of $1.15.

The restatement was necessary due to revelations of investment activities linked to a personal account maintained by Chief Technology Officer Stan Firestone.

"We are disappointed by this necessity but confident that this one-time restatement will put to rest any concerns about our go-forward strategy," said John A. Wallace III, president and chief executive officer of Vantage. "We remain committed to serving our customers and growing our business."

Details regarding specific operational units are available on the company's Web site.

Vantage PLC is a North American leader in insurance and financial services, operating across the United States, as well as in Canada and Mexico. Vantage services commercial, institutional and individual customers via widespread property-casualty and life insurance networks. Vantage is listed on the National Stock Exchange, with the ticker symbol VPLC.

This press release contains forward-looking statements concerning future economic performance and events. It is possible that Vantage PLC's actual results and financial condition may differ from the anticipated results and financial condition indicated in these projections and statements. Vantage PLC is not under any obligation to update or alter its projections and other statements as a result of new information or future events.

APRIL 2008

TUESDAY, APRIL 1

"How far has it dropped now?"

John does not look up from the report he is reading. "I don't know," he says. "Watching it isn't going to change a thing."

Dave sighs. "You're right. We need to get a press release out today, about Stan's resignation."

"Yeah. Whatever you want to say. We'll promote Angela, I assume."

"I'm sure that's the right way to go."

John leans back in his chair, staring at the ceiling. "I need to say something positive about the rest of the leadership team, I guess."

Dave nods. "Now would be a good time to stress our bench strength."

"And I'm sure you guys are planning an all-hands meeting?"

"Yeah, for Monday." Dave's voice is hesitant. "I think there's something else you should know. You're not going to like it."

John shrugs. "When has that ever stopped you?" But then he recognizes the tone of Dave's voice and the peculiar, guilty set of his mouth. This will have something to do with *her*.

"Matt Parsons was in on it with Stan."

John cannot speak for a moment. He races through the last several months in his mind, searching for any indication that Amanda was keeping a secret of this magnitude. He is certain she is capable of it — and equally certain that she knew nothing about what Matt was doing. He had driven such a wedge between the two of them, keeping Matt at the office or sending him out of town; it was perfectly reasonable that she had no idea. No matter that he had claimed no need to be calculating; that was before he realized how much she meant to him and how painful it would be to lose her.

"Okay."

"That's it?" Dave rises from his seat, shocked. "I told you she was dangerous; she probably put him up to it."

John shakes his head. "She had nothing to do with it; I can guarantee."

"Do you think you're in love with her, John? I mean, seriously. Is that the problem? Because I can promise you; you will get over it."

"Leave her alone, Dave." John looks back at the report. "I don't care what you do to him, but don't touch her."

"Your ego is going to destroy you, John. You are so fucking blinded by it."

John's head snaps back up. "My *ego*," he spits out, "is what has made it possible for every employee with a director title in this firm to be driving the German sports car of his or her choosing. My *ego* is what has made it possible for entire retirement funds to split and double their returns to investors." He slams his fist on the surface of his desk. "And my ego has paid for every fucking vacation you have taken for the last ten years, your wife's tits and Botox injections and your kids' fucking private school tuition."

WEDNESDAY, APRIL 2

"They walked me out of the building," Matt says from a corner of the living room. The house is dark; blinds turned tightly closed against the afternoon sun. "Security."

And that was not even the worst part of his day. The worst part had been Anand's scorn, delivered in low tones at his desk, before Security had arrived.

Did you honestly think you could just dick around with something it took us years to create, and we'd never notice?

Matt had no reply. He simply looked at Anand, waiting for the next words.

You were put in here to find companies for us to buy. Period. You have no idea what we do or how we do it; and that was by design. If we needed someone who understood finance at this level, we could have sneezed at the employee cafeteria and hit someone more qualified than you.

Amanda stands just inside the front door, still holding her bag and keys. She clears her throat, as if to jump-start her entire body, and then moves to place her things on the console table in front of the stairs. That morning on television, she had seen Stan Firestone escorted from his home in handcuffs.

"I'm sorry," she says quietly, entering the living room and sitting on the end of the sofa closest to his chair.

"And the Feds already have Firestone. I'm sure I'm next on their list."

She nods. "Have you called an attorney yet?"

"No."

"I'll do it," she offers. "I can be more objective."

"Yeah." He waits for her to say more; to get angry or to tell him that she had warned him. But nothing comes. After a few minutes, she rises from the sofa and goes to retrieve her planner, with all the phone numbers she does not trust to technology.

"Mandy?" He calls after her as she leaves the room.

She turns to face him. "Yeah?"

"I'm sorry. I'm really, really sorry."

Amanda nods again. "I know. We'll deal with it. We'll deal with it the best we possibly can, and then we'll move on."

As she stands at the kitchen island, flipping through her planner until she finds the right page, a single tear slides down her cheek. She looks up, eyes focused on nothing at all, and brushes it away before bending her head over the book once again.

THURSDAY, APRIL 3

"We are going to take John Wallace down with us," Stan asserts. He and Matt sit across from each other at his kitchen table; he had posted bail the previous afternoon. Tomorrow will be Matt's turn to do the "perp walk," according to his attorney.

"Why? What difference will that make, now?"

"For one thing, we can reduce our sentences if we can give them Wallace." A stern look. "We are going to prison, Matt. There's no way around it."

Matt's shoulders slump. He knows Wallace had nothing to do with any of this, and now the man and his company are going to suffer because of Matt's stupid move. When Stan's side arrangement with Prometheus had been uncovered, Vantage had been forced to pull the entire fund out of the two previous quarters' earnings releases. The net result was minor — just as Matt had known it would be — but it had set off a major crisis in confidence for the company, and the stock had fallen apart as investors started selling off their holdings.

"And, for another thing," Stan pauses, searching the young man's face for any glimmer of knowledge as he stubs out his cigarette. "He and your wife...."

"What?" Matt's tone is defensive, as if he cannot believe the insinuation. He feels the anxiety rising as his stomach drops to the floor beneath his chair.

"Jesus, Matt. You must be the only person at Vantage who didn't know about it." Stan shakes his head. "Why the fuck do you think you were moved into the lab? Because of Fox Trade? Because you're so much smarter than everyone else?" He starts laughing, actually slapping his knee at Matt's expense.

Matt has no response. Something that has become distressingly common over the last few days.

"And all those trips to meet with the transition teams." Stan is still laughing. "Shit, Parsons. You did everything but turn down the bed for them."

#

The museum door opens with a bang, hitting the wall behind it. Matt storms inside, fury twisting his face. Amanda turns to the teacher leading the school group.

"Would you excuse me for a moment, please?"

The teacher nods, apprehensive, and leads her students to another part of the museum, far away from Matt and Amanda. Amanda walks to her office and Matt follows. She closes the door and turns to face him. His breathing is rapid and heavy, as if he has perhaps run the entire way. They do not speak; neither wants to go first.

"Tell me it isn't true," Matt says at last, his voice pleading.

Amanda shakes her head and for a few seconds he has hope.

But she tells him, "I can't."

He staggers under the force of her simple words. He would have believed her if she had just lied. He wishes that she had. Matt sits heavily on the sofa and buries his face in his hands. Amanda does not move or speak. Nothing she says can fix this. For once in her life, she does not have a plan in place.

"Every bit of this," he says. "Every bit of it, I did for you."

Amanda shakes her head. "Then that's the problem, isn't it? You shouldn't have done it at all. And certainly not for me."

Her words bite through his skin and he stares at the floor again, stunned into silence.

He stands after a few minutes. Walks past her without making eye contact and says, "Don't bother coming to the trial. I don't want to see you again."

But at the door he turns and looks at her one last time. "You're just like your father," he says. And then he leaves.

She watches him walk away, sees the door swing slowly closed behind him, trying to muster some emotion — any emotion — in response.

FRIDAY, APRIL 4

It is the news helicopter. The sound of its rotors chopping the air above the house. That is when Amanda knows. She almost smiles in pity for the wasted gas, because of course Matt is not at home when the U.S. marshals come to arrest him. He had spent the night at the Hyatt Regency downtown. His attorney had already notified the Justice Department that he would surrender at the federal courthouse that morning. But the public will have its drama; and if it must take the form of the alleged perpetrator's young and pretty wife standing forlorn in her front yard as the Feds duck back into their car, so much the better.

But the scene still does not play out quite the way the news directors had intended. Amanda emerges no farther than the front door and thus remains hidden under the porch that bends around two sides of the four-square house. The old architecture affords her some degree of privacy, as she explains to the marshals that Matt had stolen their thunder and is — probably at that very moment — turning himself in. They smile politely but insincerely and apologize for the disturbance.

Back inside, now, twenty minutes after their departure, Amanda's cell phone rings; the caller ID displays her father's office number.

"Hey, Dad."

"Amanda. Saw the news. How are you?"

She smiles. "I'm fine, Dad. How else could I be, right?"

"Good girl," he says; his voice crisp. "Come for dinner tonight. Lisa doesn't want you to be alone. Have you heard from your mother?" Rapid-fire, as ever.

"No. She's still struggling with it, I guess." Ann had not taken the news of Amanda's impending divorce or Matt's likely incarceration easily — although it was yet unclear which fact was more difficult for her to abide. She had become a pariah among her social set. Amanda felt terrible for her; she could only imagine what it must be like to show up at the regular luncheon and find that nobody will meet your eyes. Her mother had called once, after the news had broken, desperate to hear that it was all a mistake. That the stories in the press were about a different Amanda and Matt Parsons, existing in some parallel universe. The conversation had not gone well.

"She'll come around, I imagine. You know it takes her some time to process unpleasant events."

"I know. What time tonight?" There is no point in even a token refusal of the invitation. Ted would simply send a driver to collect her if she demurred.

"Seven-thirty. See you then."

"'Bye, Dad." She moves to end the call and then hesitates. "Dad?"

"Yes?" She can picture his hand poised above the speaker phone, his mind already on the next agenda item.

"Thanks."

He sighs, but gently. She can hear the paternal smile in the air as it leaves his mouth. "Of course. You're still my girl, no matter what. You know that."

Amanda pushes the button without another word. Her throat is prickling, and it would not do for her father to hear emotion in her voice.

#

Lisa hugs Amanda when she arrives. It is the last thing Amanda wants, but she endures it, just as she endures the meal and its superficial conversation about everything but Matt and Vantage. They discuss the presidential campaign; her father, as ever, amused by ability of 24-hour news channels to whip even the smallest incident into a "game changer." Amanda watches him as he speaks, wondering what he will do in November. With everything that has transpired over the last several months, she would not be surprised if he made a statement vote.

Amanda's offer to help Lisa with the dishes is declined, and she recognizes that now her father will get down to business. This invitation likely had nothing at all to do with Lisa's concern about

Amanda being alone. She follows her father into the study and accepts the drink he pours, completely unaware of what it is. Her intuition is on full alert.

"I thought we should address a few things, about your future," Ted says as he snips the end off a cigar. "I don't expect the museum will be around much longer."

She shakes her head in agreement. "No, probably not. We can stay afloat through the end of the year, maybe a little beyond."

"Job market is tightening up everywhere. I don't think people realize how bad this is going to get." Lights the cigar and takes several long draws on it. The collapse of Vantage had been the tip of the iceberg; the real crash was yet to come. Mortgage-backed securities. *Ridiculous.*

"And my own, personal job market will be even tighter, I'm sure."

Ted smiles around his cigar. Amanda never has been one to sugar-coat a bad situation.

"How are your finances?"

"I'm good," she insists. "I met with Karl a few months back, and we set up a contingency account."

"Really? What made you do that?"

"Nothing concrete. Matt just made me nervous with his investment behavior." And his professional behavior.

Ted is nodding. He never liked that boy; couldn't understand what Amanda had seen in him. He had always assumed she had married Matt just to prove a point to him. And that reminds him of the other topic he must cover with her.

"Something else, now," he says, his voice almost hesitant. This is not a subject any father would be comfortable raising with his daughter. Not even the fearsome Ted Griffin.

Amanda reads the change in his mood. This won't be good, whatever it is.

"Old colleague of mine was in Baltimore last month."

The slight lifting of her eyebrow is the only signal that she understands his intimation.

"I see."

"What's your exposure there?"

"It's over," she says simply. "It was very brief."

Ted nods again. Now this one, he understands, although it is not like her to dally with someone. Still, a much more suitable match for his daughter, apart from the fact that it's wholly inappropriate. But on paper, it makes perfect sense.

"I'll do whatever I can, if it comes up."

"I know you will." She manages a smile, lips only. "And I'll do whatever I can to make sure it doesn't come to that."

"I know you will."

But they both know it is beyond either one of them to control.

MONDAY, APRIL 7

"Here's your script." Dave hands him a packet of pages, stapled together in landscape orientation. The font is enormous, at least sixteen points. John rolls his eyes.

"I hate scripts," he mutters.

"I know, but this is not the time to speak off-the-cuff," Dave reminds him. "It's not just employees who will be listening." The ire that had erupted between them last week has cooled, but they speak formally. The last few months have taken a heavy toll on their relationship; perhaps an irreparable toll.

"I know; I know." John checks the time. "I have two hours?"

Dave nods. "Roughly. Security will walk you to the Hyatt at nine-forty-five."

"Okay." He drops his eyes to the script again. "Maybe I can memorize some of it, at least."

"You know," Dave begins, "You still have the employees in your corner. This is all the stuff they want to hear. It won't matter to them if you have it memorized; they just need to hear it come out of your mouth."

"I get it, Dave." The stock has taken a steady pounding in the last week, with the final blow coming in the termination of the Fox Trade acquisition. Vantage had already been using the technology to manage its investments, and the entire portfolio had to be shifted back to the old system. The end result would likely be another drop in earnings, at least for the first month of the quarter.

John looks up again. Dave is still standing in front of his desk. "What else?"

"Just please don't go off-message." His tone is fairly pleading. "Please."

"I won't, Dave. I won't go off-message." John shakes his head. "But you have to give me some time to look at this, okay? Did Albert write it?"

"Yeah; he's got your voice down the best."

"Yeah." John nods. "Now leave me alone, please Dave. Seriously, get out."

#

"The last week has been a difficult time for Vantage. We've taken a hit in the market as the result of some dealings of one of our leaders. These were poor decisions on his part, and I do not condone or support the choices he made. *[Don't refer to him by name; move on quickly.]* And I pledge to you that we will continue to investigate the matter until we are confident that all misconduct has been identified and addressed. The health of our company is paramount — that has not changed and never will change. And my commitment to our employees remains the same as it has for the last eleven years, since I took over from my father, John Wallace II. *[Invoke the legacy of leadership; remind employees that you are not just the CEO but a part of the company's history.]* But I will need your help to move forward from this unfortunate and isolated incident. We must all redouble our efforts to drive company value and to act with integrity in our business dealings, just as we do in our personal lives. Vantage is more than a company to my family; it is our history and our legacy for the city of Houston. And I am proud to entrust the success of that legacy to our current leadership team and to each one of you present in person or via teleconference. *[Remember the remote workers; they account for the majority of our base.]* I see a bright future for our firm; we will recover from this downturn and emerge even stronger than we were.

"Now, I'm happy to open the floor to questions at this time."

John scans the audience as he utters the conclusion. The house lights come up, and he can see the first few rows of employees. The faces that greet him are relieved, he thinks. He sees heads nodding. Eventually, a smattering of applause takes off from the back of the room. Dave, no doubt. John groans inwardly: *the slow clap*. It spreads up the rows of banquet chairs until someone stands and then the entire room is standing and applauding him. For the life of him, he cannot imagine why. But he smiles beatifically, as he knows he should.

MONDAY, APRIL 14

Larry looks across the table at John. He knows what is coming. At this very moment, he reckons that his assistant is packing his personal effects into a box, his network access is being terminated, his building security card disabled. At least John has the dignity to deliver the news himself. Larry respects that. He picks up his napkin.

"Okay," he says, spreading the napkin across his lap. Café Annie is a nice touch. Discreet and exclusive but just public enough to ensure there won't be a scene. Melissa's choice; John had no worries on that front.

John sighs. "Ah, Larry," he says. His voice is miserable.

Larry shakes his head. "Don't worry about it, JW. What else can you do?"

What else, indeed? John's speech to employees had proved a temporary salve. The stock stabilized for one day and had been in a tail-spin ever since. The market demanded action; words were not enough anymore.

"And it happened on my watch," Larry continues. "Off the record, and I'll deny this later, it pisses me off that I didn't know."

John is nodding. "I know it does. You don't deserve this. And," he hesitates, "I'll deny *that* later."

Larry nods, too, his head joining the bobbing motion in front of him. The two men sit sadly, quiet in their grief over a situation that has spun so far out of control, neither can be certain that even this will be the last step in the process. When Prometheus had been discovered and the stock had begun its downward spiral, every institution that had provided Vantage with financing had pulled its support, fearing more damage. And they had been correct. Half the portfolio had been wrapped up in mortgage-backed securities. And the blame for such risky investing had to rest with the chief risk officer.

And with me, John thinks. *Why didn't I see the signs? Were there any signs? Is success something that should cause suspicion? Is profit something to distrust?*

"I'll be next," he predicts suddenly.

"No," Larry disagrees. "Vantage has always been headed by a Wallace. No way."

John shrugs. "I don't think tradition matters much anymore," he speculates. "The board will want to be clean of the entire mess, and that means I'll have to go. It's okay." He shrugs again and then smiles ironically. "Maybe I'll *retire*."

Larry laughs. "Do it soon. Hurt them before they can hurt you. Bastards." A serious look. "You'll have my things shipped to the house?"

"Yeah. Will you be okay?"

A shrug. "Will anybody? What a mess. The whole country is going to feel this one."

# # #

"How did it go?" Steve enters John's office unannounced. Melissa must be away from her desk.

John simply shakes his head. Steve can see the regret in his eyes. Neither one speaks for a moment.

"Well, I guess you and I need hammer out some transition issues," John says at last.

"Come on; let's not get carried away." Steve is alarmed. It's not like John even to hint at surrender.

"I don't think I am, honestly. This is a mess. It's going to look like I had my hand on it." The public had already turned on him; every regular city and business columnist had featured a scathing assessment of his poor leadership in the last three weeks. As far as anyone on the outside was concerned, he had already been tried and convicted and they couldn't fathom why he was still walking around free.

"But you didn't," Steve insists. "The truth will bear out in the end."

John actually smiles at this. Steve and his eternal optimism. He'll make a good leader for Vantage after John is forced out. A strong rallying point for employees.

"I don't think anyone is particularly interested in the truth of these matters. Revenge is a much more popular objective. And history does not favor my chances, there."

Steve's shoulders droop; he can't deny this. "Well, before you hand over the keys, let's talk about it logically for a bit, shall we?" He takes a seat at John's conference table.

John sighs. "Okay, let's." He scoops up a legal pad and joins Steve at the table. It is a welcome distraction, in fact. And John reasons that it is better to have his points outlined now, before he is under pressure to craft a legal defense. Because he knows it is coming. "I need you to play devil's advocate."

Steve nods. "Got it." He tears a sheet off the pad and starts a list. "Let's start with the lab itself."

"Right. Why did we need a separate finance team? What were they really up to?"

"Yeah," Steve agrees, pen scrawling across the yellow paper. He looks up. "Do you want to do answers now, or just questions?"

"Questions," John replies. One thing at a time. Besides, he knows the answers. It's the questions that pose the problem.

"Okay. So, second, Firestone's incentive structure. That's going to be a big one."

"Yep. But we all have them, in some form; make a note of that, too."

"Got it. Third … the Parsons issue."

John closes his eyes. "Which one?"

"I'll make two entries." Steve hesitates; he puts down his pen. "Why *did* you move Matt Parsons into the lab?"

John does not answer immediately. He looks at Steve, appraising what the man expects him to say. "That's a bit of a gray area, I suppose. I wouldn't have done it without Fox Trade; but I could just as easily not have moved him, too. If not for her."

Steve lets the words settle; it is a very honest answer. But that may not be enough for anyone else. "Have you talked to her?"

John shakes his head. "What would I say?" Takes a deep breath and then mutters, "What a fucking mess."

Steve nods; it is a mess.

Another pause and then John speaks again. "Let's keep going."

"Okay. Next?" Pen back in hand, poised above the paper.

"Steve," John's voice is suddenly weary. "I appreciate what you're trying to do, but I don't think it's going to help. No matter what I say or do right now, I'm the bad guy."

"You have a lot of history in this city, John. People will come around; they're angry now. They don't understand what's happening, and you're the best target. It will be okay."

John studies his friend's face while he speaks. He knows that Steve does not believe a word of what he is saying. And neither does John.

WEDNESDAY, APRIL 16

Amanda knows who they are as soon as they enter the museum. Even if they had not borne such a resemblance to the marshals who had visited her home just a couple of weeks before, she would have known. The two FBI agents are walking caricatures of themselves: dark suits, dark glasses, sensible but polished shoes.

She is seated at the reception desk when they arrive; business has been slow for the last month, and there is no need for a volunteer to occupy the chair. Amanda is perfectly able to sit in silence and wait for the minutes to pass. Her stomach tingles as they approach the desk.

"Amanda Parsons?" The one on the left — the man — speaks.

"Yes."

"I'm Agent Martin Scholes; this is Agent Vivian Black." He points to the woman at his side. "We'd like to ask you some questions about the Commerce Museum."

Really. Agents Black and Scholes. Amanda stifles a smile; they wouldn't understand, anyway.

"Certainly." She rises. "Here?"

Agent Scholes nods. "Yes, here is fine."

"I'll just go lock up, then, so we won't be interrupted." As she reaches the door, she pauses and looks back at them. "Unless I should ask my attorney to join us."

A smile from Agent Black now. "That's entirely up to you, ma'am."

She turns the lock in its chamber, ruminating. "I think I'll keep my options open," she concludes. "We can use the conference table in my office."

If she contacts her attorney now, she looks guilty before she even knows why they are here. It's a terrible game of cat-and-mouse, but she will play it for a little while, at least. Amanda walks past them confidently and leads them to the table.

"How can I help you?" she asks when they are seated.

It is Scholes' turn again. "In the course of our investigation into insider trading and conspiracy at Vantage PLC, we discovered an inconsistency with the funding for the museum."

"Okay." Her voice steady; her brain sprinting several steps ahead already.

"And we'd like to know if there is anything you would care to share with us about that."

Amanda thinks for a moment before answering. Her books are extremely simple; she has a variety of funding sources, but everything is in order. The accounting firm she had retained specializes in 501(c)3 organizations. Confident, she shakes her head. "Everything is very standard and certified by the museum's outside accounting and audit firms."

A look is exchanged between the two agents before Scholes speaks again.

"I see," he says. "Well, we've determined that the Wallace Family Foundation funds that were applied to the museum had also been used by Vantage PLC to short sell the company's own stock."

"At a significant profit," Black adds, with a severe look at Amanda.

"I see." Her face is still, but a wave of nausea has begun, all the way in her toes. She feels dizzy and forces herself to stay focused on the two officers at her table. Her breathing remains steady; she relies on her marathon training to pace her brain and her body.

Used. Artfully, expertly used. The thought erupts into her head and she quashes it immediately.

Quiet for a moment, as the two agents wait for Amanda to say more.

Scholes decides there is nothing else and presses on. "Do you know a Vantage employee named Balaji Anand?"

Good God, how much worse could this get, she wonders. And then reminds herself not to ask questions to which she does not want the answer.

"Only in passing," she responds. "My husband worked with his team for a while."

"It would appear that, in addition to your husband's activities, Mr. Anand was using his position within that team to set up the short-selling arrangement," Black has taken over.

"And we'd like to know what you might know about that, Ms. Parsons." Scholes drives home the point.

Amanda shakes her head. "Nothing," she says simply. "I know nothing about that arrangement."

"Very well," Scholes concludes, sliding a folded set of paper out of his portfolio. "We need access to the museum's financial statements, starting with the most recent and going back to its creation."

He places the warrant on the table in front of Amanda.

She picks it up and unfolds the packet. "Certainly," she says mildly. And then she shifts her eyes to the words and reads every, last one of them while Agents Scholes and Black wait.

When she has finished, she shows them to her computer and watches patiently as they disconnect the CPU from the components, tag it and set it on the conference table. Over the course of the next hour, they add folders and binders to the collection. Scholes does the lifting, packing the paper and binders into boxes, while Black ticks off each item on a receipt, which she presents to Amanda upon their departure.

"And the laptop, as well," Scholes comments, expecting that this, finally, will elicit some response from Amanda.

But she merely hands it over, nodding as Black reclaims the receipt and adds one last entry to the list. The two agents lift their swag and move toward the door; Amanda precedes them to unlock it.

As they step into the sunlight again, she hears Black mutter to Scholes, "Now that is one icy-cold bitch."

On her way home after the agents have left, Amanda takes a detour through town, near the baseball stadium. While stopped at a red light, she rolls down her window and beckons a homeless man to her car.

"Here," she says simply, unclasping the Rolex and sliding it from her wrist into his waiting hand. She speeds around the corner before he can respond.

THURSDAY, APRIL 17

Amanda is returning from a run when she sees the vans in front of her house. She hesitates, but briefly, before setting her arms and clenching her fists for the final yards between the stop sign at the end of the street and her front door, three houses in. They spot her just before her foot touches the neighbor's driveway.

"Amanda? Amanda Parsons?" The phalanx of reporters and cameras points itself at her like a guided missile. She keeps her pace steady; eyes forward. So Matt had finally dropped the bomb. She wonders how many years they had sliced off his sentence for *this* nugget.

"Is it true that you're Ted Griffin's daughter? Can you tell us what he thinks about his only daughter's illicit affair with a man who might easily be regarded as one of his peers?"

She does not even pause to tell them, "No comment." They will figure it out on their own. Eyes fixed on the door to her home, she simply keeps running. Feet echo on the wooden steps up the porch, boards creaking beneath her shoes. She keeps running right up to the door until it is open and she is inside. She turns and locks the door, then walks slowly into the kitchen, pacing around the island to warm her muscles down. She puts her hands against the counter and stretches; first one calf and then the other, back and forth. Staring out the window over the sink and into the back yard. She is worried about the roses; she'll have to call Polly and see if she might care for them from her side of the fence line for a while. Just until Amanda's fifteen minutes of fame have passed.

A click from the dishwasher catches her attention. She opens the door and begins to put away the clean dishes, frowning absently at the fact that everything inside was a wedding gift. Perhaps she can donate it all; she can get new things at Target. The thought leads her to the contents of her closet. Long overdue for a thorough weeding. She will attack it in the morning.

The telephone rings. She glances at the caller ID. Her father; he must have the TV on in his office. She ignores it and continues putting the dishes away.

A few miles away, Margaret Wallace turns off the television in her own kitchen and picks up the phone. She has had the divorce attorney on speed dial for at least four years, and it feels good to push the button at last.

MONDAY, APRIL 21

Houston – Vantage PLC announced today that John Allen Wallace III has stepped down as president and CEO.

Company spokesman David Galvan said in a company-issued statement that the move was "consistent with a change in corporate strategy agreed upon by the board of directors at its meeting last week. Mr. Wallace departs on amicable terms and we wish him the best in future endeavors."

Phone messages left at Mr. Wallace's home and The Wallace Family Foundation were not returned in time for publication in this story. The news of Mr. Wallace's departure follows last week's revelation that he had been involved in an extra-marital affair with Amanda Parsons, the estranged wife of former Vantage employee Matt Parsons, who was recently indicted on criminal conspiracy and embezzlement charges, along with former Chief Technology Officer Stan Firestone. Ms. Parsons, the daughter of Pinnacle Oil CEO Ted Griffin, also could not be reached for comment; nor could her father. Ms. Parsons is also the curator of the Commerce Museum of Houston, a major beneficiary of the Wallace Family Foundation.

Vantage stock responded favorably to the news, climbing $1.50 in early morning trading. Mr. Wallace has previously been implicated in an embezzlement scandal that was uncovered at the firm in early April of this year. Legal experts believe his departure from Vantage heralds an impending indictment on charges that may include fraud, conspiracy and insider trading.

Check our Web site for continuing coverage of this developing story.

WEDNESDAY, APRIL 23

"Surely your client can appreciate how difficult it is for us to believe that his CTO and a mid-level employee were able to perpetrate this right under his nose."

Tim Cavanaugh leans forward. "I believe that's the very definition of embezzlement, Ms. Wilcox. Mr. Wallace had no knowledge of the activities of these two individuals."

"But he reaped a tidy bonus when revenue targets supported by those activities were exceeded every quarter — not to mention his own holdings in Vantage stock."

"Neither of which is a criminal act." Tim appears bored. "Mr. Wallace never received a cent from the Prometheus trades."

"Just because we haven't found the funds yet, that doesn't mean they don't exist. We believe it's very likely he laundered them through his sizeable charitable contributions or his family foundation."

John is leaning back in his seat, looking at the table. He shakes his head. "The foundation is an open book," he asserts. "You're making noise."

Tim lifts a hand to settle his client even as he nods in agreement with John's assessment. "You've had ample time to review those books and turned up nothing. In fact, you've turned up nothing concrete from any of your investigations. Isn't it time for you to focus on the individuals who have actually committed crimes?"

"Oh, we haven't lost our focus on Mr. Parsons and Mr. Firestone," Debra assures him. "And they have been very helpful in our investigation of Mr. Wallace." She extracts one more sheet of paper from her folder and lays it in front of Tim.

He studies it for a moment before sliding it to John, who frowns as he reads it. A guarantee that Stan Firestone would never lose money on his Prometheus activities. It's absurd; nobody makes guarantees like that. No single officer of any company is that valuable.

"I've never seen this document," John states. "Never."

"So you deny those are your initials?" Debra touches her pen to the *JAW* scrawled in the margin, next to the typed version of his full name: John Allen Wallace.

John shakes his head. "They're my initials, but I didn't write them."

"Unfortunately for your client," Debra addresses Tim now, "both Mr. Parsons and Mr. Firestone remember the event of his participation quite clearly."

John rolls his eyes. "And how much time did you agree to knock off their sentences for that recollection?"

Tim raises his hand again, a matter of protocol only. He is fuming right alongside his client. "Really, Debra. This is the best you have?"

"It's all I need," she replies. "Have fun finding anyone to back your client under oath, Tim." She stands and collects her papers. "You can expect the indictment in the next few weeks. You might want to use that time to consider plea agreements."

An icy look from John. "You want an agreement from me?" His voice drops; Debra can barely hear him. "I will never plead to anything. That will be our only agreement."

Debra leans forward over the table and smiles at John. "How've you been sleeping, Mr. Wallace?" Tilts her head before continuing, "Having trouble nodding off? Get used to it. This is not going away, and neither am I." And then, as if an afterthought, "Are your kids enjoying their time in the spotlight?"

John unleashes a look of pure fury at her but says nothing. Hands grip the arms of his chair until his knuckles are white and he cannot feel his fingers. Teeth clench and jaw twitches. But he says nothing.

She straightens and turns to leave. "You'll be hearing from us," she calls over her shoulder on the way through the door.

When she has gone, Tim turns to John. "Did you sign it?"

John shakes his head as he loosens his hold on the chair. "No; look at the date for Christ's sake. It's a Saturday in the middle of February. It doesn't make any sense." He sighs and leans over to tug up his sock.

"Fucking witch hunt," Tim mutters.

"Yeah," John agrees. "And I'm sure as hell not drowning to prove my innocence."

"Legally, *you* don't have to prove anything," Tim asserts, although his tone carries a hint of concession. They both know it doesn't work like that, anymore. Juries don't work like that, anymore.

"*Could* you prove that you weren't there?" Tim poses. "Were you at the ranch in Wyoming, by any chance? Was Margaret with you?"

As the question travels from Tim's lips to John's ear, he feels his heart slow down. He straightens in his seat and looks again at the date: *February 16.* Margaret was in Atlanta. Matt Parsons and Stan Firestone were in New York. And he was at his loft, with Amanda. All weekend. It had been perfect, at the time. He shakes his head.

"I was in town. Alone. All weekend."

TUESDAY, APRIL 29

John feels sick to his stomach. How much worse was this going to get? Evidently, the document Debra Wilcox had shared at last week's meeting was not all she had. He reviews the notes Tim's courier had delivered to his loft that morning, feeling sicker with each word that passes under his eyes. Pushing the papers away, he lifts his head and stares out the window, watching a construction crane that is swinging a girder high above. Just what the city needs; probably another parking garage.

He lowers his eyes to the paper again. What the hell is going on? As if the words might have changed, he rereads the document. Anand had been lifting funds from the Wallace Family Foundation and using them to short Vantage stock, siphoning off the profits into a separate account before feeding them back into Vantage via the multitude of entities that were managed in the lab. John closes his eyes. The museum will come under suspicion now. And so will Amanda. He had seen her on the news last week, descended upon like a pot of honey at a picnic by the insects that are the media. He has not spoken to her since Baltimore, although he has brought up the museum's number countless times on his cell phone. And now it is too late. Any call he places from this day on will be taken the wrong way — by the government and the media, certainly — but more importantly, by Amanda herself. Will he never time anything right with her?

The finality of it is beginning to sink in. He feels a strange pressure in his chest. Perfect. A heart attack would be just the ticket. He shakes his head briskly. He cannot let himself be distracted by anything else. The divorce proceedings have nearly done him in already. Margaret had wasted no time staking her claim to fifty percent of what might be zero if she hesitated. His youngest son Greg had refused to speak with him for an entire week when the papers had been filed. Jack had managed to bring him around, on a visit from California. It turned out that he had been taking some heat at school already, and the news that his parents couldn't stand to live with each other anymore had been too much for the boy to handle.

His eyes move back to the screen of his laptop. To the Op-Ed he had begun writing and knew he would never submit. It is purely therapeutic, and Tim had encouraged him to try:

By now, you have probably already formed your opinion of me; and it is probably incorrect. It is most likely based, in part, on the testimonials of people you do not know, people who claim to know me. They do not. The rest of your opinion about me comes, perhaps, from the people who were paid to create me. To spin me. Interesting word, spin. The first definition is "to draw out and twist into thread." To twist. Sort of the psychological version of disembowelment, in its modern application. If you think it is less painful than the physical treatment, well, you are wrong about that, too.

The fact of the matter is that you envy me. Or at least you used to envy me. Now you wag your finger at me in a self-righteous "I told you so" that is not yours to claim.

John clicks to close the window on the untitled document; he does not save changes. Then he picks up his phone to call Tim. Might as well see what the damage from the latest grenade will be.

WEDNESDAY, APRIL 30

Carlo pops his head into the freight elevator lobby and pulls it back inside quickly. He sends a baleful look down the hall to Thomas. The boxes have arrived. Still collapsed and held together with plastic binding; but they have arrived.

"*Shit.*" Thomas hangs his head for a moment; then snaps it back up. "They couldn't do it yesterday, when it was karaoke night at the Tavern?"

"Inconsiderate bastards, aren't they?" Carlo shakes his head as the two wander in the direction of the coffee bar. So much for getting any more work done today. The entire team is still reeling from Matt's dismissal and subsequent arrest. Not a one of them had thought he was capable of devising such a plan, never mind putting it in place and actually having it work — up to a point. They had almost admired him for it, until the realization that he'd effectively taken down the whole company had settled in their minds.

Anand is already there. "Well?"

Thomas nods. "Today's the day." He looks suspiciously at his boss. "But you knew that already, didn't you?"

"It won't be me," he insists. "It will be Larry. They're not telling anyone outside the fiftieth floor or HR anything yet." At least he thinks that is why he has had no notice of terminations for his group.

Thomas fills a Styrofoam cup with coffee; screw the environment. "I've had my resume out for the last month anyway. The market's still not bad here. We'll be fine."

"Yeah," Carlo agrees. "We'll be fine."

When they return to their desks, both Carlo and Anand have messages waiting. Carlo's sends him to a conference room on the forty-fifth floor. Anand's sends him to the office of Steve McAllister. Thomas watches them both leave; he had not counted on being left behind.

###

Kate Wells reads flatly from a prepared script, avoiding eye contact with anyone in the rows of seats before her. Some three-hundred Vantage employees sit like paper dolls as she informs them that they are now unemployed. As the first words leave her mouth, a gasp of sorrow and surprise erupts from somewhere behind Carlo. He does not turn to see who it was, wondering, instead how anyone could be surprised at this point. The gasp is followed by the sound of quiet tears, and Carlo shifts in his seat, as if the motion itself will stifle the noise — like one spouse moving on the mattress to quell the other's snoring. It does not work, of course, and these tears are soon joined by others, and then a growing chorus of dismay and disbelief begins to drown out Kate's voice as the people remember that they are not, in fact, paper dolls but living, breathing humans who will be heard. Carlo looks wearily from side to side as his neighbors join the outcry, disappointed in them all.

###

Anand walks cautiously into Steve's office and is relieved to see that nobody else is present. He takes a seat at the conference table and faces Steve, expectant and yet still confident.

"Anand," Steve begins; his voice quiet. "I'm glad you came." The way he says the word makes it obvious that Anand could just as easily have left the building and waited his turn for a visit from the marshals.

Anand is nodding, lips pressed together in a grim line. "I appreciate the invitation."

"I'd just like to know what happened, so we can try to sort it out," Steve continues. He is leaning forward in his seat, willing Anand to come up with some sort of explanation that will make sense.

"I had to cover our position on the derivatives. It was the only way." He shrugs and says nothing else. He should not have said anything at all, but he believes he owes Steve, anyway. He opens the clip that connects his ID badge to the waistband of his trousers and slides the badge across the table.

Anand rises slowly from his chair and extends his hand to Steve. "It's been a pleasure," he says.

He turns then and leaves the room without another word. He does not bother to stop by his floor on the way out of the building. He cannot enter without his badge, and he knows they will send his things, eventually. Besides, he won't need any of it, where he is going.

MAY 2008

MONDAY, MAY 5

Houston — Former Vantage PLC President and CEO John Allen Wallace III was indicted in Houston federal court today on eight counts of conspiracy to commit fraud and six counts of insider trading for his role in the company's spectacular financial collapse which began in April of this year.

Federal Prosecutor Debra Wilcox commented on the indictment, stating, "This is a victory for both the justice system and the current and former employees of Vantage and their families. We are certain the government will make its case against Mr. Wallace and he will be convicted by a jury of his peers. This sends a clear message to corporate leaders that it is no longer appropriate for them to gloss over activities that have a direct impact on employees and shareholders."

Tim Cavanaugh, lead defense counsel for Wallace, issued the following statement on behalf of his client: "I have faith in the fairness of our nation's justice system and am confident that, following a fair trial, I will be exonerated of any wrongdoing in this matter." Cavanaugh further added that he hopes, "the public will await the court proceeding before passing its own judgment on a man who has unwaveringly served his community and bolstered the economy of his city for nearly 20 years."

Reaction from former and current employees of Vantage suggests that opinions have already been formed, however. "I hope he burns in Hell," said one former employee, who wished to remain anonymous. "I had my entire retirement portfolio tied up in Vantage stock. Maybe if he'd spent more time watching the store and less time screwing around, the company would still be in business today."

A September trial date is expected.

Amanda reads the article with scorn and clicks the link to the PDF summary of the indictment. Ah, technology. She skims the document for the salient information.

Misleading investors by knowingly making false statements about the company's value. Amanda had forgotten in the last several years that it's illegal to be optimistic about your company anymore.

Conspiracy to commit fraud. The catch-all of white collar crime. Intentionally vague, so the prosecution can intimidate anyone else who might have been involved and coerce them into making statements against their main target.

Insider trading. This one has to do with Anand and the foundation investments. Amanda closes the document; she is not ready yet to read the details of how the world at large believes she had been played.

Betrayal, anger, sadness. She should feel all of these, but she does not. She cannot, no matter how hard she tries; no matter how powerfully she wills the emotions to surface. Instead, she is numb. Those who know her — or think they know her — would not be surprised. They would say that she has always been like this. But they would be wrong. She has feelings; she just never shares them with anyone. Not her parents or her brother or even Matt. There was never a girlfriend to whom she revealed her darkest thoughts or brightest aspirations. A switch had been flipped in her brain the day her father left; a filter had been engaged. After almost a year of her mother's histrionics at his every coming and going, Amanda had made the connection: if you show people how you feel, eventually they will leave.

She is frustrated by the timing, most of all. Considering that she would like everyone around her to leave, it is unfortunate that she cannot bring herself to act out and scare them all away. But she has replayed every minute she and John had spent together from February to March, and she cannot identify anything — even in retrospect — that was suspicious. She cannot believe that it had all been an act on his part. Men simply don't possess that brand of deviousness, in her experience. They can lie about golf handicap, salary, stamina. But emotion? No. Even her own father, for all his appearance of detachment, cannot completely disengage when his heart is involved. Otherwise, he would have stayed with Ann.

Amanda leans back against the chair. She has a decision to make; she must choose where to cast her lot. John will resurface in her life eventually. It is only a matter of when, and she is resolved to be ready. All that remains is to determine what shape that readiness will assume.

WEDNESDAY, MAY 7

Anand supposes that he has endured much worse. The federal jail in Houston had nothing on the underbelly of Mumbai, where he had spent most of his youth. And Steve McAllister has been to visit a couple of times — with counsel, of course — which he appreciates. Out of everyone involved, it is Steve who has kept his head and insisted that no judgment be passed until the facts are known.

He is awaiting a visit from Steve today, sitting anxiously in the meeting room, along with his own attorney, Ivan Kettleman. His family has suffered terribly since he was arrested. His wife has received threats from immigration on a weekly basis. They take the form of phone calls placed to check the status on his case, but they both know the real purpose: to scare him into cooperating with the government as it builds a criminal case against John Wallace. Steve's visit today is to update him on the real status of his family's residency in the United States, as well as the progress JW has made in securing witnesses for the defense. Even though Anand had set up his scheme to implicate the CEO, he cannot stomach the idea of testifying against him and committing perjury. He honestly never thought it would go this far; if he had known what Firestone and Parsons were up to, he would have chosen a different path. In his deposition, he had explained that the arrangement had been established so that he could meet corporate goals. Nothing more; nothing less. Someone else could determine whether those goals were within the legal limits of commerce and how specifically they had been communicated to Anand.

When Steve and his attorney arrive, Anand stands to greet him with a hug. The two men sit across from each other at the table, a peculiar echo of their final meeting in Steve's office just a couple of weeks before. The two attorneys sit likewise across from each other.

"I talked to my contact at Immigration," Steve begins. "So far no formal proceedings have been filed. So, at this point, they're still just making noise and trying to scare your wife."

"Which is working," Anand interjects.

"I know. I'm sorry." Steve frowns. He doesn't like bullies; never has. "As for John, he's still struggling to find anyone to come to his aid."

Anand nods. He figured as much. Nobody is willing to take on the federal government. If nothing else, that lesson had been learned in the past seven years. He much prefers the detention center in Houston to what might await him in Guantanamo Bay, for example.

"In a way, though, it works to your advantage," Steve suggests. "It reduces their leverage on you to testify against him." A shrug. "If they don't really need you, with Firestone and Parsons."

Anand tilts his head at this; a question in his eyes.

"Oh," Steve clarifies. "*Matt* Parsons, that is."

"Ah." Anand feels a strange degree of comfort in this. He has met Amanda only a few times and has never understood the relationship between her and Matt. The way Matt had paraded her around various company events, showing her off as some sort of prize that he had won. Dangling her like a lure in front of the other men. When he had first heard the rumors of her involvement with John Wallace, it had been no surprise to him. He sighs; his mind has wandered and Steve is looking at him expectantly.

"Sorry," he says. "Lost my train of thought. You were saying?"

"I think it's possible they'll content themselves with your deposition instead of requiring you to testify in person. As long as you don't testify for the defense, I — " a quick look at both lawyers, who nod briefly " — that is, we think you'll be none the worse."

"Good enough," Anand sighs. Ivan has told him he is looking at about fifteen years, max. With good behavior and whatever else they might lop off, he could be out in seven. At which point he will most likely voluntarily return to India; he has had enough of the American dream.

"And Amanda Parsons?" He cannot leave it alone, though he knows he should.

Now Steve's attorney, Eric Bennett, speaks up. "She's set for a deposition next week. She's expected to say she knew nothing of your activities with the foundation's investment."

"It's true," Anand states flatly. "It was just a matter of pure convenience for me. But I don't suppose I'm allowed to go on the record with that, either."

"No," Ivan confirms.

"It doesn't look good for her, though," Eric states flatly. "She was romantically involved with two of the four alleged conspirators." He shakes his head.

"She'll be fine," Ivan counters. "Her daddy will come to the rescue. If anyone in Houston has the power to snatch her out of the fire, he does."

Steve and Eric are nodding. Anand supposes they are right; but he does not think she will take it well.

THURSDAY, MAY 15

"My client must be the Bruce Lee of criminal finance, the way you think she man-handled not only her husband and his boss but also the CEO of a huge insurance company and two more of its executive officers. All without any of them ever discovering each other's involvement. *Please.*" Amanda's attorney, Ron Abrams, wastes no time launching an assault as Debra Wilcox and her team enter the conference room for Amanda's deposition. He shakes his head in scorn.

Debra scowls at him. "You think she couldn't pull it off because she's a woman?"

"I think she couldn't pull it off because she doesn't have control over the space-time continuum."

The exchange is almost funny to Amanda. Less funny, however, is the death threat she had received the previous day. Ron had handed it over to the police, and she had moved into her father's house for the duration.

Debra has realized that Ron's comments are rhetorical and turns the subject toward business. "Are we ready, then?" Her voice is crisp and professional as she looks from one face to another around the table.

Seeing nods from all parties, she draws a breath and continues, "Once you are officially sworn in, Ms. Parsons, your statements will be regarded with the same bearing as they would have in a court of law. Do you understand that?"

"Yes," Amanda replies. Ron has explained it all to her; she is to treat her responses today as if she is seated in the witness box at the court house. Any misstatements on her part could be regarded as perjury. *Would* be regarded as perjury.

The attending clerk swears her in, and Debra's questions begin. Amanda answers mechanically; she and Ron have rehearsed every possible line of inquiry. At first the questions revolve around Matt and Stan and their conduct.

Were you aware of your husband's activities regarding the Prometheus arrangement at Vantage PLC?

No.

Were you aware of your husband's financial agreement with Stan Firestone, former CTO at Vantage PLC?

No.

Were you aware of the activities of Balaji Anand related to short selling Vantage common stock via funds that were related to the Commerce Museum of Houston?

No.

After several more rounds, in which Debra asks essentially the same questions with different wording, she shifts gears to John Wallace.

Did John Wallace, former CEO of Vantage PLC, solicit your participation in any financial transaction related to Vantage common stock or the Commerce Museum?

No.

Who had ultimate oversight of the Commerce Museum's operating budget?

The Wallace Family Foundation Board of Directors.

Are you now or have you ever been a member of that board?

No.

Is John Wallace a member of that board?

Yes.

Describe your relationship with John Wallace.

As a board member of the Wallace Family Foundation and the Commerce Museum's primary benefactor, he was involved in financial and operational decisions at the Commerce Museum of Houston. He appeared at media events and participated in fund-raising activities for the museum.

Did you have a sexual relationship with John Wallace?

Yes.

Was this relationship consensual?

Yes.

Did you exchange sexual favors with John Wallace for a job at the Commerce Museum?

No.

Did John Wallace use his position as your superior to extract sexual favors from you?

No.

Did you use your relationship with John Wallace to secure special treatment for your husband at Vantage PLC?

No.

When did the sexual relationship between you and John Wallace begin?

In February of 2008.

Who initiated the relationship?

Here Amanda hesitates for the first time. She and Ron had discussed this, but she is still not comfortable with the answer. As far as she is concerned, this is open to a lot of interpretation.

Mr. Wallace initiated the relationship.

Were you at any time pressured to engage in sexual acts with Mr. Wallace?

Amanda is growing increasingly uncomfortable with the line of questioning. Are they contemplating additional charges against him?

No.

And who terminated the relationship?

It was mutual.

Do you believe Mr. Wallace betrayed your trust, in his position as your husband's employer or the museum's primary benefactor?

No.

It is true, after all. She does not believe he betrayed her in either of those ways. Not anymore. And she knows Debra will not ask if he had betrayed her in any other form. The deposition lasts another two hours, as Debra rehashes the same questions, over and over, trying to snare Amanda in a misstep and extract something she can use against John Wallace. It will not happen.

#

Amanda sits at the foot of her bed, arms at her side, staring at the Picasso print that hangs over the dresser. The *Blue Nude*; her favorite of that period. Most people know only the *Old Guitarist*, but Amanda considers it too sentimental. In each fist, she clutches a wad of silk dupioni duvet cover. Eyes fixed on the print, the curve of the woman's back. Hunched forward and hugging her knees — in sadness, shame or perhaps the echo of pleasure.

When the deposition had ended and Debra Wilcox was gone, Ron had to tap Amanda on the shoulder to get her attention. She had been staring at the table, her face in the same empty expression it had worn throughout the interview.

Amanda? It's over; you can go now.

She had startled at his touch, and then looked up apologetically. It had taken another five minutes before she could gather the strength to stand and exit the room. Ron had offered to have his paralegal drive her home; he would follow in his own car and take them both back to the office. But Amanda had demurred, insisting she was fine. Just tired from the effort. Nothing more.

Did John Wallace use his position as your superior to extract sexual favors from you?

With the recollection, the nausea returns, rising like a miasma up from her gut. She does not move. There is nothing left to expel. Even the acid is gone. Her throat contracts and it is over for the moment.

Were you at any time pressured to engage in sexual acts with Mr. Wallace?

She closes her eyes. Her father and Lisa are expecting her soon; she has agreed to stay with them for a couple of weeks to let some of the furor subside. Her bag is packed and waiting beside the bedroom door. All that remains is for Amanda to get her game face on so she can leave. She opens her eyes and studies the picture once more. If only the nausea would go away, she could focus on what she had learned from the prosecutor's questions, which is that they have very little credible evidence against John. She feels more violated by the deposition than by anything John had ever done to her. *With* her.

What she needs, she realizes suddenly, is a spreadsheet. She needs columns and rows and categories of data to soothe her frenetic state. Out of habit, she glances at her wrist to check the time and then smiles, remembering. It was just as well, after all. The watch was as much about Matt as it was about John, and it was suffocating to wear them both on her wrist all the time. Her eyes slide now to the clock on the bedside table; plenty of time to collect her thoughts before she has to make the drive to River Oaks. At least she will be staying in the guest house, and not in the bedroom that had been created for her as a part of her father's new life.

TUESDAY, MAY 27

"I want her on the stand," Tim states, dropping the transcript of Amanda's deposition on the table in front of John.

John's eyes flicker to the cover of the booklet. "No."

"Have you read this?"

"I don't care," John says. "She's been through enough because of me."

Tim sits down next to John and speaks softly. "You need to read this. She states very clearly that there was no conspiracy between the two of you regarding museum funds, and that she had no knowledge of a conspiracy between you and her husband. We can put a dent in those charges. A small dent, granted; but it's a start."

"They will unleash holy hell on her if we so much as try to have a conversation. She's an unindicted co-conspirator."

Tim shakes his head in disbelief. John is not getting it. "Hostile witness."

John groans; it is almost a growl. "Leave her alone, Tim."

But Tim's wheels are already turning. "We have to talk about the ramifications, of course; it could just as easily work against you. And not just for the moral judgment issue."

As if that has any bearing in a court of law, John thinks.

"Although, if you promoted her husband because of your relationship with her, or because you were seeking a relationship with her, that would play against you." Tim is thinking out loud, now. John tries to tune him out.

"We need to steal a little thunder on this. I'm not saying we take out a full-page ad in the Sunday Chronicle and admit you're an adulterer — " He is surprised to see John wince at the word " — but we treat it as if it's a foregone conclusion. A big 'so what.'" He stands up and begins pacing, muttering to himself as he walks across the floor.

"When did you promote her husband?" He returns to sit at the table. His nervous energy is wearing on John's nerves.

A sigh of frustration. "I never really promoted him; I just moved him into a specialized group inside Corporate Finance, after Fox Trade." A pause as he stares at the ceiling, mentally groping for the date. "That was back in September or October. I'll have to check."

Tim is nodding as he takes notes. "This is good, John. Good. The timing of the end might look a little suspicious, but we can dig into that some more later." A quick look at his client. "Why did you end it?"

"I didn't. Not formally, anyway." He suddenly looks every second of his fifty-one years. "It was ended for us, when Vantage went down."

"Do you still have feelings for her?" Tim's voice is both incredulous and impatient.

John nods. "I do."

Tim laughs. The sound is unexpected and snaps John out of the reverie he was not aware he had entered. "Wow. It's pretty bad, then." He sits down at the table once more.

John rests his forehead upon his left palm. "I guess. I don't know." He shakes his head.

"John? I need you to focus."

"The last thing I wanted was for her to get caught up in this mess. I had no idea she already was, with Matt. And the foundation." A heavy pause before he can speak the next words. "I'm sure she thinks I was using her, setting her up so I could launder investment proceeds through my museum donations."

Tim frowns in surprise. "I don't think so," he insists. "She makes no mention of that in her deposition. *Read* it," he repeats, tapping the transcript sharply. "I need to know if you agree with her statements. I don't know what she *thinks* about you, but what she *says* about you is pretty clear."

John shakes his head. Typical Amanda; she would never speculate on someone else's actions or motivation. She trades exclusively in the facts that are available to her.

"Beyond all this," Tim has started talking again. John wishes he would stop. *Lawyers*. "Her testimony could set her husband up for perjury. He implicated both of you, under oath at his deposition. Besides," he mutters. "It's not as if she needed the money. Ted Griffin's daughter. You never have done anything half-assed; I'll give you that."

JUNE 2008

TUESDAY, JUNE 5

Grace Kim sits nervously at her desk, scouring the Internet news sites for word of her own fate. Vantage has been less than forthcoming in recent weeks. There had been talks of a merger with another firm, but those had broken off after two weeks of fevered negotiation. Grace had slept on the floor under her desk three nights in a row so she could be ready to help with a press release in the morning. Only a fool would make the perfectly reasonable push for telecommuting under these circumstances. She rises slightly out of her seat and peers over the top of her cubicle, to see if anyone else is prairie-dogging at the moment. No luck. She sinks back into her chair.

What a mess. She had warned Amanda; nobody could fault her in that respect. Seeing her friend — former friend, as they have not spoken since the gala — being hounded by camera crews at her own home was beyond sad. It was reprehensible. Grace had smiled a little to herself when Amanda had not even turned her head, striding confidently past them and through the front door. A lesser woman would have forgotten that it was her house; would have turned to face them as if she owed them something. Not Amanda. But it still bothers Grace, the way Amanda is being presented. As if she were somehow playing her husband and John Wallace against each other and making herself the prize. That wasn't it at all. *What a mess*, she thinks again. She clicks the refresh button on the screen and receives a 404 error. She tries another news site; the same. Apprehension rising in her chest, Grace tabs over to Outlook and refreshes her inbox. The hourglass spins and spins in an infinite circle.

Someone has entered the floor from the elevator lobby. Grace groans; an HR rep. Here it comes. The rep, whose name Grace does not recall, beckons everyone to an open corner of the building. When he is satisfied that everyone is assembled, he stands on a desk and addresses the group.

"My name is Kevin Festa; I work in Human Resources here. Those of you who did not receive a phone call last night regarding your employment with Vantage have thirty minutes to vacate the premises."

A roar explodes among the staff. Kevin lifts his hands for quiet.

"Vantage filed for Chapter 11 bankruptcy protection in federal court this morning," he explains. "I'm very sorry to have to deliver this news, this way."

He steps off the desk and makes his way through the crowd; now stunned into silence by the news. Grace looks around her, at the people, at the walls. Gone. Seventy years of history, just…gone. She sees Dave Galvan standing near the windows; he will not meet her gaze.

WEDNESDAY, JUNE 6

When the first punch line comes, Amanda wonders only what had taken so long. The bankruptcy, most likely; the writers must have been waiting for it to be official. It provides a better hook than the deliberate and heavy grinding of the justice machine. The images of former employees, milling about outside the building, boxes in hand. Embracing, weeping. And suddenly, her name is on late-night television. Part of a monologue on one of the cable networks. The host — she cannot remember his name, only that he seems to be famous for no better reason than she is, now — standing in front of a picture of the Vantage Tower in its first of many "guilty building" shots. Relegated now to b-roll.

Of course times are tough in Houston, with some 3,000 employees of former insurance giant Vantage PLC out of work after the company declared Chapter 11 bankruptcy and had to lay off about seventy percent of its local workforce.

The image shifts to a head-shot of Amanda.

It's all old news for Amanda Parsons, though, who had been getting laid and getting off in the executive suite at Vantage for months. Must be the Columbia education that put her ahead of the curve.

He points at the camera and affects a serious look.

Stay in school, kids.

"Well." Ted leans forward and looks at his daughter. "There it is." He presses the mute button on the television remote.

Amanda nods. "Yes. There it is."

"What do you think?"

She shrugs. "Not bad, I guess. I mean, it would be funny if it were about someone else, right?"

Ted studies her for a moment. "That's my girl. Chin up."

"*Nolite bastardi carborundum.*" She manages a smile. "Besides, it's only fifteen minutes." She stands up to leave. "I'm tired. Think I'll call it a day."

"You're comfortable in the guest house? You feel safe?"

"Of course I do," she insists. "Those letters are just people letting off some steam. I'm fine."

"Okay," Ted replies. "You're a tough monkey, Amanda. I'm proud of you."

"Thanks, Dad." She leans over to kiss his cheek.

As he watches her go, he wonders when she will reach her breaking point and whether even he will be able to pick up the pieces when it finally comes. For the life of him, he cannot imagine how she became so unbendable.

FRIDAY, JUNE 15

Steve's head feels heavy. Too heavy for his neck right now. His mind a muddle of facts and lies; information and misinformation. He is beginning to piece it all together; but something is still missing. He does not know what, only that it exists. Only Steve has the bird's eye view. He sees clearly how Stan and Matt had implicated John after the fact and how Anand had set him up from the start, if for different reasons.

Anand's hands are tied. His residence status has been thrown into the mix and he faces certain deportation if he testifies in John's defense.

Matt and Stan are too far gone, now; each will begin serving his sentence sometime in the next thirty days.

Amanda is in limbo. Now considered an unindicted co-conspirator. Just like Steve, himself. And fodder for late night talk shows on every channel. He sincerely feels for her. She has made one mistake and is paying for it with everything that truly matters: her reputation, her dignity, her name.

Steve's own attorney has met with Tim Cavanaugh and shared the facts they have managed to gather. It is clear to Steve that John had no knowledge of what Matt, Stan and Anand were doing. And so that one missing piece still plagues his mind. It is the answer to the simple question: *Why?*

The company is bankrupt. John Wallace's net worth a mere whisper of what it once had been. As one of two majority shareholders, along with his father, no amount of short-term hedging could ever cover his losses. Those caught in the act — Stan, Matt and Anand — would be punished. The civil court would play its part in John's reckoning, as well. So why the criminal trial?

He shakes his head to clear it and looks at the clock on his monitor. Mike O'Malley from *Bottom Line Magazine* will arrive any minute. Steve's first interview with the publication as CEO and it comes after the company has already failed. Should be an interesting thirty minutes. Perhaps they should just play Gin Rummy instead. His phone buzzes to notify him of Mike's arrival; he tells Denise to send him in.

"May you live in interesting times," Mike says, taking his seat.

"You know that was intended as a curse, originally, don't you?"

Mike shakes his head. "Had no idea. Are you sure?"

"Oh, yes," Steve affirms. "It's followed by two more lines: 'May you come to the attention of those in authority' and 'May you find what you are looking for.'"

Mike looks skeptical. "Not sure I see how that's a curse, except for the middle one."

"Well," Steve says, feeling tired again already. "Who the hell knows?" He shrugs.

Mike laughs out loud. "Well, this is already the most interesting Vantage interview I've ever conducted. What's new?"

Now Steve laughs. "What isn't new? Are we really going to do this; I mean, what's the angle?"

"For starters, how you managed to stay clean in all of this."

"Oh, a human interest piece for *Bottom Line*?" *Right.* He nods at Mike's recorder. "Aren't you going to turn that on?"

"In a minute." Mike shrugs. "I have something that might help John Wallace."

Steve leans back in his chair, eyeing Mike suspiciously. John had never liked the man. Steve himself had found him merely annoying. "Let's hear it, then. Bankrupt companies are busy places, believe it or not."

"Couple of months back I had a sit-down with an analyst named Chris Morton — " at the name Steve bolts upright in his chair " — and a snippy federal prosecutor named Debra Wilcox. That's right," he says, noting Steve's growing attention.

"And?"

"For starters, I didn't like either one of them. I'm not exactly the founding member of the John Wallace fan club, mind you, but these two were up to something."

"Is that it?"

Mike shakes his head. "Nope. It took some digging, but it seems Amanda Parsons isn't the only woman in town with a daddy complex." He slides a piece of paper across the table.

Steve looks at it. *Vantage PLC Announces Acquisition of Southeastern Mutual Life.* "This was ten years ago, at least," he says. John's first big accomplishment as CEO.

"I know; that's why it took me a while. The CEO of Southeastern was a man named Miles Oberg. His daughter's name is Debra."

"Well, shit," Steve says, sitting back in his seat again. "Is that what this is all about? She's out to avenge her father?" It was too ridiculous to believe.

"Yeah, that's what this is all about," Mike agrees. "That and insider trading, conspiracy and fraud."

An angry look from Steve. "John needs to know about this," he insists. "I can't go near him. You'll have to call him yourself."

"Fair enough." Mike leans forward and turns on his recorder. "So tell me about the restructuring at Vantage and how you're going to put your stamp on the company that emerges."

Steve shakes his head. It's all about getting the best story, in the end. Does Mike honestly think this barely relevant information will make him more forthcoming about the company's plans? There is another angle at play, Steve suspects, but he's too damned tired for the game right now.

WEDNESDAY, JUNE 20

"John; this is Mike O'Malley."

John pauses before responding. "Yes?"

"I wonder if you might have a few minutes to talk."

"About what, specifically?" How did O'Malley get his number? He would ask but knows he will not get an honest answer.

Mike sighs. When he speaks, his voice is almost submissive. "For one thing, I don't like the way you're being portrayed in the media."

John actually laughs out loud. "Seriously. What do you want?" Must be a book deal in his future. As much as Vantage had kept Mike dangling before its collapse, he may be at the very top of the list of people who want to see John Wallace pilloried in Market Square.

"I am serious. Right now, all we're reading is what everyone else is saying about you and nothing that you have to say for yourself. I'd like to give you the chance, at least."

"I don't think so, Mike. I appreciate the offer, but — "

" — but you don't trust me."

"Not at all," John agrees.

"What if I said that wasn't it?"

The sentence hangs, as if it has gotten stuck between phones.

"What else, then?" John speaks at last.

"It's about Debra Wilcox. Something personal; I don't want to talk about it on the phone."

There is a quality to Mike's voice that John cannot identify yet. It creeps in at the end of his sentences.

John's eyes move to his desk calendar. "Monday at one-thirty. I'm meeting with my attorney already; you can come, too."

"All right. Is it okay to call you at this number if anything changes?"

"It is not okay, but I don't see how that would stop you."

The call ends, and John does not move for a few minutes. He cannot remember what he had been doing before his phone had buzzed. The thought of damaging information about Debra Wilcox has taken hold of his mind and will not let go. The past two days have brought news that will play favorably for John: members of congress have been implicated in the subprime collapse now; and high-profile fund managers have been arrested for misrepresenting the value of their mortgage-backed funds. Certain elements of the government's case may start to unwind, as the extent of the duplicity on the part of lenders and fund managers is revealed. Dirt on Debra Wilcox can't do much for him, personally; but it may divert some attention away from Amanda. She has been vilified on an almost nightly basis for the past two weeks. The latest joke was that each of the seven arrested fund managers had used his one phone call to contact Amanda and tell her he would be late for their rendezvous.

MONDAY, JUNE 24

"How's the defense coming along?"

John glares at Mike across the table.

Tim clears his throat. "Did you really need a face-to-face to ask questions you know we're not going to answer?" He had been opposed to this meeting from the second John broached the subject with him last week.

Mike shakes his head. "No, no. I was just making conversation. A skill I've recently decided I am sorely lacking."

"Can't imagine why," John mutters. "What do you want, Mike?"

"Here's the thing." Mike leans forward in his seat. "I know you don't have many witnesses; everybody knows that. And I don't think it's right."

"You have a solution in mind?" John's voice is hostile.

"And this is all on background," Tim interjects, before Mike can answer.

"Yeah, background." Mike agrees hastily; it's a formality as far as he is concerned. "I'm not saying it's a solution, but what if you had a little bit of unbiased coverage? It couldn't hurt, could it? Maybe some people are teetering on the fence and we could help push them onto your side."

John looks at him in disbelief. He's still angling for a story. He sits back in his chair, arms folded, and glares at the reporter. He has never liked him.

Tim is shaking his head. "We've seen how the 'positive' angle plays out in the past," he asserts. "John comes off looking defensive — which is apparently a criminal act in this country now — and people grow even more cynical about his character."

"There has to be someone," Mike says casually.

John looks at him, noting that peculiar quality to his voice again. He is holding something back; that much is certain. But John does not know whether it is something that will help him or hurt him. And it is too big a risk, with no clear mitigation strategy.

"What do you know?" John's voice is quiet and probing.

"It's not enough for a story," Mike begins, his voice halting. "Not yet. But I think I know why she has such a hard-on for you."

"Go on," Tim directs.

"Her dad is Miles Oberg."

John shakes his head. "Who cares?" Everyone is motivated by something from his or her past. This is not what he had been expecting; it won't help Amanda at all. Disappointment is clear in his eyes.

Mike is surprised by the response. He had thought he was coming to a meeting with a desperate man. He looks to Tim for help.

"I don't know, John," Tim mutters. "It could be a start. I'll make a filing, anyway. May be enough to have her removed from the case and get an extension."

John ponders this. At the rate things are falling apart nationally, an extension might not be so bad. "Okay," he says, shrugging.

"And you," Tim says turning to Mike, now. "What do *you* want?"

"I want to see justice done," Mike asserts. It falls flat; he had suspected it would.

"He wants my story," John explains softly, shaking his head again. The balls on this guy.

Tim laughs contemptuously. "Is that it?"

Mike possesses at least enough grace to appear embarrassed. "Worth a shot," he offers.

"You keep digging on Debra Wilcox, and we'll talk," John tells him, leaning forward in his seat and showing some interest at last.

Mike nods. "I can do that. I'm pretty sure there's more, and I think I already know what it is. But I want to be certain."

JULY 2008

WEDNESDAY, JULY 11

Houston – Former Vantage PLC Chief Technology Officer Stan Firestone was sentenced in federal court today to seven years in prison for his role in an embezzlement case that set in motion a chain of events that has all but crippled the former insurance giant. Risk executive Matt Parsons was sentenced to four years for his role in the same scheme. Judge Walter Cline indicated that Parsons received a lighter sentence due to the fact that he never actually profited from the illegal activity; although that was merely because the fraud was detected before Parsons had the chance to realize any gains. It is widely held that each defendant reduced his sentence through cooperation with the Justice Department's criminal case against former CEO John Wallace, although the prosecution has been reluctant to discuss sentencing details until all the trials have concluded....

Amanda drags the mouse pointer to the X at the top of the window and clicks it to close the browser. She rubs her hands briskly across her thighs, trying to stir her blood against the numbness that has settled in her hands as she perused the Internet for news of the two men's fates. She has found three different versions, all reporting essentially the same news, including one which asserted that Matt has agreed to undergo substance abuse counseling in prison to further reduce his sentence. The only substance she has ever seen him abuse is cash. And her patience. This, and Matt's label as an "executive," elicits an ironic laugh. No wonder they were building a million-dollar home; it all makes sense now. Even her mental voice sounds bitter, she realizes.

Overall, it is a good news day, she reasons. Matt has been sentenced; and her status as an unindicted co-conspirator has been lifted. Her father's doing, she is certain. Equally certain is the fact that it will never be discussed between them. Ted has a heavy hand with an incredibly long reach. The less she knows about how it transpired the better. And last week Ron had shared the details of Anand's deposition with her; he received no direct instruction from John

Wallace to funnel money through the museum to short sell Vantage stock. It was all about funding the acquisitions that her husband was initiating. And of course, the driving force behind those acquisitions was John Wallace. It does not matter that his intentions were simply to grow his company. In the end, Anand's testimony will not help John in a criminal trial, but it gives her some degree of peace.

Her phone buzzes; a new voice mail. She never answers it anymore, although it is a new number and the calls have tapered off. She plays the message, pen in hand. It is her attorney's paralegal, informing her that CNN has called yet again for an interview, this time with Larry King. Amanda replaces the pen on the small writing table and erases the message. Ron's office has already declined on her behalf; the call was a mere courtesy. The clock is still ticking on her fifteen minutes, apparently.

She glances at the manila envelope next to her laptop. The final divorce decree. *Busy week*, she thinks. Best of all, though, she is ending her self-imposed exile and returning home this evening. She rises from the desk in her father's guest house bedroom and walks to the window, gazing at the pool. Lisa and Emily, her father's ten-year-old daughter, are splashing together in the shallow end. She smiles absently at them and begins to peel off her sweaty running gear. She had returned from the speed drills two hours ago but had been sucked in by the day's news. Dropping her clothes into the hamper outside the small bathroom, she starts the shower and studies herself in the mirror as the water heats. She can see her ribs, and her bellybutton is stretched sideways on her always lean, now practically emaciated frame. She closes her eyes and steps into the shower; fortunately the bathroom has its own small water heater and never takes long to warm.

MONDAY, JULY 16

Steve is leaning back in his chair, his body a plank making contact only at the edge of the seat and the top of the headrest. Hands behind his neck. Head toward the ceiling but eyes closed. Anand has vanished. Released on bail pending sentencing and then…gone. Steve cannot even find it within himself to be angry, although it was he who had posted the bail. One-hundred-thousand dollars, also gone, now.

Anand's attorney had called him with the news. The family is in shock, scrambling to make arrangements for themselves. Steve is confident that Anand would not completely abandon them; it was not in him to do such a thing. But for the moment, he is invisible. Back in India somehow? It didn't matter, in the end. Everything is a risk; every benefit comes with an associated cost. Steve will do what he can for Anand's family; he knows Marie will support him on this. But it will be difficult the next time someone needs help. And Steve fears that time is coming faster than anyone appreciates.

THURSDAY, JULY 19

The door bell rings, drawing Amanda from the mess in the study. She looks once more at the pile of papers she has been sorting and goes to see who could possibly be visiting her. Her heart lodges in her throat when she sees the lanky figure through the window. Always fit, he now looks gaunt; the last five months have taken a brutal toll. She opens the door cautiously; she has not seen him in person since the night he left her in Baltimore.

"Hey," he says. "I'm sorry I didn't call. I was afraid you wouldn't answer or you'd tell me not to come."

She looks at him thoughtfully before shaking her head. "I would never do that. Come in."

The signs of relief are visible as he crosses the threshold into her foyer.

"Would you like some coffee?"

"Only if you have it made already."

She grimaces. "Why do people always say that? Either you want some coffee or you don't. It's not as if you're asking me to turn lead into gold." She corrects her course and heads to the kitchen, John in tow.

"Ah, Amanda," he says. "I've missed you terribly."

She does not respond and John instantly regrets his words. Amanda fills the kettle and measures out the grounds.

"A French press; how utterly expected." The awkwardness between them is nearly suffocating. John is desperate for something to say that will erase the last few months.

"It makes the best coffee."

"Yes, it does." He tries a smile. "Have you been okay?"

She shrugs. "I guess so, considering."

"Yeah, considering."

"And you? You filed for an extension."

He nods. "And a new prosecutor. We'll see." He is not optimistic.

"I suppose we will." The water has almost come to a boil and she pours it into the press, stirring the grounds with a chopstick before placing the filter assembly on top.

"The news has been interesting, this past month."

"Yeah, Vantage is hardly alone anymore." He sighs. "But there's still plenty for the prosecution to do."

Amanda shakes her head at this. "Our tax dollars at work."

He takes a close look at her. She has lost weight, just as he has. Her jeans hang from her hips in spite of the belt, cinched roughly to its tightest setting. The heather gray t-shirt making a haze of her eyes and accentuating the darkness beneath them. He feels actual, physical pain as he regards her, standing as erect and proud and confident as she had been when he kissed her that final time before walking out the hotel room door. John forces himself to look away briefly or he will take hold of her right here, and this is not the moment. He wonders if it ever will be again.

"Are you hungry?" Her voice disrupts his thoughts.

"Not lately." A grin. "You?"

She shakes her head again, pushing the plunger into the pot now. She pulls two mugs from the cabinet and pours; no cream or sugar for either one.

"So," she ventures, after a sip. "Tell me more."

"I don't want to bore you," he says. "I just wanted to see you; to tell you that I'm so sorry for what happened."

"So am I." Eyes on the counter top.

"I feel bad that we didn't get any real…closure."

She lifts her head now. "Is that what you want?"

John searches her face for some clue of what is in her mind and then almost laughs at himself for the wasted effort. "No," he admits. "But I think it's probably all I deserve."

Amanda looks away again, through the window at her roses. Polly had done a good job while she was away. Her thoughts are spinning. She wants to tell him that everything is okay; that she had never truly doubted him. She wants to pour the coffee down the drain and lead him upstairs to prove her point. But she cradles the warm mug in front of her face and studies the roses through the steam.

He shuffles on his feet next to her, as if preparing to leave. Sets the coffee mug on the counter and takes a shaky breath. She turns to face him and is startled by the sadness in his eyes.

"I'm sorry," he says again. "I shouldn't have come. This is the last thing you need right now. You need to get your life back in order…."

"No." She speaks into the vapor trail of his voice. Offers a weak smile. "Stay. I know it was difficult for you to do this; to come to my house. Don't go yet."

He studies her for a moment; her trance seems to have restored some of her usual command. "Okay," he agrees.

"Good. Come sit with me," she invites. "Let's just talk for a little while, okay?"

He follows her into the family room, where each one claims a club chair in front of the windows to the porch.

"So tell me how things are going. I won't be bored, I promise."

But John shakes his head again. "You first. What's going on with the museum?"

"The Commerce Museum is history," she announces, enjoying her pun. "And in very messy fashion, actually."

He leans forward. He has paid no attention at all to the museum since his indictment; patently ignoring Harry Lexington's many phone calls to complain about Margaret's mishandling of the situation.

Amanda continues, "At first, the government tried to seize everything, claiming it was all ill-gotten gains." She shrugs. "Once they dug a little deeper and understood the timing of Anand's activities, they backed off. But it has no funding." And then, an afterthought: "I'm not the curator anymore. Harry keeps me in the loop."

"I guess I knew that," he concedes, mentally chiding Harry for using the museum to pester Amanda. "Sorry."

"No more apologies, okay? Things could have been much worse for me."

"How?"

"Well — and I know this will seem crazy — but if you and I hadn't…" she hesitates and then decides to skip over it altogether. "I would probably be in prison now, on some charge the prosecution had dreamed up in order to put pressure on Matt to implicate you."

John frowns. She's right; that is crazy. But most likely also true.

"So I can suffer through some tabloid nonsense for a little while." She sits up straight. "I really am okay, you know."

"Yeah?"

She nods. "I was upset for a little while, but I knew…." She draws a breath and looks him in the eye. "I knew you hadn't done that to me."

"I'm glad."

Another awkward silence. It will take more than one conversation and one pot of coffee for them to sort through the damage that had been done. If they even agree to try.

"So, what else?" John tries to make his voice brisk and almost succeeds.

"Well," she smirks, "*Playboy* called."

He smiles and rolls his eyes. "Duh," he says. "When's the big shoot?"

But Amanda shakes her head, smiling self-consciously. "I politely declined their offer."

"I'm glad for that, too," he says softly, holding her eyes for a minute until she breaks their gaze.

"Now your turn," she insists, sitting back in her chair and listening as he shares the details of his life since they had parted. When he leaves an hour later, some of the discomfort has eased, but they avoid touching each other — not even a handshake to say goodbye. He promises to call next time before he comes, and she tells him there is no need; and this is enough for the moment.

MONDAY, JULY 23

The request for recusal and an extension is, of course, denied. John receives the news as he has received all the news about his life over the last several months. With muted anger and reluctant acceptance. Tim storms around the conference room for a while, blasting whoever had drawn the short straw and placed the call to inform them. John steals a glance at his watch. He is due to pick up Greg soon for a trip to the science museum, and he and Tim have some items to cover before he can leave. He leans to the side, into Tim's line of sight and makes a winding motion with his hand. *Wrap it up.*

"Morons," Tim exclaims, tossing his cell phone on the table, where it skips like a stone before settling to a halt. He stares at the wall for a few seconds. "Fine," he snaps. "Documented for appeal." He turns sharply to his paralegal Sara Jacobs, who has observed the tirade from a safe distance in the opposite corner of the room. She nods.

Tim spins back to look at John, now. "Amanda Parsons," he begins.

"Don't go there, Tim. Not going to happen."

"It's exculpatory."

"Use her deposition. That's plenty."

"Not compelling. I want people to see her in person; to see that she harbors no ill will toward you, after everything that happened."

John's shoulders sag. Tim means, after everything John had done to her. "Honestly, Tim, I don't even know if that's true."

"What do you mean? You saw her last week, didn't you? It went fine." He holds out his hands in a gesture of confusion. "All is forgiven."

"Leave it, Tim."

Tim takes a seat and a different approach. "All she has to do is repeat what's in her deposition. Nothing more. She's said it once already. Nothing will happen to her." He shakes his head. After all these years, John Wallace decides to be chivalrous. His timing could not be worse.

"What the fuck is the matter with you?" John whispers.

"What the fuck," Tim speaks slowly, "is the matter with *you*? Do you *want* to go to prison? Are we doing the martyr thing now?"

Sara clears her throat from the corner. "Boys, same team. Okay?"

"Let me see her a few more times first," John proposes. "If she is willing to do it, she'll offer. But I'm not going to ask."

Tim recognizes this for the stall tactic that it is, but he nods. "I'm sure you know her better than I."

John glares at him, hearing two meanings where Tim had intended only one.

Tim raises his hands in defense. "Not what I meant, okay? Just take it easy." He opens his notebook for the first time since their meeting had convened. "Shall we move on to current events and their impact on our case?"

"Please," John mutters through clenched teeth, the muscles in his jaw working furiously.

"It's going to come down to the timeline of events. It's becoming evident that a whole lot of companies, even bigger than Vantage, had invested in these mortgage derivatives. If you guys hadn't collapsed in March, you'd be heading for trouble now anyway. We need to plot it all out, one step at a time, and separate the legal investment activities from whatever Firestone and Parsons were up to."

John nods his agreement. With the way events had unfolded, it will be difficult for a jury to categorize each piece accurately. As far as they are concerned, everything Vantage did was illegal because of Matt and Stan. It's the old "one bad apple" problem. Add to this the fact that Matt and Stan claim to have had an agreement with John that forced them to play in the risky derivatives market for his benefit and the picture gets murkier, still. Finally, Stan Firestone's incentive package, with its related-party agreement, is easy to misconstrue as nefarious. The terminology is complicated; Tim will be speaking over the heads of almost everyone in the courtroom unless he can find a way to dial it back — without oversimplifying and offending the few members who might grasp the concepts. And although the burden of proof legally rests with the prosecution, they have a clear advantage because legal business activities should never be difficult to explain. It was the Smith Street model of prosecution: throw whatever you can at the jury, and when they don't understand, turn up your hands and say, "Exactly."

As Tim elaborates on his timeline plan, John listens quietly, nodding when appropriate. Now that Tim is focused on something concrete, John can tolerate him. This need to inject drama into John's side of the story by putting Amanda on the stand is ill-conceived; it comes up only when Tim feels cornered, as he had after the disappointing phone call about the extension. And it is exactly why John must ensure he never finds out where John was on February 16 — and who was with him.

TUESDAY, JULY 31

Amanda sits patiently in the chair at the small conference table with Sara Jacobs. She has been called in to review the finer points of her deposition, to help John's defense team identify some minor detail that might help his case.

"Thanks, again, for coming," Sara says, as she opens a manila folder and pushes it to the side so that each of them can see its contents.

"I'm happy to help," Amanda insists. "I wish we could have had an earlier start."

Sara nods. "We still have all of next month, though. Plenty of time," she replies.

Amanda moves her eyes to the page and studies her words. Could it really have been only two months ago?

"We just want to be sure that you're still okay with everything included in here, so we can use the deposition. Mr. Wallace has expressed some reluctance at having you on the stand."

"I appreciate his hesitation," Amanda agrees coolly.

The phone in front of Sara buzzes. She frowns and picks it up to see the screen.

"I'm sorry," she says. "I need to take this. Can I just leave you for a minute to review this on your own?"

"Of course." Amanda waves her away and continues reading.

Nothing stands out as inaccurate or capricious, and she finishes quickly. Her eyes slide to the other folders that Sara had left on the table. She leans forward slightly to peer through the sidelight of the conference room door. Nobody. Amanda gingerly lifts the cover of the folder on top of the stack; John's initials catch her eye. Then Matt's name. The rest of the page comes into focus and a scowl begins to draw itself across her forehead, deepening into her eyes and mouth.

When Sara returns a few minutes later, the deposition folder is closed and pushed aside. The written guarantee between Stan Firestone, Matt Parsons and John Wallace is the only piece of paper on the table.

"Let's talk about this," Amanda says smoothly.

Sara suppresses a smile; it had worked.

SEPTEMBER 2008

MONDAY, SEPTEMBER 8

John is stoic as the first prosecution witness is called. Stan Firestone sits, edgy, in the witness chair as he is sworn in for testimony. John regards him with steady eyes.

"Mr. Firestone," Debra Wilcox begins; her voice cold. "Please describe the nature of your relationship with John Allen Wallace, III."

"I reported to Mr. Wallace as CTO at Vantage PLC from the fall of 1995 until March of this year."

"You were employed by Mr. Wallace for thirteen years?"

"Thirteen years as CTO; prior to that I was senior vice president of Infrastructure for five years."

"That's quite a tenure, by modern standards."

"I suppose it is."

"Your honor?" Tim speaks up from his seat next to John.

"Let's move along, Ms. Wilcox."

"Certainly, your honor." She nods briefly at the judge. "I mention Mr. Firestone's length of service because I believe there is relevance in how that loyalty was both rewarded and abused."

"Then I suggest you proceed with your questioning." Judge Harris has a reputation for a short temper, and John is happy to see the prosecution tripping over it first. "And limit your questions to the matter in this court."

"Yes, your honor. Mr. Firestone, can you explain a financial arrangement known as 'Prometheus'?"

Stan nods. "Prometheus was the code name for a financial arrangement that invested Vantage funds in several technology stocks. When gains were realized on those stocks, the profits were set aside in a separate entity that had been created for the purpose of maintaining the funds."

"And was this entity part of Vantage PLC?"

Stan looks down briefly. "No, it was not."

"Was it owned by Vantage shareholders, then?"

"No. I managed the entity, initially."

"And so the profits that were gained were in your control?"

"Yes, that's correct."

"And did you use those monies toward activities that were related to Vantage?"

"No, I did not."

"Then what was the purpose and use of those funds?"

Stan clears his throat and pauses before answering. "The purpose was my personal enrichment at the expense of the company's profit."

"You embezzled money from the company that had employed you for nearly twenty years."

"That is correct."

"And was anyone else at Vantage involved in this pursuit?"

"Yes, a risk analyst named Matt Parsons joined me earlier this year."

"Anyone else?"

"John Wallace."

Although he knew it was coming, John cannot prevent his jaw from clenching, his hands from gripping the edge of the table in front of him. To witness a former employee — a former friend and ally — commit perjury simply to reduce his own prison sentence; the betrayal is almost unbearable. Their sons have played together since they were babies, for Christ's sake.

"The CEO of Vantage PLC was also involved?"

"He was; he directed me to create the Prometheus arrangement and guaranteed my return."

"And did Mr. Wallace receive monetary compensation as well?"

Stan nods. "He did; my understanding was that he routed it through his family foundation. To keep his hands clean."

John moves his eyes to look at the faces in the jury box. His twenty years of work in the community, gone in a matter of seconds because of one man's choice. His character utterly destroyed. He stops listening and looks down at the legal pad in front of him, picks up a pen as if he is taking notes about Stan's testimony. But he writes only one word, several times. *Liar.*

Next comes Matt Parsons, who looks as if he may be physically ill at any second. Even Debra Wilcox keeps her distance from the witness box, perhaps to avoid being caught in the stream.

"Mr. Parsons, how long were you employed at Vantage PLC?"

"Ten months," Matt answers; his voice shaky. His youthful appearance will allow the jury to pass it off as simple nerves — as well as maybe a bit of remorse. Any young man as pretty as Matt should be afraid to go to prison, after all.

"And during that time, did you receive a promotion?"

"I did. I was promoted to senior risk analyst after five months."

"Is that a normal period of time for such a promotion, based on your experience at Vantage?"

Matt shakes his head. "No, it was accelerated."

"And was this because you had earned this promotion, as some sort of reward?"

"Partially, it was," Matt says, hesitantly. "I had steered the company's acquisition of Fox Trade, and that had gotten me noticed. But there was another understanding as part of my move."

"And what was that understanding?"

"That I would monitor the Prometheus transactions and try to extract a higher return."

"And were you compensated for this activity?"

"Actually, no." Matt's voice is flat. "At the time of my termination, I had not yet realized any gains."

John adds a word to his pad. *Idiot.*

The day is rounded out with the former CEO of Fox Trade, now bankrupt after the failed acquisition, who claims under oath that he had been led to believe he had agreed to a merger of equals, versus an acquisition, and that John Wallace had betrayed him by overstating the company's liquidity and cash reserves. Then the board member who claims to have been strong armed into purchasing his K&R policy through Vantage, at a much higher cost than he would have paid elsewhere. Finally, the former employees and shareholders, who claim that their plans for retirement had been destroyed by the greed of John Wallace. That he had somehow coerced them into investing every cent of their 401(k) contribution into his company's stock so that he would receive performance bonuses when the share price rose. That he had lied about the company's stability over and over, all to line his own pockets with their hard-earned money. They all seemed to have forgotten the significant value his leadership had created for them as the stock price climbed before its sharp and ultimate decline.

John sits through the first day of testimony with no expression on his face. Watching the trial as if it is happening to someone else, someplace else. Not the change of venue his team had requested and been denied, but another world altogether. A world in which a man is no longer presumed innocent until proven guilty but is in fact presumed guilty for proclaiming his innocence.

Amanda endures it, too, watching from the back row of the court. She had arrived five-thirty in the morning to secure a seat in the main court and not the overflow room. Sitting just as still and silent as John, as if their thoughts are connected across the expanse of the hall.

# # #

"I wish you wouldn't come until it's necessary," he tells Amanda that evening as they sit on her back porch.

"You try to shield me too much. I don't like it." A subtle reference to his failed attempt to keep her off the witness stand.

He sighs. She is right; there is no reason for him to protect her. She is capable of taking care of herself, as she has proven to him several times over.

"Are you staying here tomorrow?" He moves on to another topic; it is futile to argue with her.

Amanda shakes her head. "I've booked a room at the Hyatt. I don't want any distractions before my big day."

John wishes she would stay with him at the loft, but he knows it isn't possible or even wise. It's not a question of desire — he has conceded to himself that the time for that is gone and may never come again. What he wants is the calm confidence she radiates, even in the face of verbal dismemberment at the hands of the prosecutor. He wonders, almost absently, what had happened in her youth to create this in her. He draws a long and shaky breath.

She turns to look at him. "What is it?"

"Tomorrow is going to be rough on you; worse than you're expecting, I think."

She nods. "I can't even imagine. I watched some reruns of *Law & Order* yesterday to prepare myself."

He laughs; there it is, to prove his point. "And I don't know what's going to happen after that. I'm probably still going to prison. And that makes what you've agreed to do even more of a burden."

Amanda shakes her head. "It's not a burden to do the right thing."

"Only you would see it that way." He smiles at her. "But whatever does happen, I want to be sure you know how much I appreciate this, and how much I care for you."

She nods. "I know."

Other than Amanda, they have located a low-level accountant to take the stand on John's behalf, as well as an auditor from Lawson-Kent. Along with Melissa and a few character witnesses who will speak to John's work with charitable organizations and educational projects, this represents the entirety of his defense. Unless Mike O'Malley comes through. Tim has not been able to contact him again since their meeting last month. Probably shopping his book, testing the market before he begins writing. Or waiting to see how it should end.

"I need to tell you some things before you take the stand. Some things about me; my past. The stories you've heard."

"Okay."

"Okay, then. I started working at Vantage when my dad was the CEO," he begins. "I was still married to my first wife. My oldest son was a toddler. And I behaved very badly. I was cocky, the CEO's son. I played that part to a tee."

Amanda laughs lightly at this. "Who wouldn't?"

But John doesn't laugh. "I hurt my wife terribly. Some of what you've heard about me is true. It's sort of institutional knowledge; it never fades away. This is where Margaret enters the picture," he says, and then stops.

"You met her at Vantage?"

"She was an admin." A sigh. "And I made a huge mistake."

"She got pregnant."

He nods. "So, there I was, separated from my first wife and queuing up my second at the same time."

"And there were others?"

"Well, yeah." He actually looks embarrassed. "Did I mention I was really cocky?"

"Good word choice."

He grimaces. "So, I finalized the divorce with Kelly, married Margaret and cleaned up my act in a big hurry."

"But you had the reputation already."

"I did. And it never went away. Then, my dad got sick and the transition from him to me happened sooner than we had anticipated." A shrug. "Nobody was ready; nobody thought I was ready."

Amanda remembers the news. John Allen Wallace II, stricken with multiple sclerosis at the age of 55. He had held on at Vantage for a couple of years and then it became too much. She was a young teenager at the time; it had been dinner table conversation for her family. Her father had been affected very deeply by it, for reasons she had not understood then. And then, when he had divorced her mother within mere months of the announcement, it had begun to make sense. *Life is too short.*

She eyes him skeptically. "And you never once strayed again?" She doubts Ted has remained faithful to Lisa; she believes it simply isn't part of his fabric. And she worries, now, that it may not be part of hers, either. She pushes away that thought; it has no bearing on them at this moment. She is not certain it ever will again.

"I never had time," he says, his voice bordering on angry. "People think I sit at a desk and just watch the company run." Shakes his head in disbelief. "You have no idea how much that pisses me off; what people perceive as my lack of involvement in the day-to-day."

She smiles; of course she knows. That's why she — and nobody else — is sitting with him at this moment. She had learned from her mother's mistakes; the assumptions she had made and what it had cost her in the end. There is no magic wand for leadership, no matter how big the desk is or how many windows frame it.

"Besides, I don't have a lot of patience for nonsense or drama." He says this almost comically; he is surrounded by an endless stream of both, now. "And my HR team; they used to stir the pot, anytime they thought I needed a reminder. If I paid too much attention to a female employee, I would hear about it. They'd come to me with some trumped-up story about the threat of a lawsuit. Total bullshit."

"So you really stuck your neck out with me."

"Yeah, I guess I did."

They are quiet for a minute, as each reflects, and then she says, "I hope you don't regret it."

"Never even crossed my mind," he says. Quiet again; awkward this time.

At last John continues. "Anyway, I thought you deserved to know some history before you sit in the box. Some history beyond the rumors, that is."

"Okay. Thanks."

"And something else," he adds after a few quiet minutes. "I know I'm not blameless in this."

Amanda regards him steadily. Nor is she, after all.

"I failed my company; I failed my family." His voice is strained. "I made a lot of mistakes. My intentions were good, but the path I took wasn't thoughtful. I was bored; I should have moved on and handed it over to Steve a few years ago. I let us take on too much risk."

They do not speak for a moment, and then John asks, "Will you tell me something now?"

"Of course."

"Why did you marry him?" His voice is filled with skepticism. "He has no spine."

Amanda laughs softly. "I brought home someone with a spine once." A direct look. "*Once.*"

"Oh," he says. "A little too much competition for the old man?"

"Exactly," she says quietly. And then she adds, "One hell of a way to learn a lesson."

John smiles sadly at this. "Yeah."

TUESDAY, SEPTEMBER 9

"Please state your name for the record."

"Melissa Kemper."

"And your relationship to the defendant, John Allen Wallace III."

"I was his executive assistant at Vanguard PLC."

"For how long?"

"Ten years."

"And was that the extent of your relationship?"

"I would consider him a friend, as well as my boss. But that was it. We don't socialize regularly."

"And there was no romantic involvement?"

Melissa shakes her head at this. "None at all."

"In your employment with Mr. Wallace, did you ever have dealings with Amanda Parsons?"

"I did."

"Please describe the nature of those dealings."

"I provided occasional support to Ms. Parsons in her role as curator of the Commerce Museum."

"Did you find that unusual?"

"No, given that Mrs. Wallace is also involved in the museum and I frequently assist the foundation in a similar manner."

"And were you compensated for this support?"

"No. I consider my time a donation to both the foundation and the museum."

"What sort of specific assistance did you provide Ms. Parsons?"

"Travel and transportation logistics, mostly."

"And did you arrange travel for Ms. Parsons on March 24 of this year?"

"I did. I arranged a trip to Baltimore for her."

"Please share the details of that trip."

"I arranged a flight for Ms. Parsons on the Vantage corporate jet, as well as accommodations in Baltimore."

"And did Ms. Parsons fly alone on the corporate jet?"

"No. She accompanied Mr. Wallace."

"And regarding the accommodations in Baltimore; did you book separate rooms for Ms. Parsons and Mr. Wallace?"

"No; they shared a room at the Marriott Waterfront."

"Thank you." Tim looks at the judge. "I have no more questions for this witness, Your Honor."

Judge Harris glances at Debra, who waves and says, "No questions at this time, Your Honor."

"The defense calls Amanda Griffin," Tim announces.

Amanda can hear the heads tilting, feel the intake of curious breaths in the jury box and the gallery. She takes the stand and sits erect as she is sworn in by the bailiff. It had been part of the divorce settlement that she resume the name Griffin; her provision. The feeling of exposure it has created is nearly unbearable, but she could not spend the rest of her life as Matt Parson's former mate.

"Ms. Griffin, would you please describe the nature of your relationship with John Allen Wallace III?"

"Mr. Wallace and I were romantically involved during February and March of this year."

"And at the time of this involvement, both you and Mr. Wallace were married to other persons; is that correct?"

"Yes."

"And what is the status of your marriage at this time, Ms. Griffin."

"I am recently divorced."

"And was that a result of your affair with Mr. Wallace?"

"In part, yes it was."

"Thank you. I'm sure this is not a pleasant experience."

Amanda nods one time. Her eyes are fixed on Tim's face.

"I am going to show you a document that the prosecution has entered as evidence in this case, and I would like you to tell me if you find anything out of order."

He places the authorization form with John's signature and the date February 16, 2008 on the railing in front of her. Amanda studies the document for a moment, although she has already seen it.

"Yes, I do."

"And what is that?"

"The date on the document; Mr. Wallace and I were together that day, as well as the evening before and the morning after."

"And what about the two other signees?"

"One is my ex-husband," she says. "And he was out of town that weekend, on a business trip to New York. According to him, the third signee — Mr. Firestone — was on that trip, as well."

"So it's unlikely that all three men were in the same place to sign this document on the same day."

"Objection, Your Honor. Calls for conclusion based on facts not in evidence." Debra does not rise from her seat; her tone is bored.

"Sustained. The witness will not answer."

"The question is withdrawn," Tim concedes. But he has made his point. "I have no further questions at this time."

"Your witness, Ms. Wilcox."

Debra rises and approaches the bench.

"Ms. Griffin — " Debra flashes a caustic smile before continuing, " — were you deposed as a potential witness in your husband's embezzlement trial?"

"Ex-husband. Yes."

"Forgive me. Ex-husband. And was that as a prosecution or a defense witness?"

"Prosecution."

"Did you serve as a witness for the prosecution in his trial?"

"I did not."

"Thank you. No further questions."

"Re-direct, Your Honor," Tim says as he stands and returns to the witness box. "Why didn't you testify for the prosecution in your ex-husband's trial, Ms. Griffin?"

"I was told the government didn't need my testimony; that it did not help their case."

"Did it hurt their case?"

"No," she confirms. "They said it was neutral."

In spite of where he is sitting, John cannot suppress a slight smile at the word.

Debra declines the re-cross and Amanda is dismissed. She does not look at John as she walks back to her seat in the second row behind the defense table. But she can read the anxiety in his posture as she looks at the back of his head. Her testimony today was simply setting the table. It is up to John to state his own case; and Mike O'Malley to make good on his promise.

THURSDAY, SEPTEMBER 11

I remind you, Mr. Wallace, that you are still under oath."

"Yes, Your Honor."

John is seated once again in the witness box. The previous day, he had answered Tim's questions in his own defense. Today, it is the prosecution's turn to have a go at him. He has taken his oath to tell the truth, hand on the Bible, so help him God; suppressing the debate that rages in his mind about separation of church and state. He imagines only an act of God could save him now, anyway.

Debra rises and requests permission to approach the witness before advancing to the box.

"Mr. Wallace, are you familiar with what is called a 'related-party transaction' between Stan Firestone and Vantage PLC?"

Good; she's not wasting any time. John's boredom with the proceedings has grown intolerable, except for Amanda's brief time on the stand.

"I am."

"And what was the name of this transaction?"

John shakes his head slightly. "It had no name, as far as Vantage was concerned. Mr. Firestone came up with Prometheus as a code name. He used similar names for a lot of the technology initiatives at the firm. It was sort of his trademark."

"Why did he choose Prometheus?"

"Actually, I believe it was a joke on Mr. Firestone's part. The arrangement itself was simply a part of his employment contract with Vantage. The incentive structure. When we were negotiating the terms, I told him he was playing with fire. But it was all standard negotiation posturing. I wanted him to think he was getting something out of me. He wanted me to think he was unhappy with what we'd offered. It was a play on his last name. He said his wife picked Prometheus. I never knew it had a name until we had the earnings problem in March."

"So your assertion is that these related-party transactions are common, then?"

"Yes. Companies use them to create bonuses that are attractive to senior-level management. There is nothing unusual about them."

"But Prometheus was unusual, wasn't it, Mr. Wallace?"

"In terms of what Mr. Firestone had arranged on the side, yes, it was unusual."

"But you knew nothing about that, is this correct?"

John nods. "Yes, that's correct. I was unaware that Mr. Firestone was stealing from my company."

"But shouldn't you have been aware, Mr. Wallace? Isn't that part of your job? Ensuring that your company is running in an ethical fashion?"

"It's everyone's job." Leans forward in his seat. "Including Stan Firestone."

Debra smiles patronizingly at this. "Let's move on for a moment." She walks back to her table and retrieves a sheet of paper. *The* sheet of paper. She places it on the railing in front of John, just as she had the day before with Amanda.

"Are you familiar with this document, Mr. Wallace?"

John shakes his head. "The first time I saw this was the day you showed it to me and my counsel, in June of this year."

"I remind you that you are under oath, Mr. Wallace. Would you like to reconsider your answer?"

"No." His voice is sharp, decisive. Several members of the jury flinch at the force of his tone. Tim frowns slightly; they will think he's arrogant.

"According to Mr. Firestone, you not only saw this document prior to June of this year, but you initiated it as a means to prevent him from reporting your firm's fraudulent investment schemes to the SEC."

John is shaking his head. "That's not true." His tone milder, now.

"Your exclusive finance team — I believe you affectionately called it the lab; I guess you like code names, too. The lab warned you that the derivatives market was highly volatile, yet you directed them to invest large sums of your financial clients' money in that market. When Mr. Firestone learned that his incentive package was tied to this, he confronted you. You offered him a guarantee that Vantage would make him whole if he lost money on Prometheus."

"No. That never happened."

"Furthermore, he threatened to expose your affair with Amanda Parsons, and you knew your wife would ruin you financially if she found out. You moved the former Ms. Parson's husband into the lab to extract his involvement and keep him quiet while you pursued his wife and your own greedy self-interest."

John draws a slow breath to calm himself. "Matt Parsons was moved into the lab because we wanted a sharp M&A representative co-located with our corporate finance team. The intent was to accelerate our acquisition activity — for the benefit of our shareholders and our clients. We were looking to expand our service offering. Firestone's actions were all his own. If you look at the big picture, he didn't even take that much. It was the timing that made it look like the two were related."

"I'm sorry; he 'didn't even take that much'?"

John winces silently. A terrible choice of words when people had lost their life savings. "What I mean is that his take versus the overall profit of the company was not significant. It didn't have a significant effect on our return to investors or our financial services clients."

Debra is squaring her shoulders for another salvo when the court room doors swing open. The judge looks up in alarm, anger clear upon his face.

"I'm sorry, your honor," says the clerk who has entered the room. "But Galveston is evacuating in advance of Hurricane Ike. The mayor just issued the order. And Houston has been instructed to recess all court proceedings until further notice."

The expected din erupts inside the room. Judge Harris pounds his gavel for order.

"Very well. This court is in recess pending further notice from this office."

#

"Should we stop by the store?" Amanda's voice bounces off the inside of her refrigerator as she gives it a final wipe with a damp cloth. It stands now, empty open and unplugged in the old kitchen — a stainless steel monument to nature's ability to put man back in his place whenever she damned well pleases. No matter how energy-efficient and shiny his appliances may be.

"Are you serious?" John is sliding his phone — an iPhone now, a gift from Jack who had told him Blackberries were for losers — back into his pocket as he enters the room. His face is weary; he had been talking to Margaret, making sure she didn't need him to stop by the house for a last check before the storm. She and the two younger boys had packed off to Michigan the day before, to stay with her parents for the duration.

Amanda shrugs. "At this point, I doubt it will be crowded. Everyone is gone or hunkered down."

"No, I have plenty of frozen stuff and water at the loft." A pause. "And wine."

"Okay, then. How about flashlights and batteries?"

He sighs. He thinks the entire city is overreacting; he fully expects to be back in court the next morning. "I don't know," he admits, bordering on exasperated with all the preparation. "But I'm sure you have some here."

"As it happens, I do." She moves to the pantry.

"Did you talk to your dad?"

"Yeah," she calls back to him, standing on tip-toe to reach the highest shelf. "He's staying put. Thinks at most we'll get some flooding along the bayous but doesn't want to come home to a hole in his roof, just in case."

Ted had already sent a crew to board up Amanda's windows; he knew better than to wait for permission. And he had asked her to stay with him and Lisa, but she preferred the isolation that John's loft would provide. She did not want to be around neighbors in the aftermath of the storm, clearing debris and making idle conversation about when the power would come back on as they scrambled to cook the contents of their freezers before spoilage could set in. That, and she did not want John to be alone; the trial's delay would be killing him.

John is nodding. "The winds could be pretty strong, I guess. But people are forgetting this has a long way to go before it reaches us. It'll weaken."

"John," Amanda says sharply, standing in front of him now. "Have you seen the size of this thing? The leading edge will be on top of us before the eye hits Galveston. This is not just a rainstorm."

"So you're a meteorologist now, too?"

"Yes. Let's go; I'm finished here." Her bag stands packed and ready by the front door. She strides past John and picks it up, waiting for him to exit so she can lock up.

"But what about the looters?" His voice a parody of concern as he passes her and waits on the porch. "Don't you have some burglar bars you want to install before we leave?"

She glares at him as she hefts the bag into the back of her Range Rover. Slams the gate shut and takes her seat at the wheel.

Once they are underway she asks him, "How long are you usually like this?"

He turns to her, startled. "Like what?"

"Pissy," she says.

"Pissy?"

"Yes. You're being pissy with me and I'm curious how long it usually lasts, so I'll know when to start taking it personally."

He is silent, staring out the windshield as she turns left on Durham. He remains silent, stewing over her words. *Pissy?* Nobody has ever called him pissy. Ever. Now she waits at the light on Washington, tapping the steering wheel with her fingertips. The streets are nearly empty on this sunny afternoon; evidence of the consensus that everyone had waited far too long to evacuate with Rita.

"Sorry," he says at last, as the light turns green and she steers them onto Washington. "It's the delay. Storm won't even make landfall in

Galveston until tomorrow night, and we have to shut the whole city down today." He is muttering; his words barely audible.

She nods; eyes on the road. "I know."

"Yeah." He lifts a hand to touch her and then places it back on his own leg. "Thanks for coming with me. I'd go crazy by myself right now."

A quick look at his face as she changes lanes. "You're welcome."

But the air between them is awkward, and she worries what the night will bring. Since John had appeared at her home in July, they have either spoken on the phone or seen each other in person every day. And, apart from the conversation on her porch, and her testimony the following day, the subject of their involvement has not been raised. Neither one can make it fit inside the frame of their lives right now; it is difficult to see anything past the conclusion of the trial. Amanda drives by the Commerce Museum without a glance and turns right on Lubbock, into the edge of downtown.

At John's loft, Amanda takes a look in his pantry and fridge. They are fully stocked with a variety of cereal, crackers, Pop Tarts, frozen pizzas and the cans of margarita mix ubiquitous to freezers in Houston. The fridge holds milk, cheese, eggs, cold cuts and more condiments than she has ever seen outside a grocery store. No wonder he had scorned a trip to the market.

"Do your sons hide out here?"

He grins. "Their mother can grate on the nerves a bit."

"Is that right," she murmurs, sliding the freezer closed and ignoring the twitch her words draw from John's lips.

His phone buzzes and he digs it from his pocket. "Cavanaugh," he says, excusing himself.

Amanda leans on the counter and listens to John's half of the conversation, mostly "yes," "no" and "okay."

"Looks like someone went to the same meteorology school as you," he says when the call has ended. "We're in recess until at least next Tuesday. I guess half the court left for the Hill Country."

He grabs the remote and turns on the TV, flipping through the local news coverage. Every last station features a rain slicker-sporting reporter, standing on a pier in Galveston and being lashed by pre-storm gusts.

"Just think how glad we'll be when the power goes out," John reflects as he moves from channel to channel.

"Well," Amanda says almost coyly. "At least they're not talking about you anymore."

He turns very slowly to face her; lowers the hand with the remote and starts to laugh. She smiles at him but does not move.

"Thanks," he says. "I guess I needed that."

Amanda pushes herself up from the counter and turns on the oven. "What kind of pizza do you want? Or would you prefer a sampling of mini eggrolls and pot stickers?"

"Pizza. Mushrooms and olives; but I'll do it." He lowers the volume on the TV and walks to the kitchen to open a bottle of wine. It is only four o'clock in the afternoon. Good thing he has a big BluRay collection; it's going to be a long night. He studies Amanda from beneath his lashes as he presses the cork screw into the cork.

She feels his eyes on her face. Turns to look at him. "What?"

He shakes his head. "Just trying to figure you out. Still."

Amanda laughs. He's not certain he has ever heard that sound from her before; it is ironic yet somewhat uncontrolled.

"Better hope for a really big storm, then."

"That's what I'm thinking," he agrees, nodding as he speaks. "Sometimes I think I get you, and then you do something that completely destroys my theory."

"Such as?"

"God, where to begin," he muses. "The fact you're even here, for one."

She takes a breath to speak and then sets her mouth, instead. Tilts her head at him, eyes narrowed. Finally, another breath and she says, "Maybe you should think in terms of the journey versus the destination."

He laughs and shakes his head, eyes closed; fingers on his forehead. He opens his eyes and pours the wine, handing her a glass and trying to squelch the memories associated with the simple gesture.

Amanda is wondering how long they will be able to play house and make small talk. It is unfamiliar to them both — with each other and in general. Each is accustomed to speaking toward a purpose or saying nothing at all; but the strangeness of the situation begs some form of interaction, if only to confirm that there is in fact nothing else for them to do.

They sit together on the sofa and watch television. The local media have still refused to acknowledge that anything else exists outside of Hurricane Ike: no war in Iraq, no presidential election, no murders or rapes to report today. For to do so would risk being scooped by a rival outlet and losing precious market share. And yet Amanda and John are completely enrapt, as if it truly is the single, biggest news story of the decade. Anything to resist the overwhelming trajectory toward slumber — or its absence.

FRIDAY, SEPTEMBER 12

When Amanda awakens, she is on the bed. John is sitting up next to her; laptop open and humming as he peruses the Internet news sites. She has slept late, later than she has managed in months.

"Couldn't take the TV anymore," he says when she levers up on an elbow and peers at the screen. He pauses to appreciate her disheveled hair and squinting, cloudy eyes. He had forgotten what an image she is made of morning light.

She yawns and stretches, nodding. "Good call. What's going on outside of Houston?" But her mind is racing. She has no recollection of going to bed. Or anything else that might have transpired.

"Nothing good," he muses, back on the screen. "Although from where I sit, it's not all bad, either." He turns the computer so she can see.

Government-Backed Mortgage Lender Receives Federal Bailout

"No way," she says. "What happened?"

"Same damned thing that would have happened to Vantage, if we'd held on a little longer." His voice is paradoxical. "Someone finally figured out that risky derivatives most likely *derive*—" a sharp look as he draws out the word for effect, "their value from equally risky underlying securities."

Amanda scans the entire article and then pushes the laptop back to John, shaking her head. Not only the government's own mortgage bank, but also two investment firms that had purchased the bundled securities and passed them along to their clientele, one of which had — until April — been Vantage PLC. The dominos have started to fall; the banks will be next, probably. She is torn between relief and dread. Relief that people will see John did nothing illegal; dread that this will upend the country's entire financial system.

"So you're not an evil genius, then?" She sounds disappointed.

He sighs. "Guess not. Is that a letdown for you?"

"I'll get over it." She smiles. "What about Ike?"

"Midnight tonight." He puts the laptop on the coffee table and grabs his phone. "I need to get in touch with Tim and see what this really means, before I get too carried away; and before we lose phone service." He has seen the satellite images, now, and finally believes there may be a reason for all the worry.

"I like this phone," he mutters as he places the call. "It *is* cool."

"Uh-huh," she says sleepily, lying back down. She listens with half an ear to John's voice, still puzzled by the events of the night. She is dressed the same shorts and tank she wore yesterday. She closes her eyes, deciding it doesn't matter. John has ended his call and moved to the kitchen; he returns with a cup of black coffee.

As he hands it to her, he explains, "You fell asleep on the sofa. I moved you."

"Okay." And then, "Thanks."

"Oh, it was easy," he insists. "And then again, not so easy."

She takes a sip and looks at him, her face serious and sad.

"What's wrong? You take it black, don't you?"

She nods. "Yes, I take it black."

"Then … ?" He is perplexed.

Amanda shakes her head and looks away, out the window. "You make jokes, but you know me."

"I know how you take your coffee," he reasons.

"No," she says. "You know me. It's more than how I take my coffee or when my birthday is, or my favorite color — or any of those things that mean nothing except when they're all a person knows about someone else. You know *me*."

He reaches out a hand and pushes her hair from her face. "Yes, I do."

She closes her eyes, now, letting him rest his hand against her cheek. The contact so slight she believes she may be imagining it. Deep breaths for a count of ten. Eyes open and she looks at him, steady now.

"What did Tim have to say?"

"That the storm of the century may have just saved my ass."

"Is that right?" Her hand covering his and she turns her face towards his palm.

"Where do you go, when you do that?" His voice tentative; this is dangerous ground.

Amanda speaks into his skin. "When I do what?"

"The trance. Where do you go?" Hand sliding from her cheek down her neck and to her shoulder.

"Nowhere," she says simply, moving closer to him.

"I wish I knew how." His lips against her forehead.

"I'll show you," she offers, sliding her arms around him and tucking her head under his chin. "We have nothing but time until Tuesday."

He bends to kiss her hair and decides to pretend he doesn't notice that she is crying softly into his neck.

WEDNESDAY, SEPTEMBER 17

John sits anxiously across from the desk in Judge Harris' chambers. Tim is at his left; Debra Wilcox and her second chair complete the group. It is their first day back in court since Ike had whipped the city into submission the previous week. And the country's entire financial system had given way at the same time, as if the storm had also eroded the pebbles and silt on which it had been standing for the last decade. Vantage was no longer alone, now. And neither was John.

Judge Harris inhales deeply, casting his eyes across the small assembly. "I received a disturbing phone call last night," he begins.

John's heart leaps in his chest. He wonders if the entire room has heard it. His face remains still. O'Malley had been completely cut off from John's defense team by the storm. FEMA had taken over the cellular network, and most of the land lines were still buried under deep and filthy storm run-off. His loft remains one of the few buildings in the city with power; the notice to return to court had been hand-delivered by a messenger on a bicycle. John hoped he was receiving hazard pay.

"Followed by a signed affidavit delivered to my office by courier this morning. Both the phone call and the affidavit came from a reporter with *Bottom Line Magazine*." He glances at John and then at Debra, his eyes resting longer on her face, John thinks.

"Mike O'Malley," the judge continues. "He asserts that Ms. Wilcox has engaged in conduct unbecoming a representative of the U.S. government in the matter at hand. He asserts that Ms. Wilcox has been engaged in a romantic relationship with a stock analyst named Chris Morton — "

John's hands flex on the arm of his chair as he tries to prevent himself from rising out of the seat. Sharp looks from both Judge Harris and Tim settle him.

" — Chris Morton, who not only owned shares of Vantage but sold those shares on the short side and participated materially in analysis of the company's long-term profitability." His voice trails off as he shakes his head.

"Honestly, I'm not sure I understand the details of this yet," the judge admits. "But I do understand that Ms. Wilcox has used information gathered by Mr. Morton to exert improper influence on — among others — potential witnesses in this cause." He shuffles the pages, looking for something specific. "And that in a previous attempt to prosecute Mr. Wallace, while he was still at the head of Vantage PLC, Ms. Wilcox used a similar relationship with a member of the Federal Trade Commission in a similar manner. As such, it is my judgment to rule a mistrial in this matter."

Judge Harris looks pointedly at Debra. "Now, Ms. Wilcox, I have some questions for you."

Outside the courthouse, John and Tim stop for the impromptu press conference that has convened on the side street.

"Mr. Wallace, how do you feel about the court's decision?"

What a stupid question, John thinks. But he says, "It's good news. Let's hope the prosecutor's office conducts a more thoughtful investigation before making a decision about a retrial."

"And what about the current financial crisis? Have we failed to learn the lesson of what happened on Smith Street?"

John shakes his head. "Until someone decides to *teach* the right lesson, we can't expect much progress there." He draws a breath, as if preparing to say more, but then pauses, distracted by a figure standing confident and patient behind the small army of media. He lifts a hand to indicate he has finished with them and ignores the chorus of dismay, walking through the ranks without a care for whom he is brushing aside. They have their sound bites; that's all they need.

He reaches her side and grips her shoulders, holding her at arm's length for a moment before pulling her into an embrace. She laughs and squeezes him tightly before breaking the contact.

"Come on," she says. "I have a surprise for you."

He is intrigued. A surprise from Amanda is something worth seeing, indeed. She leads him to her car.

"Let's go," she invites.

"Where?"

"The park, of course."

She drives them down Rusk and then onto Avenida de Las Americas, skirting Discovery Green. She parks at a meter on Dallas and leads him to a quiet flower garden in the park, a packet of papers in her hand. They sit on a bench, knees touching.

"Here," she says simply, handing him the papers.

John purses his lips, puzzled. The first page is a statement of brokerage account activity dated a few months before. It details the sale of Vantage shares at the bottom of their value; just prior to bankruptcy. The gains were enormous; the result of short-selling. His eyes shift to the top of the statement. The account is registered to an entity named St. Agnes Holdings. He flips to the next page. An account statement from a bank in the Bahamas dated today. In Amanda's name. The balances are nearly identical.

"How soon do you want to leave?" she asks him.

"What?" He is trying to force the connections in his mind, but he is numb. "How did you do this?"

"At least *I* learned the lesson." She winds her arm around him and plants a kiss at the top of his collar. Her voice is coy, intended to please him; but it doesn't. Not this time.

He pushes away from her; something he has done only once before. Her face is frozen with worry; eyes searching for some sign of what is wrong. She cannot fathom why he is upset. She had done this for both of them.

"You bet against me?"

"No, I bet against Matt." Her pulse begins to race; this is not the reaction she had expected.

John's thoughts wander back to the warning Dave Galvan had delivered, half a year before. She *was* dangerous. Had she known all along what would happen? Had she somehow steered both Matt and him — and by extension Anand — so that they delivered exactly what she wanted? He studies her face; the wrinkle of her brow and the worried set of her eyes. He thinks of their days and nights together and wonders if she had simply been playing a part.

"A shameless opportunist," she says gently, almost pleading. "Remember? That's why you like me so much."

But for the first time in her life, she has played it wrong. John shakes his head sadly. He touches her face.

And then he stands and walks away.

ACKNOWLEDGMENTS

When I was a junior in high school, I worked at Neiman Marcus at Town & Country Mall in Houston, Texas. This was during the collapse of the oil business, and the store was all-but empty, every night of the week and most Saturdays, too. That was my first experience with how devastating the downfall of an industry can be to a city, although I didn't appreciate it at the time. I also had no idea that I would be thinking of those lonely evenings twenty-something years later as I struggled for words to explain why I chose to write about corporate disaster. I suppose it's simply a part of my personal history, just as it is a part of my city's history.

Which leads me to Vantage Property, Life and Casualty. It doesn't exist, but it could. It is merely a handy amalgam of any number of big companies that have come and gone in the corporate landscape of Houston and the United States.

Which leads me to the Commerce Museum. It doesn't exist, but it should. Houston residents trying to figure out where it's located: In my mind, I situated it in the old Heights State Ba nk Building on Washington Avenue at Heights Boulevard.

Which leads me to my lengthy list of acknowledgments. Thank you:

Stephen Cullar-Ledford, for designing my cover and setting up the book block, which I only just learned is the technical term for the inside of a book. Check out Stephen's work at *www.cullar-ledford.com*. And then pause to reflect on how lucky I am to know him.

Rebecca Fite and Samantha Fite, for reading, re-reading, talking me in off the ledge in my head countless times and basically kicking me in the pants until I finally did something with this writing thing. I just don't know what I would do without either one of you. Love you; mean it.

Katie Mullins, for being my photographer, publicist, editor, Web master, sanity checker and fountain of information. You are possibly the only person in the world who knows more about useless and arcane subjects than I am. And I love you (and yet also hate you a little) for it.

Stasa Cushman, for your support and encouragement, for "Turkey and Trauma," for vetting my marketing materials, and for being my *capo di tutti capo* of readers and coming at this with those all-important fresh eyes! And I say, heck yes, you can put that on your business card. You rule, LG.

Martha Dehaven, for also reading and re-reading and providing the endless encouragement that needy, artistic types like me need so desperately.

Peter Hayes, for letting me pepper you with ideas and insecurities and never once telling me I'm nuts (even though we both know I am).

Mike McConnell and Rick Shapiro, for your feedback, guidance and tremendous support.

Mom and Dad, for forty-plus years of support and love and everything else I could ever have possibly wanted or needed. Which is quite a lot, actually, when you add it all up.

And finally, Rodney and the beautiful children you made with me. Thanks for leaving me alone enough to get this done — and for not leaving me alone when I needed some gentle prodding to get this done. And thank you, especially, for not being like any of the messed-up, misguided men in my book.

ERIN K. RICE

Erin K. Rice began writing novels when she was 10 years old. Thirty years later, she published her first one. Erin was born in upstate New York and moved to Houston, Texas with her family at the age of five. Erin attended The University of Texas at Austin, where she earned a Bachelor's Degree in English Literature. She returned to Houston in 1995 and worked for several energy companies, including Enron, before and during the 2001 crash of the energy market. Erin now lives in The Woodlands, north of Houston, with her husband and children and their hyperactive dog.

For *What Happened on Smith Street* book club discussion questions, please visit www.erinkrice.com.

Breinigsville, PA USA
21 August 2009
222667BV00002B/1/P